To Hayley B,
a delightful and sincere friend who is not only a
beautiful genius but a true joy to know.
As you reach for the stars may some fall for your
dreams.

Chapter One

"Get up," the male voice came from beside her. "Come on, let's get you inside."

She wanted to get up but her body felt so weak and the cold hard ground beneath her was hardly a place for a lady to lie on. She *was* a lady, wasn't she? Her eyes wouldn't open and she heard people running back and forth, murmurs or something to that effect.

"*Am* I lady?" she asked wearily into the semi darkness.

The male voice, young and not overly crass, replied close to her ear. "I'd say you were as good as one as any," he said plainly. "You're a girl and your dress is not too shabby."

Intentionally pressing her eyelids a few times, she forced her vision to return. On first glance the sun was soon to descend behind a nearby business and it appeared she was behind a building of sorts.

The young man looked at her, somewhat worriedly but curious.

She studied him intently, trying to work it out. What had gotten her there? "I'm sorry, who are you?"

The lad, perhaps in his early twenties, squinted discernibly and removed his jacket, folding it and placing it under her head. "Well that depends on who *you* are," he said with a dry smile.

She frowned; she could feel it etched on her forehead. Was he mocking her? "I'm afraid you're mistaken," she said, clearing her throat to improve her diction. "You are who you are with no encumbrance of the truth. My identity doesn't impinge on that one way or another."

A smile crept on his slender face and his green eyes lit up with amusement as he tipped his cap at her, exposing his floppy brown hair. "Who are you, then?" he asked as he shifted his feet, uncomfortable in his crouched position.

She wanted to rise onto her elbows and at least implement some level of proper etiquette but it all eluded her. She opened her mouth to respond and then panic arose inside of her. "I don't recall," she said, reaching out for his arm worriedly. "My name, it should be something that comes to mind immediately but it is lost."

He pressed his hand on the top of her head in an odd sort of way and looked into her eyes as if doing some sort of assessment. "You don't remember who you are?"

Wearily lifting her arms upward, she studied the sheer lace sleeves that hung down like a bell from her elbows, but there was no jewelry on her slender fingers.

Surely there had to be another explanation, she would just need a moment to collect her thoughts, but staring mindlessly at her hands, there was nothing. "No," she replied deflatedly. "Do *you* know who I am?" she pleaded.

He looked past her to the building behind them. She could hear people talking inside but it was mumbled and unclear. "I found you here," he said. "I thought those Hanley boys got hold of you. These are late hours for a lady to be walking around town. Could be one of them got your purse."

Quickly struck with a unique terror, she sat up and checked her body. Pink embroidered flowers adorned her tiered white dress which was noticeably unmolested. Her white pumps were free of markings and lifting her hands to her head, she could still feel a curved wide brim hat pinned on top of her well kempt hair.

"I don't appear to have experienced an altercation," she surmised quietly, not knowing who was around.

His eyes turned downward, politely scanning her surroundings.

It was then that her hopes were dashed as she too realized no purse was on her person. "Supposing they had taken any item from me, I'm now without clues to assist me," she noted.

She worried he would leave her but he seemed prepared to remain. "May I help you?" he offered courteously.

"Yes, if you don't mind," she said, reaching up so he could guide his hands underneath her back and pull her towards him.

She sat still, clutching onto his white buttoned shirt sleeves as she gazed at him in deep contemplation. "Could you perhaps guide me to a police station?"

His eyes widened as if the prospect frightened him and she wondered if he had been in some sort of trouble. "There is a small station across the way from the Hartford Bank but we don't trust them, Miss. I'd fear they'd take advantage of the likes of you," he said, sincerely worried. "What if they told you something about you belonging to one of them and then took you in to do their domestic duties or the like?"

She smiled, amused by him, yet intrigued by his apparent sincerity. "That is quite a theory, young man, but they would fare poorly if they deceived me then armed me with a weighty mop head."

He laughed heartily as he reached behind her for his coat. As he did, his expression changed immediately and she turned slowly to follow his gaze to a circle of blood on it. "Oh no, am I injured?"

He met her gaze so she knew he was earnest in his handling of her, and then he reached around to check the back of her head. "It doesn't look like it got your hat, but you've got quite a cut back there. It might be from the cobblestones, they need to fix this road up and flatten it out like the main strip."

She felt around to the back of her head, and it still felt wet so it had to have been recent. "Did you see anyone come from here?" she enquired.

"It had to be them," he said. "They're mother passed on and they've been thieving just to get food." He shook his head and stared down at his coat.

—

4

"Oh I am sorry for your coat; please allow me to pay for its laundering—," she stopped and sighed. She must have had money for such a thing once; otherwise it wouldn't have been a statement that ran so freely from her mouth. "When I discover who I am I will find a way to compensate you," she corrected.

"I don't mind," he said with a mischievous grin. "I'd say that with blood on my coat, no one will want to roughhouse me."

She laughed then gestured for him to help her stand. Together they slowly raised her body and looking around she was surprised to not recognize anything. "Where did you come from?" she asked as she spotted an alley that allowed her a glimpse of what she assumed to be the main street and trolley lines.

"Ah, I was just checking in on Ms. Anderson down the road. Her brother didn't make it through to morning but she's still eating," he replied as if she knew who he was referring to.

"Oh, your friend is very ill?" she enquired, thinking to herself that he seemed like a very sweet young man.

He looked worried and quickly foraged his pants pocket to pull out a white mask. "I had this on, don't fear it, it's not in me at all."

She studied him curiously. "Your friend has something contagious?"

His pained expression showed that he was worried about her and now as things settled inside of her, she too was concerned.

"You don't remember the Martin's yard or anything?" he asked quietly.

Before she could reply in the negative, a loud bell sounded throughout the town as the sun began to settle behind the nearby buildings. "Is it Sunday?" she asked, wondering why church was so late.

He tipped his cap up a little and then crossed his arms and got closer to her, though not in a manner of encroachment. "It's the death bell," he explained in a whisper.

A wave of recognition went through her but she couldn't place it at all. "Because of your friend's brother, because he died?"

He shook his head. "No, Ma'am, the bell tolls because *anyone* died," he said seriously. "That's when the men take the dead out to the old Martin's general store where the big graves are waiting around the back. So many die in the nights they have to put them in together before they spread it."

Her heart started to race. She didn't know what he was talking about but it made her feel immediately vulnerable. "You make it sound like the plague from the Middle Ages," she said worriedly.

Nodding he reached out and touched her arm lightly. "It's the Spanish flu, you see," he explained. "A couple of the soldiers came home from war about a month ago and they already had it, died in days and then got a good part of the town sick too."

She stared into his sincere youthful eyes, attempting to derive some kind of memory but it was as if everything was in darkness. "There is a war here?"

He shook his head but she could tell he pitied her. "I think a lot of them are in France now but it's a world war."

"All of the world?" she asked, suddenly feeling a sharp pain in the back of her neck from laying in a poor position.

"A good lot of it, I think. Most of the men and lady nurses are across the ocean now. All of the rest of us are left to look after the sick," he explained.

"I did wake to grim times, didn't I? I don't suppose you have any reports of good fortune to recount?" Checking her forehead again, she was satisfied that she didn't feel very ill but her fall or knock had taken its toll.

—

"You don't look well," he noted as he put his hands in his high pants pockets.

"I *am* quite fatigued," she explained truthfully. "You would think having laid there for some time, my rest would have been sufficient," she joked.

He laughed but then his expression evened and he cocked his head as if considering options. "You can come rest at the theater," he said pointing to the tall dark stone building just feet from them. "They are the best people I know and they take good care of everyone they come across."

"You are closely acquainted with them?" she asked, considering it. He was a stranger but no doubt everyone she met with would be considered as such for now. Just the same she had to keep her wits about her. "Perhaps you should direct me to the police station; I wouldn't want to burden you further."

A strange expression of rejection came over him and she regretted saying it. "I don't mean to speak ill of anyone, Ma'am, but a lot of the lawmen were shipped out as soldiers. I swear I wouldn't lead you astray, I can work you out just by looking at you," he stated cryptically. "You're all goodness and the men who took over aren't too honorable."

"They misuse their position?"

He nodded. "I've been acquainted with the theater folk longer than most people know anyone and I'm just saying; good people belong with good people; that's just what makes sense."

She tried to rationalize her senses but decided to trust her instincts even without evidence of their reliability. Convinced of his sincerity and sweet nature, she nodded. "Perhaps you can ask if they don't mind allowing me to rest there for a moment."

"They won't mind, I know they wont," he assured her with a big smile on his slender face. "I promise you're safe with me," he offered further as he gestured for her to follow him to the dark gray windowless door at the back of the theater.

Opening the door for her, he seemed to be checking on her balance and she was grateful for his concern. They immediately entered a long narrow hallway with high ceilings.

Flames flickered in the Victorian era sconces allowing them to see just enough to get through. "Has electricity been introduced here?" she pondered aloud.

They walked past a closed door and he stopped at the second entrance on the right. "Some of the main rooms are wired but they're trying to conserve resources for now," he explained as he placed his hand on the round brass knob of the plain wooden door. "We like to say that it's the lighting of the ancients."

She smiled as she followed him in to the dark room. "I find it calming, there is nothing like fire to settle the spirit," she said as she listened to him walk across the cement floor and then stop, searching with his hands.

He lit the pretty floral oil lamp which sat atop a wooden filing cabinet next to an old white brass bed that accommodated one. "It's no palace but I call it home," he said with a proud smile.

Glancing around discretely, hoping not to offend him with any resonance of observation, she made sure to smile. "How long have you lived here?" she asked, noticing the many advertising posters that aligned the windowless brick wall behind him.

"Longer than my memory can catch up to," he replied as he shrugged and then placed his jacket on the unmade feather bed.

Noticing a small primitive advertisement, she got closer and was surprised to find it dated. "This is from the seventeen hundreds," she said, surprised.

"I've gotten quite a collection over the time for sure."

"Do you work for the theater people?" she asked, clasping her hands in front of her.

He nodded but then tilted his head as if it wasn't the full story. He looked around the mid sized room which had a lot of old newspapers and costume pieces in it as well. Finally his eyes stopped at the corner on his left and he quickly went over to remove a pile of old books from a chair before dusting it off and gesturing for her to sit.

"I'm sorry it's not queen worthy but it's better than sitting on the cobblestones," he said.

She nodded and sat on it graciously, unconcerned for the dust and glad to rest her feet. "No, please don't fuss. I am very grateful for your hospitality," she assured him.

He looked like he was going to sit on his bed across the room but then reconsidered as if he remembered something. "Oh, as for what you were asking, the theater folk took me in when I was just a pup and I pay for my keep by my doing errands for them," he explained as he opened the door just a crack. "I make deliveries for them and do what they ask and they treat me like I was one of their own."

She smiled at him, warmed by his sincere appreciation of the good people he spoke so highly of.

Staring down at the door handle, he caught her glance. "I am going to talk with them now and tell them you are here," he said with a reassuring smile. "I'm betting you aren't planning on staying long but just in case you are forgetting for a while; I'm sure a nice lady like you would be best set up in a room of her own."

She wanted to object but was fatigued enough to realize that a private area without prying eyes would indeed be a better option. "Thank you," she said genuinely as he smiled and left with the door open slightly.

The sounds of voices further down the hall were so faint they sounded like the humming of a trolley car.

She thought she could hear music, maybe someone playing a piano but she was so tired it was almost too difficult to concentrate on it.

As her eyelids grew heavy she was suddenly startled to realize she hadn't asked the young man for his name.

The stillness of the room made her sleepy as she clasped her hands in her lap and studied her thumb as it pressed on her other one in an action that seemed familiar to her. What had happened to her? She recalled hearing voices when she woke before, it was definitely likely those young men had pushed her and taken her purse.

She remembered reading once that a man had been knocked down by a carriage horse and he had lost his memory for many years. Would such a thing happen to her? Surely she must have lived locally and someone would look for her soon, she shouldn't worry she reasoned.

Her eyes wearily studied the wall where the slightly ajar door was and there were more posters there. Why did this young man like advertisements so much?

Seeing the colorful half masks sitting on top of a wooden crate, she realized that they were organized as if on display. Perhaps they were special to him, memories that he cherished from these people he prized.

She wanted to be cherished, but perhaps she was. Closing her eyes she thought hard, trying to remember why she was out there behind the theater, outside as the sun was going down.

A shiver ran down her spine as she realized that the sun had likely descended and it would be completely dark outside now. What if they couldn't help her? She would go to the station, she thought, nodding in affirmation to herself. There were always choices and she wouldn't crumble.

Spotting a hand painted fan with birds on it, she reached out for it, where it lay on a typewriter on the floor. Even though her dress was thin and silky, the heat was a little stifling and contributed to her weakness.

Suddenly the door opened and the young man was there smiling at her. "My friends are discussing a place for you," he said soothingly as if consoling a child. "Don't you worry at all; we'll take care of you. We'll look for who you are. If you can't remember you are safe here."

She fanned herself and smiled at him. "You are very kind," she said sincerely. "What is your name?"

"Oh!" he said with a laugh as if it hadn't occurred to him either. "I must have forgotten my manners when I found you there. I'm Gilpin," he said, with an intentionally theatrical bow.

"Gilpin? Is that your true name?"

He nodded. "It is the truth as far as any of us are concerned," he said, walking over and sitting on his bed and leaning forward. "When I was a little boy the folk here found me and took me in, and that's when they gave me that name. My friends said I deserved a name with meaning because I was a little darling," he relayed with a coy laugh.

She smiled along with him. "Then do you know your parents at all?"

He shook his head but didn't seem very saddened by it. "No, no one knew who they were but I don't remember them to miss them anyway."

"I am sorry to hear it just the same, but if these thespians care for you the way you say, they are bound to be your true family in your heart. I can see how you must have been a very darling little boy. What meaning is applied to your name?"

"Trusted," he replied as he clapped his hands together gleefully. "See, that's why you can rest easy, Ma'am. My very name means that you can."

She laughed and fanned herself more. "I do trust you, Gilpin. Maybe I don't remember who I am, but I do feel that my sense of judgment is valid and I'm glad to have met you, even under these sullen circumstances."

He beamed but then placed his hands on his knees and stared at her. "Is the heat bothering you?"

She shrugged slightly, trying to minimize any display of discomfort. "A little, but I am content. Is it summer now?"

He nodded. "Right at the center of August, but my friend Clarence says the sun will lose its power for some time soon," he said before reconsidering his statement. "Well now, he's got an idea for things, if you are the kind to be believing in mystics and such."

She nodded, knowing the meaning of the word. "I don't know how I remember what I do, but I don't doubt such things," she said, noticing the surprise in his eyes. "We can not just dismiss an idea for the mere lack of evidence. Many things existed before they were discovered, were they not?"

He laughed and clapped his hands together again. "Yes! You understand! Just like a giraffe, see?"

She smiled and nodded. "I gather that when some first saw the sketchings of one, there was much conjecture regarding mythological creatures, but they were finally seen by the eyes of the skeptics and then suddenly accepted to be real."

He removed his cap and ran a hand through his brown floppy hair as he smiled. "You are a wise lady," he said, obviously impressed.

Leaning back against the creaky wooden chair, she smiled but then it faded. "Yes, I must be a wise lady, whoever I am."

Before he could further the discussion a light knock came at the door and then opened before Gilpin could invite the visitor in.

A pretty brunette lady, likely in her early thirties, lifted the bottom of a fancy southern belle type dress and stepped into the room, closing the door behind her. Handing Gilpin a rolled up poster, she turned and looked at the stranger in the room.

The lady with no memory stood accordingly, but the pretty lady gestured for her to sit again.

"Oh no, please don't fuss with formalities," she said, reaching out and patting her hand. "Don't be fooled by my coverings, it's made out of some French lady's draperies. Just a costume, that's all. I'm as plain as a sidewalk when I'm not on the stage."

"I doubt that you are plain," the stranger assured her. "Beauty can't be created with apparel, it must derive from the wearer and I can see you are grander than French draperies."

The pretty lady laughed as she explored her own face with her hands, her high cheekbones and her large hazel eyes that were painted with pink cosmetics. "I'm sorry to hear about your fall, sweet one. You are in safe keeping with us, we wont do you wrong so don't fear any such thing," she said gently. "What is your name?"

The stranger shook her head. "I don't recall," she replied.

Gilpin unrolled the poster and held it up for them as he whistled. "You got me a real pretty one this time, Gleda," he mused as she went up to it for study.

"The soap ads are sometimes nicer than the coca cola ones," Gleda agreed. "I hear they get ladies of high society to pose for them and an artist paints them that way, as if they are surrounded by beautiful misty colors."

The pair now looked at her and she studied the pretty lady on the poster, believing they wanted her opinion. "She *is* very attractive; she looks as if she is on the way to a fair of some kind. I think I may have used Palmolive soap before."

Gleda tucked her long ringlets behind her ears then clamped her petite hands onto Gilpin's arms. "Well I'd say this girl here is just as beautiful as any of these soap girls. I suggest we give her a name like one of them."

"There's no real name here, Gleda," Gilpin explained. "We would have to name her Palmolive if you were going to do it that way."

Gleda turned and laughed as she looked at the stranger. "We must call you something, would you like perhaps to be addressed as the shortened version, like Olive?"

The stranger shook her head, but she did worry that she would offend with her resistance to their jovial suggestion. "I can not recall why, but I get the feeling I dislike that name for one reason or another."

"What about Olly?" Gilpin chimed in.

Gleda scowled as she sat on the bed next to him. "No Gilpin, that's not polished enough for a proper lady."

The stranger stood, still fanning her face, and feeling a touch giddy. "I will accept it," she offered with a smile. "It does not remind me of anything therefore will give me no grief to compare it. So good day to you, Gilpin and Gleda," she said, nodding at each of them respectively. "My name is Olly, pleased to make your acquaintance," she added with a very careful curtsy.

The pair on the bed exchanged a glance of appreciation as they both laughed. "Perhaps you would do well on the stage, Ms. Olly," Gleda said as she made a show out of looking her over.

Olly shrugged, feeling more relaxed. "I am not aware if I have experience or not, but I dare to presume that feigning the character of another is much easier when you are not certain of your original countenance."

"Indubitably," Gleda agreed as she smiled at her warmly. "You are a delight."

Olly's smile faded as she looked around the room. "Please, do you have a mirror?"

Gleda stood and looked at the many boxes aligning the borders of the room. "Do you still have the Cleopatra box from last April?"

Gilpin scanned the room as if he could see into the boxes themselves and stopped at one near the main door. "Yes, it's there under the Hamlet box," he said.

Walking past Olly with a smile, Gleda quickly went for the box and lifting the one on top of it, removed the lid and pulled out a large dresser type mirror. She handed it to Olly who was surprised by its heaviness and assumed it was likely a repainted one from the Victorian period. "This is beautiful," she noted as she placed it on the chair she had just been sitting on and crouched in front of it.

"You can keep it in your room, Olly," Gilpin said cheerfully as if he liked that he was the one to suggest her name.

Olly glanced up at him then down at the mirror, painted in hues of auburn and gold. "That is very kind of you, Gilpin. I'm not sure how long I will be staying here but I will admire it for the duration."

She took a deep breath before committing to looking into it and when she did, she could see Gleda hunched over her. "Do you see anything you recognize?" she asked her.

Olly could see the furl in her expression, the seriousness in the large blue eyes that looked back at her. Reaching up she touched her slender face and pressed her finger to her soft rose colored lips. "I see that I am blinking at the same time as the girl in the mirror but she is a stranger to me," she replied solemnly.

A knock came at the door, a harder more determined knock. "Gleda," the male voice called out insistently.

Gleda looked at Gilpin then back at the door. "Please come in," she called back.

The man cleared his throat and shuffled on the spot as if considering it. "I ask that you come here," he asserted from the other side.

Gleda nodded at Olly apologetically and left the room, shutting the door behind her.

"Is she in trouble?" Olly whispered her enquiry to Gilpin who was staring at the door.

Gilpin shook his head then placed his cap back on his head. "No, it's not like that at all. Things have been hard on him lately, that's what it is. He would never speak harsh to Gleda; we just have to help him right now. He needs us to help him now."

Olly decided not to ask further on it for now but did return her gaze to the mirror. Her brown hair was well kept and silky, tied into a loose bun, curving around like a border that framed her face.

Her hat had pink and white lace in it, tilted and glamorous, matching her tiered dress. Her skin was pale but healthy and for her age, perhaps somewhere in her thirties, she had not been affected by too many age spots or creases.

Just the same, she could not reconcile the absence of recognition. She felt Gilpin's eyes on her and looked up to see he was upset to see her that way. "I am sad for you," he said frankly.

She was touched by his words and was going to say as much but Gleda returned and went to the wall to the right of the entrance, opposite the bed. There she began carefully removing some posters, revealing a door into another room, the first room they had passed in the hallway.

Gilpin didn't seem distressed as he began to help her to put the advertisements aside in a neat pile on the Hamlet box.

"He said she can stay in the room next to yours," Gleda said to Gilpin who nodded in response. "If she needs anything, you do what you can for her, Gil."

"I will," he promised.

It sounded like boxes were being moved about in the room next door very quickly and then some other commotion suggested they were arranging the room for her.

"This door is for you," Gilpin said to Olly as she stood to look at it. "You come to me for anything at all, any time."

"Thank you," Olly said, hoping he would get from her tone how much she appreciated it.

—

Minutes later, Gleda led Olly through the door that adjoined the two rooms and pointed to a wooden bed in the left corner. "One of the boys put my extra nightgown in there for you, it's clean and I believe it will fit you."

One tall floor lamp was beside the bed, appearing as if it had just been placed there now; the dim bulb only allowing them to see a small bit of the room.

"Are you tired?" Gleda enquired further as she closed the door to Gilpin's room.

Olly nodded. "I am very fatigued," she replied, realizing she was holding the Cleopatra mirror.

"Here, let me take that from you, poor girl," Gleda said, taking the mirror and putting it on top of an ornamented burgundy table, likely a set piece.

Olly went for the bed, a carved claw foot walnut bed that looked scratched up, probably from being used on stage. Some nice large pieces of silk and velvet fabric pieces had been laid out to make it look nicer but she could tell they had put it there in haste for her.

Sitting down she took in another deep breath and felt dizzy from it. Gleda came up behind her and began removing the hair pins from her hair. It fell down Olly's shoulders, and rested at her slender waist.

Gleda pointed to a gold goblet on the floor beside the bed and explained it was room temperature water if she should get thirsty in the night. With that, she left the room through the door that led to the hallway.

Olly used every last bit of her energy to put on Gleda's nightgown and sink into the uneven feather mattress, covering herself with a thin crocheted blanket that was also on the bed. In less than a minute she fell into a deep slumber.

Chapter Two

She could hear a bell ringing, a church bell, or had it just been something she heard in her dream? Looking around the room, Olly noticed that the lamp had died out. She couldn't tell if she had slept long, only that it was a heavy sleep and it was still very dark in the room.

The only light that she could see was that which was coming from the moon. When Gleda had first let her in the room, she hadn't noticed the narrow misted window beside her bed. The moonlight was strong, casting blurred shadows onto the velvet blanket.

Fortunately the window was nearly even to the height of the bed so she didn't have to lift her body much to touch it. Feeling clammy from the stuffy room, she was glad to have her fingers locate a large latch at the side of it.

With some effort she got it unstuck and opened it, immediately allowing a soothing cool breeze to flow in. Leaning her head against the bricks beside the window, she gazed out only a small way as the window itself was not quite the width of her face.

Her fatigue was still present and she felt as if her head actually hurt more than it had before. What was her true name? She tried to concentrate on her circumstances but no information presented itself; for now she was still Olly.

A door suddenly shut with an abrupt bang further down the hall, perhaps towards the theater area. Though she didn't have a pocket watch, there was something in the air that had a definite midnight feel to it.

Her eyelids grew heavy as she stared at the side of a two storey brick building some distance away. Cobblestones aligned the area outside of her window as well and she pondered what had happened to her.

Deciding she couldn't enlighten herself any further, her thoughts turned to the banging door and the hours these theater dwellers kept. She heard some murmurs and mused that perhaps they were rehearsing. Bringing her head back into the room, she realized she could also hear a female singing.

None of it bothered her; the sounds were pleasant and comforting. Not just that, but no manner of commotion would keep her awake long in this moment.

Closing her eyes, she was about to return her head to the pillow when she was surprised by a group of people approaching the side of the building. It was dark enough that they wouldn't have likely noticed the open window but they were close enough that if she made a sound they might hear it.

Keeping her breaths shallow, she listened intently. With only the moonlight, their majestic fanciful figures cast sharp silhouettes on the stones but they were facing away from her.

By their dress, she observed four men and one woman, all of them engaged in low serious conversation. She couldn't ascertain why, but even though she could hear their voices, their language seemed like an indeterminable hum.

Worried that her injury had caused some kind of confusion with her comprehension, she tried harder to identify words. Briefly studying their mannerisms, she thought that perhaps the woman was Gleda, but why would she not be asleep now?

Why would they stand outside to talk and why did they seem so worried? There was something grandly mysterious about the whole affair and she worried they would detect her witness of them but they seemed too preoccupied.

Even though the light breeze was offering some relief, she decided to close the window quietly for a more sound rest.

As she let her body fall back onto the bed, she closed her eyes and thought about Gilpin and wondered how his parents could give up such an endearing boy.

Almost immediately a dream was making its way into her mind. Not an ordinary dream but one of crisp vision and clarity like a glimpse of a distant memory.

She felt aware of the fact that she was dreaming but was so tired she couldn't analyze the semantics of how that could be.

A breeze was pushing against her skin, it was warm but it wasn't in the room, it was there at the bottom of a grassy hill. Not being able to intentionally look down, she couldn't see what she was wearing but could feel a long dress press against her legs.

Glancing around there were more hills around her, around *them*. There was someone with her, a man. She couldn't see him but knew him to be in front of her.

She got glimpses of him but just flashes of a darker color on his clothing, just the corner of his dark shoe but she couldn't control where she looked.

He placed his hand on her face and a wave of love went through her, intense and undeniable. He loved her and she knew she couldn't be without him, the feeling was overpowering.

She wanted to kiss his hand, in gratitude for the way he made her feel, to bring herself closer to his heart but his hand moved and pointed to the blue sky.

Looking up she noticed what he was pointing at. A large bird, perhaps the size of a child, flew above them, stretching its vibrant iridescent feathers so wide that it momentarily blocked their view of the sun.

She smiled, how impressive, what a beautiful bird and how fortunate they were to witness it, but then the man kissed her. His lips were familiar, those of her love, the man who was all to her and he kissed her as if she was everything to him.

She thought she heard a loud sound echo in the hills; but no, it was another door in the theater.

Olly opened her eyes into the darkness and realized that the dream had felt brief but it was likely that considerable time had passed. Gazing to her right, it appeared that the faint hue of orange meant that the sun would soon be on its rise, but not quite yet.

Who was the man in her dream? He felt too real to simply be a mirage. If he loved her, where was he now? Would he come looking for her?

She loved him, this she knew, whoever he was. Had he left her and broken her heart or perhaps he died or went to war, then how would he find her?

Her eyes were closing but then quickly opened as the door to her room, the one from the main entrance, opened wide. Light flooded in from the hallway. A very tall man stood there, a man with a face of a creature, small eyes on a goat like face and he looked upset on seeing her.

Gasping loudly, she barely had the nerve as her body shook with panic. Somehow she got the energy and sprung up out of the bed and ran across the room, right past him, to Gilpin's door.

With her hands shaking, she fumbled with the knob then flung it open, only to spin around and slam it shut again.

Gilpin looked like he had woken recently and his lamp was already lit as he jolted upward on her approach. "A chair!" she shouted frantically.

He sprung out of bed and ran to get the chair she had sat on the prior evening. She quickly grabbed it and jammed the top of it under the door handle, shaking and shivering.

Gilpin ignored regular etiquette and seized her arms, forcing her to meet his gaze. "What's the matter, Olly?"

She placed her hands on his shoulders, wanting to be held and consoled but not forcing such a responsibility on the young man. "There was a man, and he came into my room," she explained, backing away from the door nervously.

"A man entered your room?" he asked, not quite as alarmed as she thought he should be.

"Yes, he had a face like a goat, I've never seen such a person before and he looked most upset at my presence."

"What did he say to you?" Gilpin asked straightly.

Olly brought her waist length hair forward to cover her front, suddenly conscious of the thinness of her nightgown. "When a goat-faced man enters your room without invitation you do not remain for idle conversation."

Gilpin studied her expression, and then ran a thin hand through his tussled hair before laughing loudly. "There's nothing to be frightened about, Olly," he insisted as he went to the door and removed the chair.

She watched him, flabbergasted. "You're not going in there are you?"

"Yes, I won't be absent long, you can sit on my bed if you like," he replied as he opened the door that joined their rooms.

She quickly rushed over and slammed it shut. "He might hurt you."

"I promise you that he won't," he said, opening it again. "You are safe, you have my word," he added as he entered her room and shut the door behind him.

Quickly rushing across the cold wooden floor, she took a tentative stance beside the hallway door in the event she would need it for a quick escape.

Calming her breathing enough so she could listen, she heard two men talking and realized that Gilpin was with the man and he sounded like he knew him. She quickly flattened the many hairs that had strayed from her style throughout the night then reached for one of Gilpin's blanket to cover herself for modesty.

Minutes later, the door opened and Gilpin walked in alone. "That was Clarence," he said cheerfully. "He was out of town for a bit so he didn't know about you yet, that's all. No one got the chance to tell him because he got in late and he said to say he's sorry, he didn't mean to startle you."

—

22

Studying his face she knew him to be telling the truth but the concern hadn't left her completely. "Why would he come into my room?"

He walked over and sat on his bed, adjusting the long sleeves of his own white nightgown. "We keep extra toiletries in that room," he explained. "He just wanted to clean himself up after a long carriage journey."

Her shoulders slumped and she got closer to him with remorse in her eyes. "Oh, I'm sorry to have insulted your friend in your presence. I shouldn't speak ill of anyone, it undoubtedly places me in poor standing to your thoughts of me."

A look of surprise came upon his face. "No, Olly. You're good, there's no disputing that. Clarence does look something like a goat, just like the others, but they're as good as gold, believe me on that."

"There are others?"

He nodded. "Yes, he and one lady and three fellows, they are all related to each other and they have something in their blood that makes them look like that. But they're as smart as anyone I know. Clarence is probably more bright than most people, and you would like him."

She closed her eyes, feeling dizzy all of a sudden.

"Are you not feeling right?" he enquired worriedly.

"I may have just rushed in here with too much haste," she explained. "I have such an unpleasant taste in my mouth." She quickly opened her eyes, embarrassed. "Oh, I do apologize, I forgot myself. I probably shouldn't speak so openly about such things."

Standing, he straightened his slender body and smiled at her. "As I see it, you're my friend, and I wish for you to express to me the thoughts as you think them. I pass no judgments."

"Thank you, Gilpin, you really are quite endearing. I appreciate your candor, and I *am* your friend, be assured."

A wide smile appeared on his face and his green eyes beamed as he searched the room. "I have Altoids mints, a whole crate if you want a packet?"

She frowned at him, trying to place his reference. "I had thought they were used for intestinal upsets?"

He nodded but then crouched down and pulled out a large cardboard box from under his bed. "They were made for that but a good many use them for bad tastes, especially in the morning. We all have that, see?"

She nodded as she watched him open a half used box and put one his mouth before handing her a new packet of her own. She lifted the hard papered lid and took one to put in her mouth gratefully.

"Mrs. Wilkenson from the general store further out of town, died and her son got sick so he said we could take some of the foods," he explained his unusual stash. "Are you hungry?" he asked.

"I am rather." She stared at the ends of her long brown hair in deep contemplation. "Is there a washroom here?"

"Yes, it's there at the end of the hall, the last room and Gleda put a nice dress in there for you and some of her fancy soaps. She likes to take care of people," he said with a smile.

"Oh she is very kind; I will have to thank her when I see her. I would like to go there first if it's all the same to you?"

"No need to hurry, I'll be here when you are ready and then we can eat something."

"Thank you," she said as she left the room through the hallway door while looking around discretely. She hoped if she came across Clarence, she would be prepared not to appear apprehensive and counteract their last meeting with warm hospitality.

He wasn't there however; no one was, but the wall lanterns had been lit recently. She turned to her right to go towards the end room he had mentioned but noticed there were two rooms on the right and one on the left.

Tall burgundy velvet curtains hung at the end of the long hallway. She listened out for activity but all she could pick up were maybe two or three people talking in the room she assumed to be the theater beyond the curtains.

The door to the first room on the same side as her and Gilpin's rooms was open and she glanced in, seeing that it was a laundry room. Three large basins dominated the wall under a very small window while buckets and mops ornamented the corners.

No one was in there but a grouping of wet undershirts was strewn along a makeshift line above the basins.

As she came up to the next room on the right, she could see a counter with plates and cups and realized it was the provisions area. Finishing her mint, she was going to go to the room across the way, but found herself staring into the food room.

Losing herself in random thoughts, she gazed wearily at the scuffed wooden floor and thought for just a moment that she might have experienced a memory. Maybe it was a smell in the room. She must have eaten every day of her existence; the scent of food wouldn't help her remember anything she reasoned.

"Were you looking for something to eat?" a male voice enquired in front of her.

Her head shot up and her eyes widened as she realized she had been staring into an occupied room. The biggest misfortune was her thin nightgown and tussled hair that lessened her presentation. Even worse still was the fact that the man who spoke to her was incredibly attractive.

Perhaps close in age to her, his strong jaw briefly moved in a grinding motion as he concentrated his gaze on her.

His blue eyes were large like hers but had a fleck of steely gray in them and yet he looked upon her kindly and curiously.

His brown medium length hair was not common for the men she remembered seeing, though he had likely kept it that way for theatrical performances. Just the same he wore it down as if he too had just risen from sleep.

She opened her mouth to speak but momentarily lost her train of thought and had forgotten why she was standing there.

The man himself appeared to have light around him like a glow. She quickly searched the room for where the sunlight originated that should give him this appearance but the window behind him was not the cause.

She blinked and looked again but found his radiance to only be that of the serenity on his face. "I do not mean to stare; I was encountering a true moment of forgetfulness. I could not recall my direction at all," she relayed honestly. "I had been directed to the washroom but have found this not to be it," she explained. "Please forgive my intrusion." She began to leave in a hurry.

"Please wait," he pleaded.

Awkwardly turning to him, she now wished she had never left her room in such a state of undress.

"You are the lady who young Gilpin discovered," he noted with a smile. He didn't relay any offense to her appearance but she was discretely horrified nonetheless.

She nodded as she studied him in brief and realized that he was wearing a velvet costume robe. She crossed her arms to minimize her discomfort. "Yes, he is a sweet boy and—, are you the gentleman who allowed me to stay here last night?"

"I am not sure I would term it that way," he said with a laugh. "Yes I am an owner of this theater but please do not think on it as a distinctly charitable act. You were in need and our friends here are always in their element when in the midst of assistance. You are a welcome guest, not a stranger."

Tears threatened to fall and she closed her eyes hard for a moment to prevent an emotional reaction to his statement. "I have no remuneration but my sincere gratitude," she said, shaking her head. "The kindness of you and your companions is like a light in a fog."

He took a few steps forward with a china cup of tea in his hands. His expression was surprisingly solemn and she remembered Gilpin mentioning that they were helping him. She now wondered if he had lost someone to the flu. "I thought perhaps in your gaze, you had some familiarity with me," he said, looking down at her only slightly for he wasn't much taller than her.

Studying his face more openly she looked for recognition but was at a loss. "Should I?" she asked quietly.

He sipped his tea and seemed tired as if he hadn't slept. "I am often about town and many people know me here," he explained.

"Oh," she responded quickly, embarrassed she thought he meant something else. "I haven't the benefit of recognizing my own reflection and it may be that I do not originate from this town to begin with."

"I do not envy you your predicament," he said honestly. "Please know that you are most welcome to remain here as long as you please, you are no burden to us. Gilpin will tend to you and he is valued by us."

"Thank you," she said without looking up at him for fear of showing her vulnerability.

He sipped his tea again and she could sense his contemplation.

"Some of the men have spoken to other residents regarding any hearsay of missing women but nothing has come of it yet," he relayed regretfully. "I hope this will not dissuade you from hope as there are many reasons such an absence of enquiry might exist."

She nodded and looked up at him, wanting him to know that she did understand. "Between the war and sudden illness I imagine there are many scenarios," she stated straightly.

"I have heated the kettle. Would you like some tea?" he offered placatingly.

She sighed, looking back into the hallway. "No thank you, I intended on bettering my form before venturing any further activity."

He laughed warmly and quietly. "You are not unpleasant as you stand now but I understand the need for refreshment," he agreed. "Incidentally, my name is Ehren."

Meeting his gaze she felt suddenly relaxed around him and imagined she could talk to him about anything, he exuded personability. "Ehren? I like that name," she said with a smile of her own.

Now his eyes remained holding her in his vision. "I am glad it pleases you. And what has Gleda and Gilpin concocted for you? They mentioned a nom de plume of sorts."

Apprehensive at his potential reaction, she tilted her head as she announced it. "The three of us have agreed on a derivative of a name found on an advertisement, so for now I shall go by Olly."

"Olly!" he said with a laugh. "Oh it's hardly a name that is befitting a lady."

Turning her gaze to him coyly she smiled at his teasing. "No perhaps you are correct in that deduction but should I be called out from a group of ladies, I should never fear being mistaken for another."

He laughed and nodded, his smile bringing his handsome face further radiance. "But that is not wholly in part due to the name. I would assume you to stand out on your own merits."

Smiling at him, she had nearly forgotten her reason for being there but was happy to remain. "Will you be putting on a show soon?" she enquired divertingly.

Seemingly thinking on her words he shook his head as he realized her meaning. "There have been no plays for a few months due to all that is going on," he explained. "For now our profit has been wounded by the predicament and both local seamstresses have succumbed. That is why I am costumed as such now, but it does make us seem somewhat mysterious, does it not?"

She nodded. "I rather think wearing a costume at all times does increase the interest of the general population," she agreed. "I wish I knew who I was just so I could tell my confidants how interesting you and your people are."

His smile faded quicker than she expected. "Now Olly girl, I ask of you not to be afraid."

"I am not afraid," she defended quickly.

He smiled again, amused by her. "No you do not seem timid to me. I meant to say, please don't fear that you will remain as you are. Instead you could perceive this as a blessing in disguise."

Studying him curiously, she resisted any further defense. "How so?"

Sipping his tea, he placed his cup on the long counter beneath a row of white cabinets. He appeared as if he wanted to touch her or hold her arms but he didn't.

"There is a beauty in ignorance," he said slowly. "While you are unaware of what is, you are allowed the fortune of discovering joy in simple encounters. You may now find yourself to appreciate many things that you may have once taken for granted."

Suddenly in wonder of his intelligence and perception, she found herself even more consumed by his presence. He was unlike anyone she could imagine. Even without memory of others she knew him to have rare qualities.

"You suggest then that I could distinguish things as if with new eyes," she echoed his sentiment enthusiastically. "Without the sense of attachment to people or that which is material, I can now uniquely value them without resistance. Perhaps without clinging to a sense of belonging I am gifted with greater compassion."

His expression evened immediately and he stared at her without inhibition. "You have the meaning utterly," he confirmed. "I see you have much wisdom, Olly girl. Many of our wayward clan could benefit from your counsel no doubt. You are not without use due to one handicap."

She reached out and briefly touched his arms before pulling back, worrying he would misread her. "In your words alone I find so much hope that in this moment you have given me everything."

He stood back a little as if her words had affected him physically and he placed his hand on his chest, solemn but grateful. "Hope is a strong foundation, Olly; I know this to be true. Do not let go of it, for it is then that you truly lose who you are."

The loud church bell echoed out in the nearby streets and was a somber reminder of all the woes many were suffering at this time.

Taking a deep breath she was about to explain that she would heed his advice but a younger woman entered the room and the spell of the moment was now completely broken.

The lace around the neckline of the young woman's Jane Austen style dress highlighted her youthful beauty.

"Good morning, Mi lady." Her pink cheeks and eager eyes gazed over Olly as she curtsied at her playfully then went for the copper kettle on the old Victorian stove. "Is there any tea left, Ehren?" she asked sweetly. "You promised you would get me the one I like most, do you remember?"

Olly, suddenly remembering her nightgown and unfastened hair, felt terrible standing in the same room as the pretty young woman. Obviously the girl was very friendly with Ehren and her flirtatious mannerisms where not without notice.

As Ehren went to turn and reply to the pretty one, Olly quickly left the room and made a beeline directly for the door opposite; the washroom.

Chapter Three

Standing in the washroom with the door closed behind her, Olly sighed loudly and surveyed the large but semi-congested room in front of her. By its contents, it appeared that men and women alike were serviced by these facilities.

Four leather-top humidor boxes were sitting on an old wash stand in the corner next to the door, each with a male name on it; one belonged to Gilpin. She didn't see one for Ehren and then chastised herself for thinking of him so readily.

There was a key in the door lock above the knob and she turned it, checking that it locked so the door couldn't be opened. The mixed scents of various perfumes and powders sat in the air. To add to the soothing atmosphere, the sun shone in through the thick-glassed window above the claw foot tub in a way that made the whole room look misty and ethereal.

Removing her nightgown, she realized she hadn't taken off her corset, which she was grateful to part with. Undoing the drawstring on her silky drawers, she let them fall to the floor and stretched her body out with a hushed yawn.

A covered green hamper at the left corner beside the bath was obviously for communal laundry. Nonetheless, she couldn't see any name sewn onto her own undergarments so she decided she would hold on to them for now so as to not lose them.

Her bare feet almost matched the paleness of the cream colors of the mosaic tiled floor which were slightly yellowed but she could tell they were cleaned often.

On the left wall she found a pull chain toilet which she used in haste whilst studying a wider wash stand which was on the other side of it.

On the shelf beneath it were five more feminine containers for the female residents, also with names on them.

The yellow one belonged to Gleda and had been hand embroidered with flowers over a quilted satin lid.

It was then that she saw a pink glass-jeweled wicker box with the name, *Olly*, on top of it. After tending to what was necessary, she excitedly bent to retrieve the box and stood so she could place it next to the oversized bowl and pitcher that rested on the wash stand.

Opening it up, she suspected Gleda had gifted her some of her own personal toiletries and they were very nice. One paper wrapped Palmolive soap was inside of the box and she smiled, assuming it to be intentionally ironic.

Beside the soap was a pink washcloth with a full glass-bottled perfume and atomizer with an ornate Victorian era hairbrush, gold with angels on it.

Olly's own hair pins were grouped on the side of the brush which was a great relief to her as she wanted to feel fresh and new again, no matter what the day brought.

Raising her gaze just a little, she noticed the bath tub was full of folded towels but she was grateful to find water in the pitcher so she could use the washcloth to freshen her body.

As she poured the water into the large floral bowl, she noticed another note on the bottom of the wash stand and realized that it must have been under her toiletries box.

Replacing the pitcher to the top of the stand, she bent and retrieved the note. It explained that the covered hamper beneath the large gilded mirror, opposite the toilet, was for communal use.

A store had been closed and all the women's undergarments in the hamper had been donated to the theater in many sizes so she was welcome to use and keep them. Of course it was additionally recommended for her to place her name on them once the sufficient ones were acquired.

Olly was filled with an overwhelming sense of gratitude as she bathed and stared quietly at the room around her.

The people she had so far encountered were very sincere and were very trusting to take her in, but there was something mysterious about them.

So many types of people were coming and going she had to wonder whether the theater acted as a hostel for the lost and weary.

Then there was their enigmatic leader, Ehren. He had looked at her in such a way, but no, perhaps his expression could be attributed to his nature alone. Certainly his handsomeness and wit, sincerity and mysteriousness were what attracted many girls around here.

Such a dashing figure was sure to be entangled in many a love affair, though he had his secret, his current need for comfort for some assumed loss that no one uttered aloud.

Wringing out her washcloth, Olly poured the remaining water out of the bowl and into a small basin attached to the wall. Turning to the large gilded mirror she studied herself, her pale skin, slender waist and the curves of her bosom and hips.

From her days as a child until now at this age, whatever it may be, the skin had stretched in growth and created faint lines on her stomach. Her long hair hung down creating a frame around her body like a Grecian water nymph. None of what could be seen in the mirror would determine whether she was loved, or could attract love.

Perhaps the man she had dreamt of, the man with no face who gave her such feeling might have been a memory from her youth. He may have moved on and married another, how would she be aware of it? Even now he might see her and not recognize her for she might have aged since she had seen him last.

She closed her eyes against the emotion rising up inside of her. Why cry for something she could not confirm? He could have been a dream but the love she felt was as real as the hardened soap in her hands.

Quickly drying and placing the towel in the hamper, she put the soap in the wicker box and the washcloth on the side of the bath to dry. Taking out the hair pins, she only brushed her long hair for a short time then braided it and pinned it in a twirled bun at the back of her head.

She decided she would refine her style when she got back to her room but didn't wish to occupy the washroom too long in case another was in need of it.

Retrieving her corset and drawers but also selecting some new ones from the kindly donated hamper, her eyes caught a glimpse of something that surprised her; another gift.

Laid out on a small wooden bench beside the undergarment hamper, was a beautiful red damask dress, grand with gold interwoven into the sturdy but light fabric. Thin golden rope crossed against the bodice and there were slippers to match. She realized it was a costume, perhaps representing the Elizabethan era.

Her name had been pinned to a round veiled headpiece. Rushing to get on her new ivory colored undergarments, she carefully maneuvered into the adjustable costume which pulled over her head. Using the front strings she strung it tighter at the waist and the shorter sleeves were her safeguard against the August heat.

Moments later, as she left the washroom with her belongings and a smile on her face, she heard a great many voices in the theater behind the curtains. Holding her head high she felt suddenly grand in her costume and realized why actors enjoyed to dress as such, for it offered a sense of an otherwise untapped confidence.

Swishing the long skirting with satin panels, her bare feet made her feel youthful and liberated. She closed her door behind her, feeling hopeful but still with an intermingled worry that one possesses in the face of continual uncertainty.

She placed her nightgown on the bed then tidied the silk and velvet covers to make it look more presentable.

Folding her prior undergarments she placed them on the floor, just in sight so she could ask Gleda for a pen later to label them.

Though she knew Gilpin was likely waiting for her and she was hungrier even more so than before, she wanted to gift him something. Finding a smaller swatch of red silk on her bedding, she decided to make something from it.

She twirled it around with her fingers, narrow at the end then scalloped at the top to the point of fashioning a convincing version of a rose. Removing one of her thick hair pins, she found it long enough to hold the fabric in place.

Straightening the netting over the back of her braided bun, she shuffled her cold feet into the matching velvet slippers and knocked on the door that adjoined Gilpin's room. "Gilpin, are you there?"

"Yes, Olly I am here," he responded with a laugh as though it was obscure of her to ask him without giving a reason for the question.

"The washroom is unoccupied if you are in need of refreshment before we eat," she revealed.

"No I had been in there before you," he explained. "Would you like to come in?"

She smiled wide in anticipation of his response. "I must inform you for preparatory reasons that I am in possession of a gift. Would you please offer some astonishment accordingly?"

He laughed readily. "Are you asking me to act surprised, Olly?"

"Yes," she confirmed loudly against the door with a laugh of her own.

"You are quite funny," he said and she could tell he was smiling, as was she.

"Yes," she agreed, suppressing her giddy silliness. "I have discovered that I am delightful."

Now he laughed louder, and she couldn't help but join him.

—

She was under the spell of the beautiful costume and was so happy to be acknowledged in that moment that she couldn't suppress her joviality.

"Very well, Olly, consider me prepared," he called out amusedly.

With glee in her eyes, she took a deep breath and pushed the door open, but then stopped mid-step at the sight of Ehren beside her friend. "Oh, I do apologize; I did not know you had a guest."

Ehren's smile mirrored Gilpin's and it warmed her to see that he was glad for her presence.

"He's not my guest, Olly," Gilpin elucidated cheerfully. "As it stands I'm more alike to his."

Olly lowered her gaze for a moment and nodded. "Just the same I am sorry to interrupt your small assembly."

Ehren, who was sitting close to Gilpin's bed on the chair Olly had pushed up against her own door in haste earlier, laughed heartily. "I wish to see your gift," he urged her with a smile. "Gilpin promised me a thorough display of being high spirited and stunned."

She smiled at them both, each of them now dressed differently than before. Gilpin wore thin green tights and a short sleeved tunic top while Ehren was clothed in a long purple satin king's robe with a gold bejeweled crown which suited his mid length hair and sandals.

"Oh I see we are all monarchy today," she said with a smile. "Gleda had left this dress for me."

"She chooses different themes sometimes," Gilpin elucidated. "It was when she placed me as the back end of a donkey's form last winter that I didn't go outside on the day."

She laughed with Ehren as she took a few steps forward, closing the door behind her. "I dare say the requested anticipation was much too majestic for the insignificance of my offering," she said to Gilpin. "But I hope you understand that if I had anything truly in my possession I would give it to you."

Having said that, she handed him the handmade rose and curtsied.

He ventured with widened eyes to be dramatic in his response but when he actually looked at it, immediately offered a more subdued reaction.

Studying the rose in a moment of silence, it seemed to mean a lot to him and he looked up at her but then down at the floor coyly. "Aw, Olly. No one ever made something for me with their hands before. Can I wear it?"

"Wear it?" Ehren laughed.

"I would be honored by it," Olly said as she reached up and took one of her thick hair clips out and used it to fasten the rose to the neckline of Gilpin's brown tunic.

She glanced at Ehren and he too looked touched by the gesture though she was a little embarrassed by encouraging Gilpin to be eager prior to opening the door.

"They're going to eat in the hall now; do you want to come with me there?" Gilpin asked enthusiastically.

"She is not ready," Ehren interceded quickly. She concluded him to be a decisive man with a keen sense of all matters. "Would you please bring a plate to her to eat away from all of our residents?" he asked gentler. "She needs time to integrate, Gilpin."

Gilpin nodded as he stood and smoothed his hand over his thick recently brushed hair. "Gleda wanted to see her," he said in a whisper as if Olly couldn't hear him.

"You can tell her that she can visit with Olly once she is done with her own meal," Ehren said gently as if indulging an eager child.

"I will," Gilpin said as he smiled at Olly before leaving through the hallway door.

Ehren stood abruptly then took the few steps to Gilpin's unmade bed and sat on it. "Please be seated," he said, gesturing to the chair he just vacated.

She walked over and sat closer to the edge, keeping her stance poised. "Thank you."

She could feel his eyes on her and she clasped her hands in her lap and glanced at one of the Coca Cola posters on the wall.

"It was a thoughtful gesture for you to create that flower for Gilpin," he noted, waiting for her to look at him. "At times he feels left behind and your presence lifts his spirits."

"Oh, he is a dear boy," she said sincerely, trying not to look upon him too intently. "You are good people to take him in. I feel the angels have also led me to these safe confines," she mused aloud. "Do you know where I can find employment?"

His expression registered shock. "You are thinking of work at this time? Do you have any particular skill?"

She shook her head. "No doubt I have my own expertise in some occupation but I'm not aware of it," she replied with a sigh. "I am dexterous and intelligent; surely I could be made use of. It is my hopes to pay you for my board and perhaps purchase a proper gift for Gilpin."

"You display a unique selflessness, Olly." His teasing smile faded as he contemplated options while holding her in his gaze. "Most in your circumstance would be justifiably concerned by their sudden loss. Even while you have no knowledge of yourself or your family, you endeavor to please a stranger."

Glancing at him, her pulse raced, affected by him and his warm voice and earnest flattery. "Even without access to any specific recollection I know that kindness is not in the nature of all men," she said quietly.

Shifting on the chair, she leaned forward slightly and continued. "In my opinion, those who lead their endeavors with their heart should be aptly rewarded, simply because it is deserved. Your compassion for my situation will never be forgotten. As for Gilpin, for even if it is in this moment alone, he is the only family I can own so my consideration of him stems from sincere affection."

Ehren appeared impressed and humbled but he didn't get the chance to speak for the sound of cutlery falling on the hallway floor ceased his reply.

They turned their heads to see Gilpin standing in the doorway with an ornate tray of food. Carefully bending to retrieve what he had dropped, Olly noticed that he was blushing considerably and she realized he had heard her remark.

Ehren must have realized it too and quickly offered a light distraction. "Is that Jell-O you have there, Gil?"

Gilpin wiped the spoon on the side of his tights and grinned. "Yes, the iceman came yesterday so the girls made some up for us," he explained as he handed the tray to Olly.

She looked down and noticed that the homemade lemonade had a hint of coolness to it which she was grateful for. The china bowl was quite full of red Jell-O while a generous amount of crackers were beside the bowl on a fabric serviette.

She held up one of the sweets baked in the shape of a camel. "Are these Barnum's Animals Crackers?" she asked, wondering if she had actually remembered something.

Gilpin nodded as he set two crates in front of her so she could place her tray on it. "Yes but we just call them animals," he said with a laugh. "Clarissa, who you met this morning, gave you more crackers than the others because she feels sorry for you and thinks you're real beautiful."

Olly placed the camel cracker in her mouth and stared at him, stunned. "She thought that of *me*?"

Gilpin sat on his bed beside Ehren and they exchanged a surprised look. "Why shouldn't she think such a thing?" Ehren enquired seriously.

Sipping her drink, Olly shrugged and avoided their stares. "Oh I don't know, I suppose I hadn't anticipated such a statement to come from a young beauty like herself," she said straightly. "Never mind," she added, embarrassed that she aired her insecurities in their presence. "It was very kind of her to give me extra; I'm rather famished I must confess."

"I'm sorry we could not offer you more," Ehren said, leaning forward and playfully taking one of her crackers, which made her laugh. "The food cart will arrive in town within the week and our supplies will be replenished then."

She swallowed a spoonful of Jell-O and was soothed by the taste of the sugary gelatin. "Oh no, please, you have been too generous already, you need not apologize. I would still like to know if you could tell me where I might find work."

Ehren wiped the crumbs from his hands then crossed his arms, asserting his kingly stature. "I can not offer you financial remuneration but if you are willing to barter for your residence, we are in need of certain assistances."

She politely swallowed her cracker and sipped her lemonade and nodded. "Please, I am not too proud for any position. I do not wish to be a burden and would be grateful for the opportunity to compensate you."

Ehren shook his head. "You are no trouble to us, Olly. You bring new life to these old walls; please know you are a welcome presence."

Olly nodded shyly. "Thank you," she said seriously before taking her last cracker and handing it to him cheerfully.

He took it and laughed, surprised by her strange timing. "Since the Spanish flu has begun to take its toll, we are very conscious of keeping the contagion from this building. If you could please clean the theater area and the side rooms, it would benefit us greatly."

"Of course," she said, dabbing her lips with the serviette.

Gilpin discretely tugged on Ehren's sleeve as if he opposed the idea. Ehren pat Gilpin's lap to pacify him and the exchange was left without further issue.

Suddenly a knock came at the door and they all turned to it. "Gilpin, is Ms. Olly in there with you?"

"Yes, you can come in!" he called back to her.

Ehren stood and nodded at her. "I have business to attend to, Ms. Olly but it has been pleasant making your acquaintance," he said with a smile. "Gilpin, I would like to speak with you, if you may?"

He nodded and followed him out of the room, closing the door behind them.

Gleda, who was wearing a mid length white toga, looked back at the door then offered her a big smile. "Handsome, is he not?" she asked as she loosened the rope belt at her waist then tapped the end of the poster she was holding against her flat white shoes.

"Ehren?"

She nodded before taking a place close to her on the corner of Gilpin's bed.

"I agree he is quite striking," she said with only a modest smile in the case of him having attachments she was unaware of. "Though I'm certain that all women here make the same observation," she added carefully. "I have seen how he is looked upon in admiration."

Gleda's expression evened and instead of being jovial in her delivery, seemed contemplative at Olly's remark. "His skin is just that which holds his good spirit. It is not only all that we see that makes a person attractive."

Olly sincerely liked her and smiled, showing her agreeance before expressing it. "I concur wholeheartedly. I must say that he has done well in both respects for he is also very gracious and amiable."

"That he is dear girl," she said as she pat Olly's hand with a smile in her eyes. "Do you think you have a love somewhere?" she asked.

Staring at the rolled up poster on Gleda's lap she shook her head. "I can't be sure, Gleda," she said quietly and seriously. "I dreamt of a man last night."

Gleda's long eyelashes lowered somewhat over her pretty hazel eyes. "What happened? Do you think it was a memory?"

Olly shrugged. "I couldn't know, but the way I felt being there with him is something that remains with me still. We were surrounded by beautiful green hills, it was like a memory but dreams are often nonsense."

Standing now, with an expression of true interest, Gleda adjusted her rope again and thought on it. "What of his appearance? Did he speak to you?"

"No," Olly replied solemnly. "I did not see his face or much of him; it was only a sensation, a feeling. Still, I do not know what to make of it."

"You will find your way home." Gleda said as she looked upon her sympathetically before changing her tone. "I have a present for you."

"Oh dear." Olly's smile faded quickly. "If I had known, I would have created one for you in return, I feel terrible for it."

Gleda laughed as she smoothed the top of her waist length hair that was styled into one braid. "Like the flower you created for young Gil, perhaps?"

Olly frowned, worried she was mocking her. "Well, that would have been likely I am not sure what else I can create," she explained.

"Oh Olly," Gleda sighed as she reached out to momentarily place her warm hand on her face. "You touched his heart and with that, his smile touched ours. He showed all of the girls and every man there what his wonderful friend, Olly had made, God bless him."

Tears fell from Olly's eyes in a way that she was unable to control the flow of them.

Gleda, shocked, quickly raced to push away the crates and knelt in front of her, taking her hands in hers. "Please don't cry, sweet girl. The news was supposed to make you happy."

Olly nodded as she reached past her for the cotton handkerchief to wipe her face.

"I'm sorry, Gleda. I don't know what came over me. I feel so honored to have him as a friend in such a short time but what if he is the only friend I will ever know?"

"I am your friend," she insisted with a smile.

Olly looked down at her, finding her sincere but she shook her head. "But you have just met me," she said, sniffing lightly.

"You just met you too," Gleda said with a laugh. "And you can tell you are a good person I'm supposing, and so do I. Don't worry that you won't be liked here, Ms. Olly, I only give presents to Gilpin and the loveliest of Queens."

Looking down, Olly smiled as she remembered her costume. "I feel very grand in this dress, it is very beautiful," she said, suddenly feeling very pensive. "Will you remain my friend should I leave here and discover who I am?"

Gleda stood and curtsied. "It is a promise because your spirit shines through all your uncertainty. I can't help but like you. You remind me of an angel."

"Perhaps I will never find my way home if it were true. It is a long way to fall from the heavens," Olly said with a laugh.

Gleda laughed too as she pointed to the poster. "You must look at it now."

Unraveling it carefully, Olly stretched out the poster of a beautiful lady in a flowing gown, holding her hand to her temple. It was an advertisement for Tarrants Seltzer Aperient. "Oh Gleda!" she said with a laugh, pointing to the woman. "Are you making light of my condition?"

Gleda clapped her hands together and bent over with a loud but feminine laugh. "Oh, how could it be helped? What better than to gift you with something appropriate? This poor lady has a head ailment as well."

Olly stood and feeling brave took a step to hug her new friend who was happy to reciprocate warmly. "It is unlikely the seltzer will return my memory but when I look upon this advertisement I will always smile so for that I am grateful."

"Laughter nourishes the heart," Gleda said smiling at her.

Looking down at her dress she remembered Ehren's offer. "Oh, Ehren said I could clean the theater and adjoining rooms. Do you have anything more appropriate that I could don for the task?"

"This is what I wear while I clean the linens and such," Gleda said, presenting her toga costume. "If it is no bother to you, I have another you can wear so you do not clean as a queen."

"Yes, that would be better, thank you."

"I will bring it to you," Gleda said, walking to the hallway door. "In the interim, you'd best put that on your wall; seems like the room needs new life in it."

Chapter Four

After removing her grand medieval costume, the feeling of the plain feed sack fabric of her white toga costume seemed rather lackluster. Nonetheless, she re-pinned her long hair into a low pompadour style.

Looking around without going through the boxes, she saw a strand of pink plastic flowers and carefully picked one off to manipulate into her hair. She enjoyed color, she liked how it looked, and even the lady with the headache on her poster was at the forefront of a colorful background.

Taking a deep breath, she left her room, stopping briefly to adjust the fit of the slightly large low white shoes that Gleda provided with the costume.

She pushed the clunky wheeled mop bucket and balanced the mop inside of it, careful to not allow the water to splash out of it as she moved. Having tucked the feather duster into her own rope belt that was tied around her slender waist, she slowly approached the tall velvet curtains.

A strange sensation came over her as if each moment of newness was the beginning of a chapter of a book, a discovery. Should she have had her memory, she would be more apt to experience it differently, with the confidence of one who stood by her personal truths. This however was not a luxury afforded her and anxiety built up inside of her along with nervous anticipation.

She was just cleaning, it seemed a simple enough task but what would these theater folk think of her as she dusted in the shadows? Would she go unnoticed and fall into a feeling of being lesser? She couldn't allow it.

Gleda insisted she was her friend no matter what, and surely Gilpin was. She could hold her head high. After all, Gleda was washing linens in a similar outfit and she didn't seem like the kind of woman to feel lesser even if someone suggested she was.

Ehren didn't treat her like that either, she mused as she pulled the right side of the curtain open enough so she could get herself and the bucket through. He treated her as an equal and was sincerely kind in his approach.

She immediately noticed the wide broom leaning against the right inside stone wall, where Gleda had said it would be. Reaching for it, knowing that it would be more sensible to start with sweeping, she pressed it into the crevice that bordered the wall and the shiny wooden floor.

A great deal of dust was gathered there, along with fabric threads and other particles. Intentionally not looking up straight away, she suddenly liked the idea of sweeping. To distract herself with a menial but determined task would surely occupy her mind.

As she made her way with the broom, sweeping everything into an organized pile along the first wall, she looked around for a dust pan. It was then that she glanced up and was surprised at the vastness of the room.

At the center of the gilded cherub painted ceiling was a multi tiered glass chandelier and to the left was a grand stage with wooden floors and a couple of chairs upon it, as if having been abandoned a while.

Unknowingly, she had been thinking so hard and intently, that she hadn't paid any attention to the talking around her. The wooden chairs were all stacked up along the other walls, and opposite the curtains was a large table with food on it.

She realized that this was not only the place where the audience would sit, but also the place where the mysterious theater dwellers ate. A couple of young men were removing the food as she watched them, and one winked at her and she smiled back.

It was then that a small group of people caught her eye as they stood talking and eating in front of the table. Three ladies, one being Clarissa in her pink dress, and the other two being in white nurse like aprons, were talking with Ehren jovially.

All three of them, the pretty Clarissa included, had very radiant skin, almost to the point of it emanating an electrical type glow. Two men in white coats and white pants were standing close to them, discussing something of an apparently serious nature.

Three tall people, two men and one woman, were standing closer to the stage near the wall. They had goat like features like the man who entered her room yet each with their own distinct differences. The lady wore a long modern dress and hat while the men wore business suits rather than costumes. While holding each others hands, they exchanged glances but no words.

Ensuring not to be caught staring nor be lax in her duties, she quickly spotted the dust pan against the left wall of the curtained entrance and quietly ventured to retrieve it. As she bent to pick it up, a pair of shiny black shoes stopped directly in front of her.

Jumping back and gasping, she held her hand to her chest and looked up to see the man from earlier. "Oh gosh, I do apologize," she said sincerely. "My thoughts were so consumed in other things that I was not paying attention to my immediate surroundings. Please forgive my reaction."

A glint in his pale green eyes showed his amusement and he smiled at her. It was not as if he had fur on his face, he did have a short beard and moustache, but just a very goat like face. Just the same he looked upon her kindly and she relaxed in his presence.

"You mustn't hold your actions in such contrition," he said with a light chuckle. "If I were burdened with your circumstance, my thoughts would also be in permanent preoccupation.

"That is very understanding of you," she said, taking a shallow but intentional breath while taking the dust pan handle into her left hand and straightening. "I wish to explain my earlier actions—,"

He ceased her sentence with a wave of his hand and she briefly noticed his attire to be very seventeenth century, with a silky blue vest and dark blue pants. "Young Gil detailed me on your situation and your reaction was highly understandable. I hope my appearance does not hold you in guarded diffidence."

She shook her head but kept her voice low. "I should be the one offering you such a statement," she said sincerely. "You are the one attired as a lord while I am but a castle maid."

He laughed louder now and she felt a wave of true appreciation as if joy had sprung from his body. "The manner of garb is hardly an indicator of status." Lifting one of his hands to his head to run a hand over it, she realized the gray color of his hair contradicted the youth in his countenance. She would have guessed him also to be close to her age.

For a moment she felt compelled to comfort him further for maybe other people in the outside world weren't so kind to his uniqueness.

Reaching out her right hand, she timidly placed it on his and looked up into his eyes. "I find you thoroughly personable; I imagine you are even more regal than what is presented in your costume. I will now greet you with equal reverence should you approach me again."

His smile faded a little and she felt that her remark had detained him in a moment of poignancy. Swallowing hard, he took her one hand into both of his and looked into her eyes. "I am Clarence, Milady, and if you should not address me thus, please call me friend."

"I shall call you both perhaps," she said with a laugh. "My substituted name is Olly; my prior moniker is unbeknownst to me."

"How do you find the theater, Olly?" he asked with a smile in his eyes.

She glanced past him briefly before responding. "I have little experience with it so far, but I find it to be quite magnificent in presentation," she replied honestly.

He nodded, obviously agreeing. "And you have befriended the ever joyful, Gleda and the debonair, Ehren as well?"

"Yes they have been very kind, I am fortunate to have been found where I was."

Clasping his hands behind his back, he tilted his head to look her over. "Perhaps it was by providence. When memory loss is forced upon a duchess, it is only in the most convenient of locales."

She laughed lightly, enjoying his creativity, something that she sensed about her own personality. "Do tell me, Clarence friend, was a duchess *known* to be in this area recently?"

With only half of his lips smiling to one side, she anticipated a spot of mischief in his nature. "Not at all, but perhaps you were in disguise to flee from the arms of an unscrupulous duke."

Laughing again, she looked down to make sure that dust was not falling from the pan onto her toga. "Unfortunately my disguise was so convincing, *I* was also fooled by it."

Amusement and appreciation was all through his expression and suddenly she couldn't even see any difference in him at all. "Oh you are a joy, Milady. I wish for us to talk one day. Perhaps between the two of us we can muster a tale worthy of a play."

"I would not shy away from the challenge," she encouraged. "Please, do tell," she now whispered. "Why are those people dressed that way? Are they doctors and nurses?"

After a few steps, he turned his body so he now stood beside her and she looked up at him as he gazed at the people across the room. He was about to speak to her but stopped as he glanced down at her and smiled. "Why do you look at me so?"

Tugging the front of her toga discretely for comfort, she decided he was approachable enough to be frank with.

"Because since I lost my memory, I am consciously seeing things in their initial timing," she explained sincerely. "I want to remember this moment when I first looked upon the lovely face of my fascinating friend, Clarence."

With a glisten of impending tears in his eyes he nodded before speaking. "Your words are like flowers from the beloved duchess. Such sentiment has now prohibited me from forgetting this moment also."

She smiled at him, feeling this moment in equal gratitude, thinking upon Ehren's words about seeing the beauty in simple things. "My words are all I can give but I am glad to form them in a manner that is deserving of you."

"Beautiful, truly," he stated graciously, glancing at her before setting his eyes on the white coated men. "They are not doctors by qualification but their roles substitute for many healers that are absent," he explained stoically. "There were only two here in town and one succumbed to the flu while the other has not returned from the war."

"So these men do the work of doctors?" she enquired quietly. "Do they leave here for a specific facility?"

He shook his head. "They do their best and are quite talented in their care. The ladies that you see are often with them to tend to the sick that are laid out inside the restaurant beside the theater."

Gazing only briefly on the radiant women as they spoke to Ehren with dazzling smiles; she stopped to think on Clarence's words. "Why are they in a restaurant?"

By the grave inflection in his tone, Olly assumed it to be something personal to him. "The good people who had ownership of the restaurant had taken ill only a week ago and have now left us for heaven. Their children were dispatched to their elders in a distant city but the towns people agreed it to be the best place to confine the ill," he explained quietly. "It is rather large and open and many of us can tend to them more easily due to the vicinity."

Olly tried to be discrete but watched him as he talked, noticing she somehow observed feelings underneath the words. "Has anyone at the theater taken ill?"

"No, we are blessed," he said, looking down at her with a warm smile.

"Yes indeed you are," she agreed while she pondered the situation. "I would like to assist them once I am done here," she added seriously.

Suddenly more alert and less interactive he straightened his stance and nodded formally at her. She had seen him glance behind her and she wondered if he was meant to be doing something else. "I will broach the matter with them and offer awareness of your presence should you choose to venture there."

"Thank you, Clarence," she said with a nod of her own.

"It has been an honor to make your acquaintance, Duchess," he said with a ceremonial bow before walking over to the men.

Olly realized she hadn't gotten much work done and decided to put her efforts into it more wholeheartedly. Obviously the cleaning so far had precluded the residents from becoming ill so it was a matter of importance.

Turning around quickly to seize the broom, she found it to be in the possession of a man directly behind her.

In that moment, equally as startled as before, she briefly gasped and took a deep breath consecutively, coming out as an audible scoff. "You would think with my other senses so engaged in activity that I would be in need of eyes at every angle," she said abruptly. "I am sorry I did not hear you approach."

Somewhat shorter than her, and displaying considerable age, his long gray hair and beard suited the biblical appearance of his long white robe.

In spite of this, he had no wrinkles and the serenity in his face was calming as he subtly smiled at her. "Men were not created with eyes at their backs, for they must always look forward and never be conflicted by the vision of what they leave behind."

He held the broom out for her and she took it quietly. "Yes there is considerable wisdom in that," she said seriously. "And you look like the kind of man who would know better than most."

Smiling wider now, she was grateful he was receptive to her humor. "You wish to aid those who suffer in our midst?" His deep blue eyes looked her over quickly. "Perhaps such a virtue will be met with the recognition of another should you go there."

Frowning, she contemplated his words, not having thought of that when she proposed it. "My offer was sincere, I assure you. I suppose there is a chance that someone will know me, but I want to help. Those poor people are in much worse condition than me in this moment. They know who they have lost and their suffering is great. I want to help them *and* the people who live here."

He nodded, not conveying any judgment in his expression; rather she felt that he was appreciative of what she said. "Your honor is not in question, dear lady. I will take you and the lad there tomorrow, he brings smiles to them. I am certain your compassion will not be discarded."

"Thank you, I am grateful for your trust," she said while lowering her gaze a little, feeling the need to offer him a sign of respect. "May I ask your name?"

Initially not responding, she looked up to see him smiling in a way that showed he was entertained by her actions. "I am Aylward and that is the name you may address me by."

Unsure of whether to mirror his amusement, she studied his face. "That is quite an interesting name," she said.

"I *am* interesting," he confirmed with no particular tone of mockery, yet she felt he was being playful. "What name has been assigned to you?"

Realizing he must have had prior knowledge of her situation, she was glad not to have to explain her presence. "For now I am called, Olly."

Smiling, only with his eyes, he persisted in his straight-fowardness. "Mr. Clarence addressed you as, Duchess."

She nodded, unable to argue his point. "Yes, this is indisputable. I can only say that my true name eludes all of us so any title is sufficient as long as I am aware of it in advance of being called upon."

He laughed low and raspy but she knew his reaction to be genuine. "This is fair."

Assuming him to be the owner of the theater, she wanted to ask him more questions but he looked at her in such a peculiar way she couldn't help but study him openly. With just a slight smile, it was as if he was reading thoughts from her expressions. "How many people are stricken by the flu?" she asked, pushing her strange thoughts aside.

"More than half of those who resided here and a third have perished prior to that number," he replied without seeming somber about it. "I approached you for the intention to offer you further occupation," he said as he clasped his thin hands in front of him with his robe sleeves hanging down like bells.

"Oh, yes of course. Do you wish me to clean something else after I have finished with the hall and theater?"

He nodded, but not overly so as if the act itself was not serene enough unless offered in moderation. "There," he said, pointing to the table, which was now cleared of food. "No, past that," he added.

She followed his gaze to a wide arched opening behind the table that led to a lobby beyond it. "When you enter there, you will find an indoor walkway. There you will journey to your right and the second door will open into a dressing room. This is the one employed by the female tenants."

She nodded, making sure to pay close attention. "Do you wish me to clean that room?"

"This is so."

With her hands occupied with broom and pan, she wasn't able to extend any physical gesture of acknowledgment so she smiled intentionally. "I will tend to it and ensure I will be thorough in my actions."

Gazing at her with a glint in his eyes, he nodded but smiled slightly as if his serious nature belied less staid traits. "We will meet tomorrow, Questa," he said, turning from her."

"Please, wait," she urged quietly but adamantly. "Is that your name for me or is it simply a word that I do not understand?"

He stopped but replied without looking back at her. "It means, *seeking*, and until you have ended your journey with the haze consuming your knowledge, I will call you thus."

Unsure of how to reply, she let him walk away without furthering the conversation. Now more fixated on the job at hand, she was still wary of those around her, given the two scares she had in a short span of time.

The hall seemed quiet as she began to sweep again, but she still heard some murmurs and felt she was being watched. Turning her head ever so slightly, she could see Ehren, standing where he had been before.

The two apron wearing ladies had left, obviously with the doctors, and Clarence and his friends had also departed, leaving Clarissa alone with him.

Thinking again of Gleda and her confidence, she made sure to smile at him politely but she was very conscious of her drab outfit and couldn't help but look down at it reactively.

She refused to look up again, too vulnerable in his sights, too weak in comparison to the younger prettier girl whose clothing and countenance likely outshone hers.

Believing their chatter to be done with, she assumed they had departed from the main hall, leaving her there alone and she was relieved for the solitude.

Perhaps an hour or two passed as she dusted swept and brushed it all into a large cardboard box provided for her. Her toga costume was clinging to her clammy skin as she polished furniture and set pieces and wall trim.

Strangely she found herself humming but wasn't sure of the tune or why it was there for her to access. Nonetheless she found words forming and she was singing loud enough for it to echo against the stone and wooden walls.

"*After you've gone and left me crying, after you've gone there's no denying. You'll feel blue, you'll feel sad. You'll miss the dearest pal you've ever had!*"

Her step suddenly felt lighter and knowing she was not being witnessed in this moment, she spun around gaily using the broom as a dancing partner. Tears sprung to her eyes as she realized she remembered a song. Perhaps Gleda would recognize it.

Finally, she stood beneath the old walnut trimmed frame of the wide entranceway and looked back into the theater, studying her handiwork.

Suddenly very conscious of her smile, a chill ran over her body, making her feel beautiful in that moment. Even though it was just cleaning, something mundane and by all accounts, insignificant, she felt proud of how shiny the floors and wall trim were.

—

She had looped the very heavy green damask stage curtains onto their original brass hooks in a way that gave it a stronger grandness and beautiful symmetry. Staring now at the stage she liked how she had placed the furniture pieces as if invisible people sat on the antique chairs talking to each other.

For a moment her thoughts turned to Ehren and she wondered if he performed in the plays. Certainly such a man would attract the attention of the women in the audience, likely the lovely actresses that performed with him too.

The main hall was very large, and this was not only confirmed by sight but also by just how long it had taken to clean it, but it must have been amazing to see filled with people. She envisioned someone seated at the piano on the main floor to the lower left of the stage, playing enthusiastically while the actors expressed their prose in beautiful regalia.

Yet as she momentarily leaned against the doorframe she realized how wonderful it was to be enjoying the theater in its moment of silence and abandonment.

That is who she was now; an empty theater. She was strengthened by her barrenness and solitude for she was not shackled by drama or conflict. Any person or event that had caused her pain prior to this moment was gone from her mind; there was comfort in her ignorance.

Smiling, she thought about the beautiful red and gold velvet table runners she had found behind a dusty bench backstage. It appeared they had fallen behind it some time ago and after polishing the bench, she brought them out and gently set them up on the back of the antique chairs to ornament them.

As one final gesture for the unsuspecting actor who would find it, she found a gentleman's silk brown handkerchief. With this she created another rose and tied it neatly before placing it on one of the chairs.

After taking one more look, she turned back to the hallway and noticed an extended narrow hall area with five or six rooms running off it. She mused that perhaps Ehren slept in one of them but decided it best not to let her thoughts lean to him too often.

Just as Aylward had mentioned, she found the ladies dressing room, addressed as such, on the first door on the left. Knocking on it first, but receiving no response, she slowly opened the door and let it swing open all the way around to take the full view of it in.

Dresses, gowns and all variety of costumes were hanging on racks from ceiling to floor. There were so many of them that they were crammed tightly together yet the affect of all the color was inspiring and exhilarating.

This room was considerably larger than the storage rooms her and Gilpin slept in. Large extended wooden counters extended out from the stone walls between the racks of dresses.

Bringing her broom in, she swept up the light dusting on the old wooden floors but found the room to be quite clean already. Large canisters of theater cosmetics sat on the counters between grand jewelry pieces and hair pins.

She made sure to lift every piece one at a time, ensuring to place them back exactly as she found them after polishing the counters. The room was filled with floral fragrances and the light scent of people who had occupied it at various times.

Certainly during a performance, there could be many of them changing in there all at the same time. Olly smiled as she thought about how they must gaily chatter when they were not in performance.

There was something fanciful and festive about this room and she imagined she would love to be part of such a place, such a lifestyle. Only a short time passed and she had already cleaned the room entirely and allowed herself a moment's indulgence to look at the costumes.

Running her fingers along the long princess type dresses, she wondered what kind of lady she was. Had she been a part of high society? Would she have once shunned the likes of these theater people?

She couldn't know and a sudden feeling of guilt overcame her in reaction to her thought. Certainly if she was too reserved to appreciate the openness and creativity of such compassionate people, then she was glad to have her memory rid of such a notion.

Staring into a large oval mirror on the wall, she made a promise to herself to never stop showing her appreciation for these people and to never treat them lesser no matter who she was.

Even with her pale skin clammy and glistening, she was pleased with her appearance and her large blue eyes reflected a special type of vigor in them. She was proud of herself in this moment.

She would concentrate her efforts on making others laugh and smile and heal and perhaps the angels would allow her to find the man from the hills in return for her good deeds.

Either way she wanted to do good for others. She wanted to be helpful and return the kindness already shown to her in this brief time. Glancing at a counter behind her in the reflection of the mirror, something shiny caught her eye.

Spinning around she quickly approached it. On the second counter, between a large modern day Edwardian hat and a faux pearl crown, laid a gold ring with a large round ruby at its center.

She didn't know much about gems but by the look of it, the ruby was real rather than one of the costume pieces and it was shiny and captivatingly beautiful. There was something so unusual about it. The gold band that held it was twisted and ornate and it appeared to be considerably old, yet well loved.

For a moment she experienced a feeling she couldn't explain. Did she have a ruby once? She couldn't be sure, but the color warmed her and for just a second she thought of the man in the hills. Who could he be?

Reaching for the ring to look at it better, she quickly pulled her hand back as the door opened and two ladies entered the room. They were young and attractive like Clarissa, and equally radiant and ageless.

They stopped in the doorway, surprised to find her there, but in no way perturbed by her presence. They both smiled at her graciously, and sincerely and then nodded respectfully which she gathered was custom around the theater.

"I am sorry to startle you," Olly apologized, as she moved aside so they could enter without being compelled to greet her. "I was told to clean this room, but I am done now."

The girl with the long brown hair and auburn peasant dress looked around appreciatively. Meanwhile the one with the blonde hair tied in incomplete braids and similar dress in blue, approached her with joy in her eyes. "It looks very well. Thank you for returning life into this room. We were hoping to find something new to wear before we venture into town. Would you like to stroll with us to the park?"

Olly considered it but felt it would take too much time to better herself and acquire an appropriate outfit for such a thing. "It is very kind of you to offer, but I must decline for I am not quite attired for a princess stroll at this moment. I do hope you both enjoy your walk."

"Thank you," she said, politely and genuinely. "Please do not discredit your reflection, Mi lady. Ehren and Gleda have said you have a magic about you and as I look upon you, I feel kindly toward your countenance also."

Olly could feel her expression even; in fact she was certain they could see the shock on her face. "That is a remarkable thing to note of a stranger," she relayed honestly as she reached for her broom coyly. "What is your name?"

"I am Lillian and my dear friend who stands at my side, is Esther. We are quite engaged by what has been told to us about you and please do not fear your acceptance here. All of us have our daily mundanities and domestic requirements. Esther had glimpsed you in Gleda's favored queen dress earlier and had remarked that you cast quite an elegant shadow."

"I would have thought you were genuine royalty had I not recognized the dress," Esther chimed in jovially.

Olly laughed, relaxed by their sweet natures and hospitality. "I am grateful for you saying so," she said honestly. "I believe one of the ladies here has left her ring behind," she added, pointing to it. "It doesn't appear to be costume at all."

Lillian and Esther exchanged a quick glance at each other before looking over at the ring. "Thank you," Lillian said with a smile.

Olly nodded politely before approaching the door and smiling at them again before closing it behind her.

Chapter Five

The following morning, Olly woke just before the sun rose completely. With only a faint light coming through the thin window beside her bed, she assumed it to still be relatively early. Nonetheless she was excited to see what they day would bring.

After having cleaned the theater the previous day, she had gotten quite tired and she cleansed herself briefly with her washcloth then retired to her room. She had not seen anything of Gleda or Gilpin to occupy her time that afternoon so instead concentrated her efforts on tidying her room to make it look more inhabitable.

In the early evening, one of the goat men had brought her dinner, which for now, he apologized, was the same as breakfast, but he was in quite a rush and had left without introduction. The fatigue of her work and the dullness from the lack of activity had her retire early.

Fortunately she had slept through the entire night without incident and awoke now to feel more vibrant than she had the previous day. As she reached for an Altoids mint that she placed on the small burgundy table beside the bed, someone knocked on the door.

She quickly sat up and looked over at the wooden crates that she had pressed up against the hallway door for safety reasons. "Hello?" she called out curiously.

"Ms. Olly," came a whisper. "It's me, Gleda. I have a gift for you. Are you awake?"

Olly got out of bed and tidied her silk and velvet pieces, hoping that after yesterday's efforts, Gleda would be impressed by the room's organization. "I am awake now that you have mentioned a gift," she teased.

"I wouldn't doubt it." Gleda laughed. She sounded as if she was struggling with something.

"Well I have a gift for you too," Olly announced, glad that she had created something for her. "Did you bring me a poster?"

"No, it is something larger than that," came the amused reply.

Olly looked down at the silk flower in her hands. She had used a thread and needle to painstakingly thread a few of the animals crackers onto it. "I'm not sure I should let you in then, Gleda. You might be disappointed by my offering. Perhaps you should slip my gift under the door and I will decide if I should hastily create you something better."

Gleda laughed loud but then reduced it to a snicker, probably due to the early hours. "Oh you silly girl. Let me in before I lose feeling in my arms."

Olly pushed the crates aside and eagerly opened the door to be greeted by the large hand-painted horn of a beautiful gramophone. Gleda pushed past her politely, dropping a heavy leather bound album of records in the process.

Olly bent to retrieve the album and placed it on the empty crates near Gilpin's door, which she had covered with some blue silk fabric she had found in one of the boxes. She then quickly rushed to remove her glass of water and Altoids from the burgundy table near her bed so Gleda could set the gramophone down.

"Oh, Gleda. I do love music, you make me so happy," Olly said as she gazed at the vibrant brown funnel horn that extended from the one edge of the wooden box.

Gleda smiled then walked across to the get the album to flip through it. "How can you be sure you like music?" she asked curiously and genuinely as she pulled a record out of the sleeve and placed it on the turntable.

"I was singing," Olly announced excitedly. "I don't even know how I knew the words but I sang them with a melody."

Gleda seemed very pleased with the news and smiled at her before setting the needle on a thick record. She then adjusted the rope around her toga dress and Olly realized that she must have intended to clean again this day. "I am sure you sing very well too," Gleda added.

Olly blushed and then even more so as she realized that she was in her nightgown. She brought her long braided hair forward for the sake of distraction and modesty. "The theater was empty so regardless of my skill, I was well received."

Gleda laughed loudly as the crackling of the piano music surprised them both. She fidgeted with a couple of pins that kept her long hair out of her way then sat on the edge of the one chair in the room, a plain wooden one, quite old and unornamented.

"I am sorry to have called upon you so early. I have another dress for you; it is one of my favorites," she divulged excitedly.

"I love to see the costumes," Olly enthused. "What color is it?"

"It is green," she replied dismissively. "But shall I tell you the story first?"

"Oh yes, please do."

Gleda leaned forward with a smile on her face that gave away the tone of her tale before she spoke it. "I was the last to wear it in a Shakespeare play this past fall and just as a handsome actor was about to make all manner of love professions for me, I tripped right over the front of it!"

"You did?" Olly asked, trying to hide her smile, even though Gleda recalled it with amusement. "What did you do?"

"Nothing at first, but then the lovely man on stage with me remained in character and got onto the floor in front of me as if it was part of the play," she replied with a shake of the head and a blush filled chuckle. "I am certain the audience was not convinced, but when he laid down on his stomach and reached his hand out to me, it was a moment I'll never forget."

"Oh that is a wonderful memory, what a sweet man," Olly said but she sensed something melancholic in the delivery of her story. "Where is he now?"

"Who?"

"The kind man who was on stage with you that day."
With her smile fading, her voice croaked and she cleared it as she spoke. "Nathaniel has been gone some time now. His work has kept him from here for many months."

Olly watched as her eyes lowered, covering tears that threatened to fall and she spoke to her gently. "Even though I see that all things occur from necessity and for reason, I can not completely console myself regarding the unfairness I encounter in many things."

Gleda shook her head, and immediately tried to regain her composure. She reached behind the table where she had set the gramophone and gave the pretty sage green dress to her. "Olly, don't give up hope. We all experience pain and fear but hope is important to keep even when there is nothing but pain and fear in sight."

Olly nodded as she touched the fabric of the sturdy silk on the top layer of the tiered lace-trimmed dress. The long sleeves were dainty and bell shaped and the waist had ties attached at the side so it could fit different women. "Thank you. I am grateful to you," Olly said sincerely. "Even though I don't remember what happened before now, I know I could not imagine not calling you my cherished friend."

Gleda pat her hand then wiped a tear from her own cheek. "You will never have to worry about such a thing, so do not imagine it."

She turned away respectfully so Olly could dress. "Today is a new day, Ms. Olly," she said more enthusiastically. "Tell me, do you remember anything at all?"

Olly gave it some thorough thought, for certainly not all memories came without attempt. Nonetheless, not one moment of relevant feeling presented itself in her mind.

"No, I'm afraid not. All I recall are my moments since Gilpin found me, but none before that time," she replied solemnly as she finished fastening her camisole and drawers before pulling the dress over her head. She then put on her white shoes from the previous day, not seeing any alternative around.

Gleda, sensing that she was finished, turned back around.

Olly suddenly noticed the unique beauty in her new friend's face and the cheer in her pretty hazel eyes. She seemed on the outset, a very personable and relatable woman yet Olly could sense from her a strong intelligence, as if it was a trait she was undervaluing.

"Did you dream of the man again?"

The jovial music was relaxing Olly in quite a literal way as she sat on the edge of the bed. The beauty of the flattering long dress gave her a distinctly confident poise as she tugged on the ends of it to cover her bare ankles.

"Why yes, I do think I did, but nothing particular stood out from the last time," she said thoughtfully before meeting Gleda's curious gaze. "Do you suppose then that such a dream would no longer be considered happenstance?"

She nodded considerably. "Providence is in every moment, Ms. Olly," Gleda said, as she leaned forward, her white shoed feet neatly placed together. "To dream of the same man *twice*? He must have been in your heart to find his way to your mind more than once, certainly."

For a moment, Olly's heart raced a little. Perhaps this man was real and she would be able to find him. "Are there any grassy hills close to here at all?"

Contemplative as she stared at the small window near Olly's bed, Gleda considered the question quietly. "None that I recall," she replied apologetically. "But my travels are not extensive. It's not to say there aren't any."

Olly nodded, believing that her friend was trying to console her but the likelihood of him being near was not in her favor. Not wanting to seem ungrateful, she quickly changed the subject by handing Gleda the silk flower she made.

The smile on her face was reward in itself. Studying it, she finally let out a heartfelt laugh. "How did you do this?"

"I discovered a box of many trinkets and domestic tools," Olly replied. "Of course there was a needle and thread in there and it was the only decoration I could find to ornament your flower."

Gleda tilted her head ever so slightly and gazed upon her with true appreciation. "You are like no other, Olly," she said seriously before straightening and evening her tone. "Should I eat these crackers that you have toiled to attach to my gift?"

"I wouldn't recommend it," Olly replied cheerfully. "In fact, I doubt you should keep them there long. It was a matter of gesture over practicality I'm afraid."

Gleda held the silky stem in both of her dainty hands and smiled at her. "What else did you find in your hunt for treasure, Milady?"

Frowning as a reaction from a quick observation, Olly suddenly expressed her thought before she offered a response for the question. "Gleda, why do you call me that in particular?"

"What are you referring to?"

"I find so many address me as, *Milady*. Is that because I am assumed to be older than the other ladies here?"

Gleda gasped then laughed. "It is a name used for respect as I, like the others here, feel you have a sense of wisdom about you. You are a true lady without the need of confirmation in our eyes."

Olly eyed her suspiciously but in a good humored way. "I am not certain I am worthy of such an assumption but I am grateful for it nonetheless."

"And the treasures?" she asked with a smile to divert.

"Oh, I did discover a tatting hook but I believe I will try my hand at the crochet needle first," she replied promptly.

"Good," Gleda encouraged as she glanced happily at her flower. "Do you know how to crochet?"

"I am not certain I do, but I assume that if I try it enough, something will come of it," Olly replied honestly.

Gleda stood and took the few steps towards her before kneeling in front of her. "How can one dislike you, Olly? Here you are, not knowing your own name, not knowing your home, and yet you smile and create gifts. If only everyone displayed such hopeful conduct."

Taking in a louder than intended sigh, Olly looked upon her seriously. "I *am* fearful, Gleda, I won't deny it. But falling into a countenance of despair would not offer me any discovery; it would be all too easy," she explained. "And then what would I do with the remainder of my time? For being anxious and shedding tears would not keep me busy long."

"You will find home, Olly," Gleda said, placing her hand on hers. "No one forgets a lady like you."

"I hope so." Olly nodded, not wanting to dwell on the somber thoughts of her reality. Instead she had another question to offer. "I heard many people last night. Was there some matter of commotion that you are aware of?"

At first appearing uncertain, Gleda then registered an understanding. "No, it is that way every night, always," she explained. "We have many people stay here from all corners of the world. It is a gathering place for all of them so they can discuss their work."

Olly sensed some reluctance from Gleda regarding specifics so she was careful not to pry too openly. Just the same she wondered if this work was only regarding the theater itself. "Do you travel abroad, Gleda?"

She shook her head. "I have done over time but not so much now," she replied with a smile. "Me and Gil, along with Ehren and Aylward, and sometimes Clarence and the girls; we mostly remain here," she replied, standing and returning to her chair. "Once you have seen much of the world, nothing shines as brightly as the beauty of home. We like it here very much."

"I like how I feel here," Olly stated openly. "Thank you for letting me stay."

Before Gleda could respond, a knock came from the hallway door. "Olly are you awake?" Gilpin called out.

She exchanged an amused look with Gleda before answering. "Yes, Gilpin, I am awake and modest. Would you like to come in?"

He snickered low but enough for them to hear. "I have a gift for you, so you must do your best to act very astonished when I give it to you."

Olly laughed, as did Gleda. She liked that he was now returning her humor from the previous day and was continuing their silly charade. "I am already in the midst of terrible anticipation, Gilpin," she assured him cheerfully.

He opened the door and the first thing to be seen was his wide sheepish grin. Unlike Gleda who wore her cleaning clothes, he wore his usual day suit and cap. She couldn't see a gift in his hands but didn't want him to notice her inquisitive glance.

She did, however, notice the tray of food in his hand, the same offering from the past meals, but she was happy for it as he passed it to her.

"Thank you very much," she said as she placed it on the bed beside her and started eating.

He smiled as he looked around, sensing a change. "I like this song," he stated cheerfully, referring to the record playing.

"Why aren't you wearing white, Gilpin?" Olly quickly asked. "Are you not going with us to the restaurant?"

He closed the door then looked at her with a lack of recognition. "Oh, Aylward was called away in the night and will not return until very late," he replied apologetically. "He asked that you please wait until he takes us tomorrow."

Olly nodded, trying to hide her disappointment as she swallowed the crackers and sipped her lemonade. "Oh that is a shame, but I understand," she said with a feigned smile. "The time passes so slowly with inactivity," she expressed openly.

Gleda offered her a sympathetic look while Gilpin crouched in front of her. "He said that you might be anxious about that so he asked that you do some more work for him."

"Should I put on my cleaning dress?"

He tilted his cap and shook his head. "No, there is an ointment that he makes up to help all of the theater people while they tend to the sick," he explained. "He usually makes a lot at once and started it last night but soon it will need stirring and putting in jars."

She nodded, not adverse to the idea. "I would be glad to, thank you."

Obviously very comfortable around both of them, Gilpin seated himself on the floor in front of her rather than sitting beside her on the bed. "We're glad for you being around here, Olly, really we are. You've got a good helpful heart."

She shook her head as she clasped her hands in her lap. "Please, think nothing of it. I am honored to be counted among people who I think just as highly of." Suddenly turning to Gleda, she considered an alternative. "Gleda, would you prefer to stir the ointment? I can do your cleaning for you?"

Gleda's smile faded in surprise. "In all honesty, Ms. Olly, I quite like cleaning so unless you prefer it, your offer isn't necessary."

She returned a coy smile. "Oh I don't mind either, but I suppose stirring ointment would be something new for me."

Gilpin let out a loud laugh. "I believe everything's new to you, Olly."

She laughed too. "Yes I suppose it is. Well I did clean yesterday so I suppose I can at least attest to some minor experience."

Gleda reached down and playfully pulled Gilpin's hat down to his nose then turned her attention to Olly. "I would say that ointment preparation would be more suited for a duchess in a pretty dress anyway."

With a gasp, Olly then followed it with a laugh. "Did Clarence tell you? He endears me to him in many ways."

She nodded and smiled, agreeing with visible sincerity. "He is a qualified gentleman and creatively minded. We would not part with him for anything," she said. "I think the title suits you but I've grown fond of your silly poster name so it has stuck with me now."

"I like it too, it is unique," she agreed while politely finishing her Jell-O.

"Look, Gil. Olly put animals on mine," Gleda said, showing him her handmade flower.

Gilpin studied it with a smile. He opened his jacket to show that his flower was pinned to the pocket of his tan buttoned shirt. "Mine is better for my suits. I don't have anything that matches animals," he countered with a chuckle.

"Sweet boy," Gleda said as she tapped his cap with her flower before placing it in her lap.

"That reminds me," he said out of the blue. "I have a gift for you."

Olly nodded; glad she had eaten and was ready to give it her full attention.

He reached into the side pocket of his high-waisted brown pants and passed her a small object wrapped in a page from a newspaper.

"Oh I love it!" she exclaimed before opening it. "I have always wanted one just like this. You are remarkable in your selection, Gilpin. You are the grandest of all those that have ever bestowed a gift on another!"

Gleda and Gilpin laughed as he alone pointed to the small object in her hands. "You were supposed to open it before reacting," he insisted.

"That might be the case, but it wouldn't be so amusing if I did it that way, would it?" she said with a laugh of her own. "Very well, let me look here."

She slowly unraveled the paper but her smile instantly left as she stared at the gold ring with ruby center in her hand. A surreal sensation came over her and she wasn't sure how to feel but tears fell from her eyes even before she could understand why.

Gilpin leapt forward and seized her hands while Gleda joined her on the bed and placed her arms around her shoulders. "Oh no, love," Gleda said tenderly. "Don't cry, what upsets you?"

Olly shook her head, unable to stop the flow as Gilpin's hand clasped hers with true concern in his young eyes. "Don't be sad, Olly, please," he begged.

"The ring," she started as she felt overcome with emotion. "I saw it in the dressing room and for a moment I thought it was so beautiful. For a moment I thought that maybe a man gave me a ring once and if he had, wouldn't that be a beautiful one?"

Taking her into her arms, Gleda allowed her to cry, holding her as a mother would a child. "The ring is beautiful, Olly. It is yours and we are giving it to you now. We want you to be happy."

"But there is no man," she said, slowly pulling away from her caring friend. "What if I never remember? What if I am loved and can't be found?"

Reaching back for a piece of velvet fabric off of the bed, Gleda cupped Olly's chin and wiped her face with the cloth. "You are loved, dear girl. Of course you are. If there is a man that gave you a ring once, then he is looking for you I promise. You let the time pass and you *will* remember. Don't lose that hope, Olly."

Olly nodded, ashamed for her outburst. She had suppressed it since she had gotten there and supposed it had finally gotten to her. "I am sorry," she said quietly, wanting to explain, but when she opened her mouth she could not offer more. "I am very sorry."

"There is nothing to forgive," Gleda assured her. "This cleaning dress is for tears as well as laundry," she added with a smile.

Olly looked down at Gilpin who was quietly wiping tears away from his own face. It surprised her to see him that way.

"If you don't remember, Olly. You can stay with us forever. I wouldn't want you to go away," he said looking up at her with sadness in his eyes.

She realized that he too was orphaned in this strange place of the lost. Without care for acceptability, she got onto her knees and hugged him, which he reciprocated wholeheartedly. "Whether I remember or not, Gilpin. You will always be my brother."

He held her for maybe a minute, both of them needing it, her most of all. Slowly pulling back she found his expression to register a great deal of shock. "Brother?"

She nodded and smiled at him, now switching her demeanor to comfort the saddened young man. "Yes. I am adopting you without delay, just as we sit here. There is no one to dispute me the right. You are now my family."

He quickly looked at Gleda who was mirroring the joy on his face. "It is not every day you are adopted by a duchess, Gilpin. I wouldn't refuse her offer."

Returning his attention to Olly, who was still sitting on the floor, he knelt in front of her with his hands in his lap. "Who would you tell?" he asked, eagerly deriving specifics from her.

"All people I encounter of course," she replied cheerfully. She suddenly felt her sadness melt away, as in this moment she was able to give joy to someone else and he was very deserving of it.

Once again glancing at Gleda he laughed a little, though she could tell he was trying to be more reserved in his reaction. "I can be your brother in an honest way? Is it true, Olly?"

She reached out for his hands and laughed, feeling it high in her heart and sensing a unique kind of love for him. "Oh yes, Gilpin. It can not be changed now. I am a duchess after all, and what I say to be true can not be taken from me."

"I gave you a gift, my sister," he said with a wide smile.

Olly looked up at Gleda who was smiling as much as they were. "It is a beautiful ring, Gilpin, *my brother*. But does it not belong to one of the ladies that frequent here?"

His smile remained but the glint in his eyes faded a little as if he feared upsetting her. "Esther found it outside in the cobblestones; it does not belong to one of the actresses."

She nodded, understanding. "Then perhaps one of the women who passed," she noted quietly.

"Try it on," Gleda encouraged.

After attempting a few fingers, she found it to slide perfectly onto the middle finger of her right hand and it felt comfortable there. "Even if I met everyone in existence, I would still feel you are two of the most wonderful people that God had made. It is beautiful, thank you."

Gilpin got off the floor, suddenly very animated. "I must leave, but would you like me to take you to Aylward's room?"

"His room?" Olly also stood, being sure to remove the food tray from her bed.

"Yes, that is where he creates his ointments," he explained as he went for the door to hold it open for her. "He knows you will be there."

Gleda followed suit and pushed the chair back against the side wall below the poster of the lady with the headache. "I have a new batch of laundry to tend to so I will see you both later."

"Thank you for the music player, Gleda," Olly said, offering her a grateful smile. "Should I return the needle?"

Her now cheerier friend smiled and shook her head, clasping onto her cracker adorned rose. "Leave it to bring joy to your room, no one will mind it."

—

74

Chapter Six

Olly, in her swishy long green dress, followed Gilpin down the hall and beyond the large curtains to the theater. Gilpin took the tray from her allowing her to hold the sides of her dress so as to not fall over it.

She immediately recognized the same faces as the previous day. Clarence however was not there, but his friends were talking with Esther and Lillian who pointed at the ring and smiled in acknowledgment at her.

Gilpin placed the tray on the large breakfast table and took her behind it through the arched entrance way but this time to a hall on the left. When they came to the first turn, it was a large stone stairway, cold and musty.

A beautiful exotic scent filled the top of the stairway and it wound around, bringing them to a dark wooden floor with a long plush burgundy rug at its center.

Stepping up, she looked back down to see that Gilpin had stopped a few steps down from her. "Are you not showing me which room?" she asked.

"No, I am late at this time, Olly. You needn't be concerned. Just go there to the left and it's the room at the very end with the red door handle. He said he left a note with instructions."

"Thank you for the ring."

He offered her a sincere appreciative smile then bowed slightly and turned back around to descend the stairs.

Enjoying the strange aroma in the air, she stared at the stone walls that led to the high wooden beamed ceiling along the narrow walkway. The floorboards creaked beneath her feet but then she stopped mid step and a distinct realization came over her.

She didn't know all the rooms in the theater and perhaps others branched off beneath it, but if Aylward resided here, likely Ehren did too.

It shouldn't have mattered one way or another but there was only one door on the left of the hallway and the door was open. Suddenly the creaking of the floor sounded louder in the quiet hall and she was much more conscious of it.

As she came up to that door, aiming to quickly get to the end room without being noticed, she couldn't help but glance in. Her heart was pounding so hard it hurt her chest and she was ashamed for allowing herself to get so carried away for no reason.

The door was open most of the way, letting her see the majority of a very large room. The French antique furniture was grand and beautiful. A strong smell of perfume hung in the air as if it had been sprayed so often it remained in the cushions on the large French bed.

Pink and green silk scarves hung on the vanity mirror, giving Olly cause to believe that a woman lived in this room or at least once occupied it. A large gold rug covered the wooden floor and three rich colored romantic paintings of knights and ladies hung on the stone wall beside the bed.

Across from the bed, a large shield shaped gilded mirror and a pink satin chaise lounge below it.

This room belonged to a dreamer, someone who loved beautiful things and appreciated color and the vibrancy of romantic feeling. For a moment her breath was taken away, she was utterly consumed by the fabrics and curves of the furniture; the whole room was alike to its own work of art.

Startling her out of her dreams was the sound of shuffling feet from the side of the room that she couldn't see, behind the open door. Realizing someone was inside of the room, she quickly tiptoed quietly down the hall and immediately opened Aylward's door and closed it again.

Her heart was beating fast. Was it Ehren and had he seen her staring into his room? Would he think she was a voyeur? But she hadn't gone in, but he always seemed to be hiding something, would he lose trust for her at her curiosity?

Then again it could have been Gleda's room, after all she was not certain of where she slept.

Fortunately an electric standing lamp illuminated Aylward's large room so she didn't have to open the door again to find her way around.

This room lacked the whimsy of the other one she had just seen, but it had its own areas of focus and interest. His plain wooden bed was simple and unornamented. A single pillow and thick gray blanket was tucked into the bed frame and looked like it hadn't been slept in for a while.

A pair of brown tasseled slippers had been neatly placed beside the bed and a pair of rounded thin framed spectacles was on top of them.

A large long wooden table, high and sturdy, was pressed against the left wall, covered in handwritten notes, newspapers and leather bound books, likely antique. Along the right wall was a large arched window, wooden, as if carved from a tree and another table was below it.

Maybe ten crates of jars sat on the floor beside the table that was underneath the mirror. On the table were large saucepans and wooden-handled serving spoons.

She ventured to the table and glanced at herself in the tree carved mirror. The green dress flattered her, but she realized her waist length hair was still in a long braid and she hadn't gotten to pinning it up yet.

Her large blue eyes looked upon her womanly form and she felt a moment of confidence and was glad she was generally attractive. The dress aided her appeal and the closed door meant that her unstyled hair would not receive any attention.

As her gaze lowered to the table in front of her, a handwritten note on very aged paper caught her eye and she could see on the top he had written, *Questa.*

It detailed what she had to do which was generally to stir the thick white ointment and then spoon it into the jars. Then once she had done a whole crate full she would then put the lids on, allowing the ointment time to congeal better.

Deciding it best to get started straight away, she placed ten jars neatly in a row on the empty space on the long table and started to stir. All of a sudden the door opened and she jumped, startled.

She was about to turn and explain she was asked to be there but it was Ehren standing in the doorway and he smiled at her. His smile was so warm and the light in his blue eyes so inviting, every thought and feeling she had felt for him resurfaced in an instant.

His hand clasped the door as he peeked in at her but she could see he was dressed like a prince, right down to a feather in his green felt cap. "What potions are you creating for us, Duchess?"

She smiled immediately, perhaps a little too much as she didn't want him to see how easily she could be swept up by him, just like the other girls. "I see Clarence has gotten to your ear too."

"He was very impressed by you," he noted, keeping his gaze on her.

"Perhaps he is easily pleased," she quipped. "But I enjoyed conversing with him." Relieved that she was wearing a nicer dress than when she last encountered him, she positioned her body so she could look at him but stir at the same time.

He now entered the room but didn't close the door so she wasn't uncomfortable. Instead he placed his hands behind his back and she discretely glanced at his well kept physique and the way his costume flattered it.

"Aylward's ointment is his most cherished prize," he said, gesturing at it with a glance. "No other lady has stirred it for him, not even Gleda."

She couldn't hide the astonishment from her face as she began to spoon enough mixture into the first jar to fill it most of the way. "Is that true?"

"Certainly. Do I seem the kind of man to deceive you?" he asked, baiting her for a reaction.

She smiled in spite of the fact that she attempted, poorly, to suppress it. "I wouldn't think you to be undependable but I do gather you to be the type of man to frequently engage in jest."

His eyes widened just seconds before he laughed so loud it echoed throughout the large stone room. "You are a reliable judge of character, aren't you, you mysterious enchanted girl. If we do not keep our wits about us, you will have us all bewitched."

She tried not to take his flattery personally, but her heart betrayed her composure by beating faster in response to his words. "Perhaps then, your wits are already in jeopardy," she teased further.

Keeping his gaze on her face, he approached her slowly, smiling with a look in his eyes that showed he was awed by her in some sense. "Have you tried it?"

She finished placing the mixture in the third jar and then eyed him curiously. "The ointment?"

"Yes, it is very good."

Beginning on the fourth jar she turned away from him for a moment. "Well no, that would be constituted as thievery. I am trusted with this responsibility; I couldn't do such a thing."

Drawing even closer to her, he stared into the first saucepan, his vicinity unbudgingly a foot from hers. "Aylward was quite adamant you use it tomorrow when he takes you to the restaurant. I think you should try it now, with my permission, and any blame can be ascribed in my direction should you be concerned."

Not immediately taking action, she filled the fifth jar and queried him further. "What ingredients are contained in here?"

"Magic." She could sense him smiling but didn't look at him. "There is magic within."

Looking at him, intentionally meeting his stare, she ensured that she didn't flinch at his wording.

A strong sense inside of her took issue with predictable reaction. "*Only* magic? That is quite incredible for it to contain only one component."

Smiling, he showed she had surprised him by her response. "A very astute observation, Olly. Yes likely there is more than that, but he has never divulged it."

She filled the next jar and wanted to hold his attention longer so she didn't rush the conversation in anyway.

"Do you believe in magic?" he asked more seriously.

Stirring the contents in the saucepan again, she looked at him and gave it true contemplation. "I can not speak for my prior self," she said, making sure he remembered her unique situation. "But as I stand here now, with what I feel and suspect, I have no reason to doubt it without good reasoning. After all, if anything is truly and literally *possible* then magic could not be excluded from that."

At first he didn't speak, as if her words had caught him unawares. She thought he might lean forward and kiss her, and she didn't think she would stop him from doing it. Just the same his blue eyes looked at her with a strange intensity and he glanced at her lips but remained where he stood.

"You hold my attention in such a profound manner," he said as emotion caught in his throat. She was suddenly reminded that he may have lost someone, although she wasn't certain. Was his hesitance at speaking further stemming from a similar uncertainty to hers? She could be married; they were both aware of that possibility.

Not wanting him to compromise his morals in a moment of weakness or loneliness from his loss, she quickly turned her moistened eyes from him. She dipped her fingers in the first jar. The ointment had hardened a little.

Rubbing it into the top of her left hand she did experience a strange tingling sensation and also noticed that her whole body relaxed in the briefest of moments.

—

"That is remarkable," she noted aloud. "Do you suppose this really does prevent the residents here from contracting the flu?"

He nodded. "It is in my earnest belief that it alone is what saves us."

An indeterminable knowing caused her to hesitate and not enquire too much on the particulars or of why it wasn't used on the townspeople. The theater people were very kind but their guardedness was apparent and she did not want to endanger her tenure there.

Still in the midst of an impenetrable tension, she turned again and went to scoop some out of the saucepan for him. Not having anticipated it becoming hard inside, the spoon flicked up into the air and a large glob of ointment flung into the front of his mid length hair.

She gasped enough that it hurt her throat and she looked around for something to remove it. He began to laugh as her eyes finally settled on an unused piece of lined paper and she seized it, spinning around to help him.

To her surprise he was holding a small glob of his own and as she looked at him, he placed it on the top of her hair, squishing it in a little. Her mouth hung open in surprise. She wasn't sure whether to laugh or protest. "I would not have taken you for the vengeful type but I think we wasted enough of Aylward's magic!"

He laughed again, joy in his eyes, relief on his handsome face as if he had needed a moment of juvenility. Having a small bit of the ointment still on his finger, he very gently placed it on her right cheek, and then rubbed it slowly into her skin. "This magic ointment will turn you into stone. And then I will be able to come see you just as you are now, always."

Spellbound by the instance, captivated by him beyond pretence, she allowed herself this moment to hold his words in her heart and believe them. "Should you curse me to the life of a living statue, I would hope you did me the kindness not to keep me in Aylward's quarters."

His smile remained but he did not further any physical interaction. Obviously he was holding something back and perhaps his reason had returned to his mind and somberness in his countenance returned with it. "I had come to ask you a question," he stated straightly.

Using the paper in her hand, she reached up slightly to remove the ointment from his hair then gently blended the remainder. "Did you have work for me to do too?" she asked, masking any tone of disappointment in her voice.

He removed the ointment from her hair with his fingers and placed it back in the first jar. "The day after next I will be taking the carriage to the next town," he explained, clasping his hands behind his back. "It is quite a distance but it is necessary I go there on occasion to replenish supplies of food and also linens for the ill."

Worried he was making a lengthy departure she expressed her concern before allowing him to enlighten her. "How long will you be gone?"

Seemingly pleased by her tone of affect, his eyes lit up in appreciation. "The journey will be taken there and back in one day. I was hoping you would assist in the acquiring. It always helps to have extra hands."

Ashamed of having gotten caught up by what now appeared to be a request for a general task, she cleared her throat and turned her attention to the ointment. "I must be honest with you, Ehren. I am not sure I am ready to be surrounded by a group of people right now. However, I will make the journey if it is your particular wish."

"I usually take the journey alone, Olly. There will be no other in my attendance. I would like your company if you are willing to offer me your time."

She glanced at him surprised. "Yes then, I will go with you, thank you for asking me."

Happy with her response he let out a discrete but audible sigh. "Oh, I am glad," he revealed frankly. "I had also heard of your search for green hills," he added reluctantly. "We will pass some on the way there."

—

82

Her demeanor altered dramatically as he said it. Emotion suddenly rose to the surface with the reality of her situation. Nodding, she offered little in response. "Should I dress in any specific manner?"

Approaching the door, he smiled but shook his head. "Make your selection from the dressing room. I am sure you will choose wisely. Until then, Ms. Olly," he said, tipping his felt cap at her before closing the door behind him.

She briefly rested against the long table and sighed. She had been so affected by his apparent adulation that she had forgotten the man in the hills. If she was to be honest with herself, she wasn't happy that he knew of her search for the hills.

Perhaps Gleda had revealed that she had the dream, and she may have mentioned Olly's feeling for this man as well. She closed her eyes, trying to dismiss the way it held her in conflict.

Ehren had a way with words and an alluring smile. It might be true that he had some type of affection for her but she may have misconstrued its content. After all, he may have lost someone and was just looking for a secondary source of comfort. Meanwhile he now might have known about her situation and her love for a man that might not even exist.

Staring at the red ruby on the ring on her finger, she prayed that if there were a man that loved her she would find him presently. For if she was not to find him soon, her heart might fall prey to the warmth of the enigmatic theater owner irreversibly.

Chapter Seven

Staring into the semi darkness, Olly folded her pillow so she could raise her head and rest against it, letting her eyes sweep the bedroom. The sound of the town's bell had rung and woken her, reminding her of the death and sorrow that awaited her.

Before she could observe anything else, her first thought was the fresh angst that came with waking to no new knowledge. Her name, her home, the man she sought, they still eluded her so this day would once again begin in blind faith.

As her weary eyes set on the gramophone on the walnut side table, she smiled thinking of Gleda and Gilpin and their sincere compassion. She would never forget their friendship nor the way they made her feel welcome from the very first moment.

Of course then her thoughts turned to Ehren and their interaction in Aylward's room the previous day. He knew about the hills and possibly the dreams of a true love somewhere or at least her wanting to believe in it.

She had dreamt of him again but it was a glimpse of the hills, a knowingness he was there but nothing else. Unlike the previous mornings, she was opening the door to Gilpin within minutes of waking.

Dressed in a white suit like the men she had seen the other day in the theater, he brought her breakfast and made sure to point to her ring as he smiled with pride. She glanced discretely at the silk flower pinned to his shirt but said nothing of it.

He had given her a long white gingham dress, resembling a thick nightgown but with more lacework on the neckline and short puffed sleeves.

—

84

He allowed her a few minutes to get changed in the powder room and put on her white shoes, pinning her hair up into a pompadour bun. She felt vibrant and hopeful in spite of her uncertainty and made sure to remind herself of how much good she could do with her compassionate spirit.

Spraying herself liberally with the lovely perfume Gleda had gifted her in the decorated toiletry box; she took a deep breath.

After entering through the long burgundy curtains to the main theater, she found Aylward standing beside Gilpin. He was also wearing white, a long robe with roman sandals and a rope belt, affirming his Moses image. "Are you ready to reunite with the outside world, Questa?" he asked with a sparkle in his old but clear blue eyes.

She smiled at him, calmed by his presence. "It is more a matter of whether it is ready to take me back," she quipped.

Gilpin laughed as he bent to pick up a large crate of the ointment she had carefully canned the previous day.

"Your sister possesses your quick wit and courage, young one," Aylward said, patting Gilpin on the back as the three of them walked past the breakfast table and into the small hallway.

Olly, remaining behind them, smiled wide. She knew that Gilpin must have told everyone of her declared adoption and she deemed herself blessed for the significance he placed on it.

Turning right, walking toward the women's dressing area, they went past it to a darkened tiled lobby and a thick windowless door. Aylward turned the brass knob and early morning sunlight flooded in. It was only then that Olly truly realized she hadn't been outside since her fall.

A strange sensation came over her and she stood in the lobby staring out. A light warm breeze wafted through her hair and against her pale skin.

Gilpin put the crate on the ground to prop the door open. He then quickly returned to her with concern on his face. "What's the matter, Olly?"

Aylward lowered his gaze refraining from judgment or impatience.

"I don't know," she replied honestly. "I suppose it just now occurred to me that I had thought I would be found by now," she said straightly.

Glancing at Aylward, Gilpin looked at her worriedly as he reached for her hand, the one with the ruby ring on it. "There is nothing to be frightened of," he said gently. "You will be found; it's just not time yet. Maybe the angels just let us borrow you for a while."

Her glare had been set upon the cobblestones outside of the door but she quickly looked at him in astonishment. Reaching out to hold his forearms, tears sprung to her eyes.

"Gilpin—," she wanted to say that she loved him, that he was her family even though she knew him for such a short time. Squeezing his hands and looking into his eyes she wanted him to know how much his words gave her hope. "How could I ever be sad when you are taking up all that room in my heart?"

Aylward, who had been watching from outside, came in to be beside them. His eyes showed that he was affected and she gathered it was for his love of his young ward. He smiled at Gilpin then looked at her, speaking straightly but not harshly. "You had said to me that you wished to help those that were ill," he said.

Swallowing hard, and embarrassed that he would have seen it, she nodded and raised her head, forcing her heart to follow her head. "Yes you are correct. They need to be tended to and I am prepared to do all that I can," she said.

Surprisingly he offered her arm, which she took, and Gilpin went ahead of them, lifting the crate from the ground and watching her protectively as she navigated the cobblestones.

Crossing the walkway, Olly recognized where Gilpin had met her for the first time, helping her off the ground and offering her shelter as the sun went down.

Glancing to the left she could see the main street. It was quiet outside, only the faint sounds of horses pulling a couple of carriages. A streetcar had been left abandoned on its line mid run. Obviously some people had gotten sick and there was no one left to operate it.

Two men wearing masks were talking as they removed wooden advertising posts from a blacksmiths workshop. The air was thick with a somber and silent resonation

Approaching the side of a low rise building directly opposite the side door of the theater, the three of them stopped beneath a metal awning. Gilpin kept the crate in his long slender arms, looking at Aylward for guidance.

"Take Questa to the kitchen and show her how to prepare," he instructed him as he nodded quietly in acknowledgment.

"Be brave and serve without strong emotion," Aylward continued, now looking at Olly. "You will be aware of who will meet with the angels today. These are the ones that I wish you to attend."

A chill ran over Olly's body. Of all that could be requested of her, that seemed like the most significant of all the responsibilities. "What shall I say to them?" she asked very quietly.

"Do not express what dwells in the mind. Your heart will speak the words for you," he replied vaguely.

She wasn't about to question him further as he was not the kind of man you defined specifics with.

Following them in, she was surprised not only by the sheer quantity of people, but how such a large group could be so quiet.

There was a general murmur coming from the theater folk dressed in white.

Otherwise the only other sounds were the clanging of bed pans and the low talk of a handful of relatives beside their sick loved ones.

Lowering her gaze, Olly obediently followed Gilpin to the right hand side of the room where a restaurant counter was covered in linens and bloodied cloth in metal bowls

The occasional person in one of the many military cots would cough loudly and wheeze to the point where it caused Olly pain to hear it. Gilpin walked around to the back of the main counter and smiled at two of the theater men who were cleaning metal bowls for reuse.

Olly also acknowledged them and tried not to appear as overwhelmed as she felt. They smiled at her warmly and it comforted her. So far everyone she had met from the theater really made her feel like one of them without hesitation, such generous spirits.

The men both reached for the jars and began to put the lotion on their hands and on their necks above their white buttoned shirts.

Gilpin dipped his fingers in and gestured for Olly to put her hands out. "You have to rub it in and not miss anything," he instructed in a whisper. "Then you have to put some onto your neck and such to keep it from where you breathe in the air."

She nodded and took it from his hands, being certain to follow his suggestion of thoroughness.

Gazing into the main part of the restaurant, Olly noticed a handwritten menu on the wall to the left of them. The windows were blackened out with heavy curtains, likely to contain the illness but also to keep the sun from the eyes of the sick people.

Dining chairs were stacked high against the white painted walls, a grim reminder of the previously jovial usage of the building. A great many mechanical fans were placed intermittently throughout the room but it barely satisfied the need to rid the entire of it of the stifling stale air.

—

A medium sized tear dropped chandelier hung at the center of the ceiling and the light from it was hazy and subdued.

As Olly applied the tingling lotion on the skin on her neckline, she caught sight of Esther and Lillian. They too were in plain white dresses and had masks over the lower part of their faces like the others. Both of them were dipping cloths into water and applying it to the foreheads of patients who seemed to be awake and coherent.

Esther nodded at her and she could tell by her eyes that she was smiling. Olly waved discretely and her smile was equally non-ceremonial, considering the nature of their circumstances.

Her thoughts were suddenly interrupted by a welcome voice from behind her. "Duchess, I see that they have coerced the nobility to the role of a lowly attendant."

Olly spun around and smiled at him, happy for another friend. Now upon seeing him, a rush of warmth went through her as if she had known him a long time. "I am grateful they let me assist in this important role," she whispered in return. "Of course, it is of utmost importance that on occasion I mingle with the peasants, for they are many while I am but one."

Clarence smiled wide, impressed by her parallel wit. "An uprising would be quite displeasing I agree," he said as he wiped the inside of a metal bowl. "Do not forget the usage of the paper across your face," he added more seriously.

"Where can I get a mask?" she asked, not seeing one.

A hand reached over her shoulder and waved a mask around in front of her face. She took it from Gilpin and turned to smile at him. "Who should I go to first? What do you usually do for them?"

Clarence came to their side and placed a mask over his own face. "I must bid you a brief farewell for now, Duchess," he said to her. "Gilpin, the man in the far west corner near the newspaper rack, is your first point of call."

Her young friend smiled and nodded as he too placed a mask on his face, looping the string over his ears and tying it at the back of his head. He helped Olly with hers and she could see in his young eyes that he was grateful for her presence.

"It's my job to help people with coughing," Gilpin replied plainly. "Some of them get quite bad and the blood comes out. I try and help them because the blood gets in the way and they can't breathe."

"That sounds terrible," she said quietly. "Are they in much pain?"

He nodded, though hesitant to express it. "I'm afraid in most cases; death is their first moment of peace."

She looked out at the people in the cots, so close together there was barely room for the helpers to stand. A couple of the cots were vacant. She leaned closer and got up to Gilpin's ear, ensuring no one heard her bluntness. "Have any survived?"

He nodded. "Just a handful of the old folk," he said. "Seems it gets to the ones about your age but it doesn't stick with the old and the very young. No one knows why."

"It all seems very strange doesn't it?" She shook her head. "Who do you think I should go to?"

With a very discerning look in his eyes, he scoured the room. "Look for someone who is alone, someone who isn't coughing so much. It means they don't have the strength for it, you know what I'm saying?"

Nodding, she knew exactly what he was saying. Taking a deep breath she discretely placed his thin hand on hers and squeezed it. "I hope none of you get sick," she said quietly. "Promise me *you* won't."

He lowered his gaze as if avoiding a declaration of sorts. "We're safe, Olly. Don't worry for me. I have to keep living so I can look after my sister."

Smiling, she knew he understood her gratitude. "Very well, let us begin our healing, brother."

—

"This helps with the fever," he said, handing her a bowl with water and cloth in it.

Taking a bowl and dry cloths for himself, he then went into the main room. Clarence, standing over a man in the center of the room, pointed to the corner and Gilpin nodded, obeying the gestured request.

Olly's eyes gazed politely over the many cots until she came upon a man about a quarter of the way in. His chest was rising but stiltedly and he wasn't coughing. Alone and unattended, he seemed to be the type of person Gilpin described.

A couple of ladies, who were lying down and didn't look as ill, glanced at her wearily but in a way of acknowledgment and she nodded at them accordingly.

Approaching the side of the cot, she knelt down beside the man and decided to get onto her knees to balance better. Placing the bowl in front of her, she dipped the cloth in then rung it out. "I am going to place a cold cloth on your forehead," she said very close to his face so as to not attract the attention of others nearby.

He turned his head ever so slightly as if he had heard her but he did not speak. She placed it on his head and gently touched the side of his face. His skin was substantially warm and she hoped the water would soothe him.

In spite of the fact others were speaking in the room, it seemed unusually quiet in that area close to the ground beside him. His chest was rising very low as if it hurt him to let his lungs fill properly with air.

His hands lay at his side and the coloring of his skin was almost gray on some angles. On quick study she assumed him to be close to mid twenties, similarly aged to Esther and Lillian.

Even though the illness had caused his face to be sunken in quite a lot, she could tell that he was once a pleasant looking young man. She thought in other circumstances he might have been a good match for one of those girls, but who would love him now?

No family was next to him and she wondered if they had already passed. Perhaps they were away at war. Was it more of a mercy for him to die now rather than heal only to find himself alone?

A whistling sound was coming from his mouth, a low gurgling in his throat. It seemed he was trying to cough but was just jolting a little instead. "Would you like me to get you some water?" she offered into his ear.

Suddenly his hand shot up and she grabbed it instinctively. It seemed he was trying to speak and she leaned in closer to his mouth. His face was dripping with sweat, the top of his sheet damp, clinging to his neck. "Anne is standing over us," he croaked.

She looked up reactively but no one was there. She realized Anne must have been someone from his family. Surveying the room, there was no one to approach for assistance should Anne be there in their midst. "Does she live in town?" she asked.

"Died on the farm," he replied through heaving breaths. "She fell in the well because I was chasing her."

Olly closed her eyes, feeling the pain of his past experience. "She is with you now?"

That gurgling sound prevented him from an immediate reply but then he pushed his chest up to let the air in and spoke again. "She's all grown up now and she is happy. She loves me."

Olly wanted to comfort him and felt that he was truly seeing his relative. She sensed it in her heart that it was the truth even though his eyes were closed. "It wasn't your fault, she knows that," she said quietly but with intentional confidence. "Is she speaking to you now?"

"Mama's already there with her. She said, time to go home—," then a gurgling sound escaped his mouth and his chest sunk without the inevitable rise.

—

A small puff of air was the last sound from his mouth followed by a bubbling in his nose. That is when his hand dropped from hers. A tear fell down her cheek as she took the cloth from his head and placed it back in the bowl.

Looking up, she saw Aylward standing there. She hadn't heard him approach and he was looking down at her with much compassion. "There are more that need you, Questa."

She stood, using the side of the cot to bolster herself up and accidentally kicked the bowl over in the process.

Aylward appeased her emotion with a hand gesture. "His body is an empty vessel," he said quietly, stepping over the bowl and looking into her eyes. "His soul has returned and you must soothe the other ones that need to be guided there."

His wording was strange but she had no remembrance of her past beliefs. Nonetheless, she registered an understanding to his meaning. Most importantly, she grasped the heart of the matter. She didn't need to remember who she was to help these people in their final moments.

If anything, her ignorance would give her the ability to show no disbelief in anything they purported to witness. Perhaps this was a blessing in disguise for she could now trust that when her time came, those that loved her would be finally be revealed.

"The boy will clean this and the men will take him to the yard," Aylward relayed quietly. "Go to the next, you can do nothing more for this one."

She nodded and immediately wove through the tightly arranged cots to get back to the counter. Esther was there and was obviously in a hurry so Olly pointed to one of the bowls and she handed her a new water-filled bowl with cloths.

"Thank you." Olly scoured the room for the next person she could give comfort to and quickly noticed a woman just a few feet from her who was not coughing.

The woman, probably very close in age to her, was alert and even though pain was engraved in her brow, she looked serene. Olly fumbled with her bowl and crouched down at the head of her cot. "Are you feeling feverish at all?" she asked her quietly. "I have some cool water here to soothe you."

The woman eyed her appreciatively with dulled brown eyes. Her brown hair was all around her head and exposed arms and it was damp and oily. "Yes please," she rasped

Ringing out the cloth in the bowl, Olly lifted it up to the woman's forehead and was surprised her patient was still looking at her. Her chest was barely rising but her countenance remained calm. "I am returning home today."

Olly tried to hide her surprise, for certainly the condition of this woman would contradict the likelihood of her healing, especially not this day. "Where is home?" she asked, trying to support the woman's optimism.

The woman took a breath, as deep as she could, which was hardly at all, but Olly could tell she was happy for the cool compress. "My husband is already there," she whispered before coughing ever so slightly. "He is with the angels and he said he would wait for me."

Knowing that could only mean one thing, Olly diverted her gaze by dipping the cloth in the room temp water again. "Was it long ago?" she asked, being careful how she worded her question.

"Only a month," the woman replied. "We have loved each other since we were children," she explained before turning her head to catch her breath. "He saw I was stricken by it and he promised that he would get us a nice house there before I arrived," she said with the slightest smile on her face.

Olly smiled too, endeared to the woman's optimism and the love in her eyes for her deceased husband. "He sounds like a wise man to me," she said sincerely. "I'm sure there is no shortage of land there," she added.

—

The woman smiled more now, the hope in her eyes was unmistakable. "Is *your* love here?"

Subduing her disconcertion she returned the cloth to the woman's head and lowered her gaze to the tiled floor. "I had an incident which caused me to lose my memory," Olly explained, not wanting to divulge too much given the woman's obvious worsened condition. "I do not know if I am united with a man or not. But that is neither here nor there, for we were discussing your husband."

The woman closed her eyes and wheezed a little but then surprised Olly by opening them again but she looked weaker. "But I saw," she said gasping momentarily. "In your eyes, you showed me that you love someone. You are in love, I can see it."

Unsure of a proper response, for certainly where did her love lie? It wasn't an emotion she wanted to explore, especially now. If only this woman could look into her heart and tell her who the love belonged to. "I feel something," Olly whispered, looking into the woman's eyes, giving over her secret that would soon go with her to heaven. "I do feel love but I do not know if he is real."

The woman actually looked concerned for her and Olly felt guilty for so quickly voicing her own anxiety when this woman had much more to suffer.

"No, you must not doubt it," the woman insisted, reaching up and touching her cheek as she looked at her. "God never lets you give your heart to someone if they are a dream," she aid with another quick cough and wheeze. "If you really feel something so strong all the way inside of you, then your love is real and so is he."

Olly sighed but then regretted her expression of self-pity. Placing the cloth in the water, she wrung it out and looked back at the woman who was not able to keep her eyes open any longer. "I wish I knew how to find him," Olly said, mostly to herself.

"He is in the hills," the woman said, fading in comprehension.

Olly's heart stopped and she wanted to reach into the woman's vision. "*Who* is in the hills?" she asked quickly as if the woman was running from her.

"Roger has peonies," she replied as she smiled and let out her last breath.

With her hands trembling, Olly untucked the sheets beneath the damp woman's arms and pulled it over her face. She had thought she was talking about her, but she was talking about rejoining her husband. "I hope he has a nice house waiting for you."

Tears fell down Olly's cheeks and she quickly bent down and wiped them with the end of her dress. She didn't want to care so much for her own situation but she had to wonder if she would ever find the man her heart belonged to. What if it was too late?

Staunchly resolute to be a better nurse, Olly picked up her bowl and cloth and returned it to the counter for a new one. Only Aylward was behind the counter now and his mind was occupied with whatever he was writing in a notebook. "Should I clean this bowl now?" Olly asked hesitatingly.

"Leave it," he replied. "There are new ones for you."

She noticed a pile of clean bowls and took one, pouring water from a glass pitcher into it as she gazed around the room. Suddenly she placed the pitcher down and the blood drained from her face. A strange sensation came over her and she blinked her moistened eyes thinking that her tears had blurred her vision.

"Speak Questa" Aylward ordered, sensing her alarm.

"There is a woman in the back," Olly replied in a whisper close to him. "Aylward, do you see anything strange about her?"

"No," he replied, looking in the same direction. "What do you see?"

Olly shook her head, embarrassed. "Oh I am certain it is nothing to be fussed about. It just appears to me that she is glowing but I am sure it is the lamplight."

"Go to her at once," he insisted. "Make haste, take nothing."

Without hesitation, Olly took the route along the left wall and squeezed herself between the occupied cots and the stacked chairs to get to the back of the room. Stepping over a fan that was on the floor beside the woman, Olly crouched down to tend to her.

Not having water with her, she went to squeeze the woman's hand and ask her if she wanted something. Her hand felt cold and it was as if the woman was losing life in one part of her body at a time. The knowing of this was indescribable but confirmed when seconds later the woman let out her last breath as the others had done.

Worried she had gotten to this patient too late, Olly took a deep breath to prevent the strain from showing on her face. Lowering her hand to reach for the top of the sheet, it was then that she noticed the unique situation of this woman.

Not wanting to bring attention to herself, but being sure to show the urgency of her situation, she looked for her nearest friend and gestured for Clarence to come to her.

"What is it, Duchess?" he asked, mirroring her panic.

Olly signaled for him to lower his head so she could whisper to him. "This woman just died but she is with child. It might still be alive."

He quickly signaled to the two white suited men and they rushed over, quietly but quickly. Whispering to them, the three nodded and mumbled before approaching Olly and the pregnant woman.

Clarence got close to her. "We need you to help us. Are you strong enough at the sight of blood?"

She nodded, regardless of the truth. "I don't know, Clarence, but I promise I will try my best and help any way I can."

The theater men in the suits were already hunched over the woman checking her and feeling her stomach. There was no time to get her away from the other sick people.

"Take the sheet from her and hold it up," Clarence instructed her.

Olly nodded and did it, quickly, holding it as wide as possible so that anyone behind or near could not see the woman at all. Fortunately the other side of her was not occupied except for the chairs and the fans would prevent any sounds from traveling.

Just the same, when the bearded man knelt on one knee next to the woman and took a small knife from his pocket, Olly had to look away. The sound was uniquely disturbing. She knew the woman had been cut open and the squelching that followed caused Olly great discomfort and queasiness.

Aylward and an older lady appeared at their side. "I present a midwife for intervention if desired," he said quietly.

Keeping a brave face, Olly refused to let go of the sheet and could tell when they removed the baby out of the woman just by the sounds of the lifting out from the blood and stomach. The one thing she didn't hear is the crying of a baby.

The men mumbled and it went quiet for a moment. Olly didn't want to look but she suspected they were praying. The man must have hit the baby somewhat but there was no revival to be had.

"Just as well," the older lady said. "The father past on but a week ago. The child will have to be baptized though, the parents were believers."

The bell sounded nearby and sounded louder in the restaurant. Olly, frustrated and tired, reacted to the woman's words. "God would not reject a child just because it wasn't baptized," she said.

"Get me another sheet," the other suited man instructed the older lady.

Aylward came to Olly's side; she was still holding the sheet up. "Questa, calm your tide of judgment," he said sternly.

She immediately regretted openly expressing her opinions and felt ashamed for garnering his admonishment. "I am sorry, Aylward."

He looked upon her with sincere patience. "I agree that God would not shun any being but it is a matter of respecting the practices of all people in spite of your own misgivings."

She nodded, unsure of what to say.

The woman returned with the sheet and they covered the cut up woman with it. Aylward took the sheet from Olly's hands and Clarence gently helped him wrap the baby in it. He promptly handed the small bundle to Olly, who strangely got the sense that she did not have a child of her own.

Discretely walking around to the back of the room and approaching the side door, Aylward followed her, directing her to the church. The sunlight streamed in, hurting her eyes and then the door closed behind her.

Chapter Eight

Olly freed her right hand momentarily so she could remove her mask and tuck it in between her and the bundled infant. She was relieved for the fresh air and the heat was mild for the afternoon. Gilpin had noted Clarence predicted that it would be cooler but Olly didn't have time to analyze such a statement with all that was going on.

There was a whole row of brick stores beside the makeshift hospital. Most of them were closed on both sides of the main street. The tailor shop, one of the general stores and blacksmiths were completely packed up. The empty streetcar made her feel as if the world had ended but the peace was a welcome one in spite of its cause.

The buildings were substantially tall, blocking the sun from glaring into her eyes. Two men across the road were loading newspapers from an agency into the back of a pony cart. Their horse stood with his head bowed while the men did little to acknowledge Olly as she walked by.

A woman passed her but seemed alarmed by the bundle in her arms, and politely but obviously, kept her gaze low and maintained an intentional distance from her.

It wasn't difficult to see the church; it was at the end of the right hand side of the street, the same side as her, near a green park area.

She didn't recognize any of it, she didn't even know the name of the town or how she had gotten there. But for a brief moment something familiar came to her in the form of a sound; voices.

As she strode past the park, she turned her head quickly toward it, and three young men were throwing rocks into a pond. Two of them were yelling at each other and suddenly got into fisticuffs which caused her to shudder.

Adrenaline rose into her heart and throat. Their voices did sound familiar and Gilpin's assumptions that the Hanley boys had attacked her for her purse now seemed even more likely. One of them looked up at her, probably hunting for further gain but they must have seen the blood on her dress and the sheet covered infant and had sense enough to keep away from her.

Hastening her step, her flat white shoes echoed on the cracking pavement and she pondered the gender of the child she held. Coming up to the steps of the quiet church, Olly looked up at the arched stained glass windows of haloed saints.

The very tall wooden door suddenly opened, startling her and she took a step back on the platform. A haggard priest patting his wrinkled brow with a handkerchief, eyed her apprehensively.

"I do not have the flu," she explained quickly. "But the babe was born to a woman who died from it. Are you able to do a baptism?"

He nodded and opened the door for her, leaving space between them. Only a few lanterns were lit on the walls inside and the pews were empty. The air was less dense than in the restaurant and definitely cooler.

"Come to the altar," he instructed, walking slowly due to his advanced age. "The pastor has been gone only a week. I am the dean and I don't know this town well."

"I am sorry you were called her under such circumstances," she sympathized as they approached the pulpit and the table in front of it.

"Were the parents of this child wedded here?" he asked.

She shook her head. "I don't know. I was told they were believers but that is all that was divulged to me."

He nodded, obviously feeling awkward providing a service without particulars. "What is the child's name?"

Olly felt immediately put on the spot. "None was given; it died at the same time as the mother."

Swallowing hard, he gestured he was going to open the sheet, which he did very carefully, being mindful that the baby could also carry the disease. "The child is a boy; you must christen him, as God has given you the guardianship."

She looked around the room and her eyes settled on a beautiful renaissance style painting of some archangels standing over a child. "Gabriel," she said. "His name is Gabriel."

The name seemed to agree with the priest and his expression mellowed. "And what is your last name so that we can bless him with it?"

The child in her arms made it so she couldn't wipe the tears from her eyes. "I have lost my memory and I don't know my name," she replied honestly.

First looking at the child in deep contemplation, he turned his attention to her and she could see pity in his eyes. "Then we will bury him as Gabriel, child of God. Please hold him with love."

The process itself was not lengthy once he got the holy water organized. He seemed fatigued and she suspected he had taken short cuts but he didn't show disinterest either. She assumed he was the one who rang the bell at all hours and probably hadn't gotten much rest.

He covered Gabriel and took him in his own arms. "One of the men will take him to the yard and give him a proper burial when they come next," he said. "Are you of our faith?"

"I don't know, I believe in God," she replied. "But would you pray for me?"

"Are you unwell?" he asked, seeming worried.

She shook her head, her arms feeling lighter and freer now. "No, I don't believe so. I know that so many are in need of prayer now but I would really like to remember who I am. Could you please just pray for me one time?"

"I will, but God can hear you now and no matter what your faith, you should seek his counsel. Have faith that this time is a blessing from him."

"Thank you." She nodded with some level of ceremony for respect of his beliefs and turned to leave. As she ambled down the carpeted aisle, she glanced at the painting again and a strange realization came over her.

She had given a child a name but he had never taken a breath on Earth. Essentially his soul was born in heaven. She wondered if the angels heard her and would tell him that he had a name in that moment as his soul returned to the arms of his mother.

Opening one side of the church doors, Olly suddenly felt anxious to return to the hospital to help as many people as she could. Could she help with their healing too or was she going to be the last face in the eyes of those that died?

She didn't mind it. There was a magic in the witnessing of it. To hold the hands of the people as their souls left and their earthly bodies remained. They were returning to beauty, to love and reprieve. Even in its sadness, it was beautiful.

After walking past the now empty park, she drew closer to the empty blacksmiths and noticed Ehren in the street. Dressed in a very upper crust modern suit and regal top hat, his countenance was one of determination.

He hadn't seen her and she had a sense that he did not want to be interrupted so she hid in the shadows of the building to watch him for a moment.

His eyes seemed to be set upon an attractive woman passing in front of the streetcar and over to Olly's side near the empty store. She wore modern clothing, and even though it was obvious she came from money, her face showed much strain and worry.

She carried a medium sized box, likely of groceries, as she came away from the store behind the newspaper stand. It appeared to be selling many useful items and foods even though it used to be a military store.

Noticing Ehren's eyes on her, she at first looked uncomfortable until she noticed his handsomeness and wealthy status by his stature and clothing.

"Good afternoon," he said, having gotten to her very quickly.

She nodded politely though wasn't completely offended by his greeting her. "Good afternoon."

"I apologize for my approach as such," he began, standing straight with his hands behind his back; his fob watch and vest representing his apparent prominence. "But I had noticed the food you have in your possession."

She nodded, her hat being closely pinned to her head so as to not come over her rounded hair. "Why yes, I had placed an order with the Johnsons, the elderly couple who had run the watch store. I can not fathom how they accomplish the acquiring, but they honor it within two days with no issue."

He nodded very stoutly, but from where Olly stood, unseen by both of them, she noticed that familiar friendly glint in his eyes. "They are beyond reproach to be sure," he agreed. "I had gone there earlier and you look quite occupied but I wanted to ensure you had enquired on the lemons. They are donating to those that have aided by charitable nature towards the sufferers of the influenza."

Her attention was piqued immediately and she shifted the box she held. "Oh, I have been running many of the sick here using my vehicle actually," she said honestly and happily. "We have the second automobile in town and Harold, my husband, had been taking our ill neighbors to the restaurant. He is resting now but I would think they should consider us qualified."

Ehren smiled at her and nodded. "Most certainly you are! I suggest then that you tell them of your position as they mustn't have been aware of your aid. I would go now though, as I am aware of them being low on lemons at this time."

Her face registered urgency. "Well thank you for you educating me on this. We could do with lemons more than you know. I appreciate you taking the time."

Ehren tipped his hat.

She stepped away, moving away from the store and back towards the streetcar. In that very second, a horse and carriage came out of nowhere and ran onto the path, the exact place where she was just about to originally walk to.

Had she been going in her intended direction she surely would have been killed.

Olly went to scream but was so dumbstruck she just stared at the woman's shocked face as she must have registered the possibility as well.

Olly came out from the shadows frantically searching for Ehren. The horse jumped into the air and called out angrily but then shook its head and calmed as if it decided it was no longer bothered.

The woman in the street placed her box down and helped Olly look for Ehren but he had gone, he was most certainly not there or near there.

They both then turned their attention to the man in the enclosed carriage. An older gentleman, he had hit his head very hard on the inside of the carriage and had died in that instant it would seem.

"I could have been killed," the woman said, shaking terribly.

Olly nodded. "But you were saved somehow. You are well; this was not your time."

Exasperated, the woman looked around again, probably looking for Ehren's comfort or something to explain the quick event. "What should we do? This man has died. Does he have the flu?"

"No, he doesn't appear to," Olly said as she took some steps back to pat the horse which seemed strangely subdued and looked slightly emancipated. "I will tend to him; I am helping with the ill in the restaurant."

The woman tried to glance discretely at the blood on Olly's white dress, and she registered immediate concern.

"I suggest you go about your business and if you wish to show gratitude to God for saving you, perhaps you can take this horse home and give him some food and care."

She looked at the horse and actually seemed happy to do it. "Yes of course," she said adamantly, suddenly showing a true appreciation for her survival. "I will, he is one of God's creatures and I have hay for him and an empty stable so he will come home with me now."

Olly nodded. "You are a good person, thank you."

The woman went to retrieve her box, and that is when Olly looked to her left to see Aylward standing there. She couldn't be sure but she got the distinct sense that he had witnessed the whole scene yet didn't seem overly affected by it.

She wondered if he knew where Ehren was but always got the feeling that he was the kind of man to give information when he was ready and not when asked for it.

Gilpin, having heard the commotion, came out from the restaurant and rushed to Olly worriedly. The woman was unhooking the horse while Olly explained the situation to Gilpin who was just glad that she was safe.

With the assistance of Aylward, the three of them took the old man to Martin's storefront beside the restaurant so the other men already in attendance could prepare him for burial. Gilpin removed his credentials that was on his person and promised to get a message to his loved ones.

As they placed the man down, Olly took one more look around the empty town for Ehren and then returned with her friends to the solemn makeshift hospital.

Chapter Nine

The man's hand was warm on her face. She turned her head ever so slightly so she could kiss his palm. Her love for him was overwhelming, how wonderful he made her feel.

Suddenly she realized that she was dreaming yet she still remained there, standing in the sunlight, nestled at the center of the grassy hills. Immediately she knew she would have to look at him, just to glimpse his face, a detail, a sign, anything.

Unfortunately she wasn't able to lift her head. Was the sun in her eyes? So tired, so tired but why wouldn't he say his name? He placed something in her hand and closed her fingers over it. Even though she tried as hard as she could, she wasn't able to look down at her hand to see what it was.

"I love you," she said, either with her lips or her heart, she couldn't know. She could tell he was smiling but she couldn't see his face, she just felt that he was. He was devoted to her but he hadn't said it. He loved her too but his voice was silent.

"I miss you," she said, wrapping her arms around him. His arms took her into him but she couldn't see what he was wearing.

Suddenly he started coughing. It was such a loud cough. Did he have the flu? His image was fading, was he dead? The coughing kept going and she sat upright, and was now awake. The sound remained; it was knocking on her door.

There was no coughing, it was the knocking that had interrupted her sleep, she surmised. "Hello?" she enquired, wiping the tears from her eyes.

"It is me, Ehren, did I wake you?"

Springing up she cleared her throat before offering a reply. "I apologize. I hadn't forgotten our arrangement, but somehow I slept longer." Looking around the room she knew she didn't have time to get into a dress that quickly.

"I must be leaving, Ms. Olly. It is quite a distance."

Closing the narrow window by her bed, she called out to him apologetically. "Well perhaps you should journey alone? I could always go to the restaurant if you must make haste."

"No please. I do not wish to go alone," he said. She caught a tone of neediness in his voice and she felt sad for him, for whatever caused his pain.

Feeling more fatigued than normal, she threw the bedcovers back and stumbled over to the hallway door. Opening it only a small way, she looked up at him.

His attention immediately turned to her wet cheeks and she knew he had noticed that she had been crying.

"I did not want to continue our conversing through the door in such a manner like cattle calling," she joked divertingly.

He nodded and smiled. His hat was in his hands and he wore a modern suit but not as grand as the one he wore during the previous day's strange occurrence. "Gilpin has filled a small box of food for our journey," he said. "Would it bother you to consume a meal in such a manner?"

She smiled at him, once again embarrassed to present herself with such an informal and untidy appearance. "I think that sounds quite liberating actually. I am open to an adventure. Is it cool outside?"

Looking back towards the theater curtains she could tell he was pondering her question. "In this moment it is and I apologize to call for you before the sun has risen. It will warm later of course."

"What do you propose I wear?" she asked straightly.

Looking her over, his observation was not as discretionary as most men she encountered.

"Gleda has put your dress in the powder room, the one you were found—, the one you wore when you met Gilpin."

She nodded. "So not a costume day I assume. How *is* Gleda?"

"She is well. She has taken on your responsibilities today."

"Does she mind it?" she asked worriedly.

Shaking his head, he offered a sincere smile. "She enjoys it well enough and tells me to relay that she will see you soon."

Olly quickly glanced back at her room which was mostly in a good state of affairs. "Please allow me ten minutes, will that be a fair request?"

"I am in need of a moment to speak with Clarence," he said easing her concern. "Please meet me outside of the side door past the ladies dressing room. You had used that door yesterday I was told."

She nodded. "Yes very well I will be there momentarily," she said closing the door.

Ten minutes passed very quickly with all that she had to do. Her dress, her modern white tiered dress with pink embroidered flowers and lace sleeves, was hanging up in the powder room as she was told it would be. After freshening up and using more of Gleda's donated perfume, she organized her hair into a manageable slightly rounded bun and checked herself in the mirror.

Her feelings were mixed and her head was still full of the man in the hills but whenever she saw Ehren her heart was immediately conflicted. Nonetheless, she would make the most of this day and she was open to remembering something.

A short time later she ventured out through the side door of the theater to see Ehren standing alone beside a horse and cart. The cart itself was open and long with a raised bench in the front.

The cool breeze caused her to shiver but she was happy to see Ehren paying some attention to the horse, as she too was very fond of animals. Glancing up again, she wondered if she should rush back for a blanket.

Ehren was obviously anxious for them to leave and reached his hand out to guide her onto the rounded iron stepper so she could get up to the raised platform. Just seconds later he was seated beside her and with a flick of the reins they began to move forward, over the cobblestones and out to the breezy empty township.

"Are you cold?" he asked, seeing the way she held her arms. Even though her lace sleeves came over her elbows, the chill easily penetrated the light fabric of her dress. "It will warm soon enough," she said, trying her best not to hunch in any way he would find noticeable.

Sitting very close to her, he reached behind them and seized a quilted blanket. Gesturing for her to move forward, he placed it around her shoulders and pushed it a down a little behind her back. He smelled nice, she thought as she smiled at him. "Thank you, this will place me in a comfortable state before my body catches up to the temperature."

He laughed as he glanced at her but then stared ahead as the horse slowed for a small pony cart crossing in front of them. "You look very nice, Ms. Olly. Your hat is very stylish; I don't think I have seen another like it."

She reached her right hand out of the blanket and traced her fingers around the brim of it. The feather sticking out from it was soft and she agreed, it looked well kempt and grand by most standards. "Yes, it is very nice. Now if only we could find the milliner that created it, she might be able to identify me."

As she said it, she wondered if that could be an option. She quickly looked at him but he sighed in a manner that he was apparently sympathetic. "The one milliner passed this last week and I do not believe there is one in the town we are visiting but I can make enquiries for you."

Not knowing what to say in response, she nodded and took a discrete breath, accepting, as she had been doing, that her fate was unknown for now.

The horse carefully turned the corner onto a gravel road on the border of the town center and apart from a few houses intermittently placed; a long uninhabited road lay ahead. Trees and grass lined their journey and the sun had risen a little more, allowing them a better view of their open surroundings.

Olly breathed in the fresh air and with the blanket around her shoulders, she enjoyed the cool of the morning on her face and briefly closed her eyes. Ehren must have sensed her melancholy for he reached back for a small cardboard box and opened it up on the platform in front of them.

"Let us see what your brother has provided," he said, gesturing for her to open it.

She tried to hide her smile as she opened the box, but even still, the mention of Gilpin being her brother amused and comforted her in equal amounts.

"Oh!" she called out with a laugh as she straightened her stance and showed him the ceramic bowl in her hands. He peered inside and looked at all the Animals crackers placed in the Jell-O in a fashion that made them look like they were a carousel ride.

"I gather that one is for you," Ehren said to her with an amused smile.

She smiled back at him and plucked out a camel cracker and handed it to him. "Gilpin is like a sunny day when you are walking around in a rain cloud."

He laughed as he placed the cracker in his mouth. "You should tell him that. He enjoys your praise particularly."

Sensitive to sentiment, she decided to search through the box instead of remarking on the topic as tears flowed too easily of late. She took the other bowl out along with a plate with two slices of bread on it, which she placed on her lap.

Ehren glanced at it through the corner of his eyes. "He is a good young man," he noted. "He probably rode his bicycle all the way out to Mrs. Mansfield's home to get that and he would have had to tend her garden to acquire it."

Olly felt guilty as she looked down at it, but her stomach was so grateful it could have just as easily been gold for its value to her. "Oh, Ehren. He can have my piece; I wouldn't want him to work like that."

Ehren frowned at her as he seized one of the pieces from the plate and took an appreciative bite. "You would offend him if you didn't take it and enjoy it," he said seriously. "He wanted to give you a gift because he likes you very well and wants to impress you, so all you need give him is your gratitude."

Taking a bite, she chewed slowly to savor it. "I would like to at least save him some."

He shook his head as he finished his piece. "Mrs. Mansfield is very generous to him and makes sure he is fed enough that he is apt to waddling home on his cycle from momentary gluttony."

Olly laughed as she bent to retrieve the glass of lemonade wedged in the box with fabric to hold it in place. She gave it to him and he nodded in appreciation.

"I feel better for it with that knowledge," Olly said with a sigh as she finished her piece of bread and looked at the bowl of Jell-O. "Now that we discuss gifts as such, I had already made something for Gleda and Gilpin. I didn't wish you to feel neglected in any respect so I have made you something too."

Bending down to place his glass beside hers in the box, he eyed her curiously. "You have created something for me?"

She nodded and lifted the top tier of her dress on the side facing away from him. She had wrapped it in a swatch of velvet and tucked it underneath so he hadn't seen it. Passing it to him, he took both reins in his left hand and accepted it from her.

He placed it on his lap and opened it up but his expression did not automatically give away his thoughts. Holding the hand made silk flower he held it up and smiled appreciatively.

"What have you done here?" he asked, pointing to the silky gold fabric hand sewn at the base of the flower.

She reached across and pulled it out a little. "It must have been flattened. It is supposed to be a crown," she explained coyly. "You always remind me of a prince."

His smile faded and so did hers. She wondered if he had taken her flattery to be too forward. "I am sorry; I hope I did not offend you or your situation in any way."

He gazed at her with surprised eyes. "There is nothing to apologize for. This is beautiful and I am touched that you should think so highly of me," he said honestly, keeping his eyes on hers. "I will cherish this above all other tokens for it has come from a mysterious angel and one that thinks of me as a prince no less."

Smiling, she was unsure of how to respond and bent to retrieve her own lemonade and sip from it as she gazed out at the land. An automobile, boxy and loud, came into their view and an older woman with a sick woman in the back passed them looking rather serious.

Olly turned back to look over her shoulder at them and was reminded of the restaurant, knowing that was likely their destination. Then she remembered Ehren and his strange meeting with that woman in the street.

As his attention was consumed with navigating the horse over a rough area on the road, Olly held the sides of the bench and placed the box between her feet to stabilize it. She thought about the previous day and wondered why he had been there and dressed the way he was.

She couldn't dismiss the uncanny moment when the lady had moved in the direction where he told her to go, and avoided being quickly killed. Was it a coincidence?

Suddenly she felt his eyes on her and she was aware that he must have noticed the frown on her face as she sat in deep contemplation.

She considered broaching the subject but somehow it seemed like it would be rude of her to ask why he was dressed nicely and such.

Was there any valid question she could pose and somehow not seem like she had been some kind of voyeur?

Slowly turning her eyes to look at him, he smiled wide as if he had forced her gaze by his silence and she smirked, coy, as if he had won over her. "The hills," he said straightly.

Her smile faded and she was puzzled. "What of them?"

He pointed out in front of them. "There, after that third tree, the hills are there. Let me know if they offer you some familiarity."

Olly was stilled by his declaration and her heart began to thump wildly. Her torn emotions rose to the surface immediately as she wanted to see the man, she wanted to find him but she didn't want Ehren to be there when she did.

As they neared the spot he spoke of, her demeanor was calmed but disappointment companioned her relaxed state. "It is not them," she said, as she scanned the low grassy expanse with an audible sigh.

No person was standing in the hills as the sun was nearing the center of the sky, but it wouldn't have mattered. "The place I saw in my dreams was much richer in color and the hills were much grander, perhaps like a valley."

"I am sorry I had raised your hopes," Ehren said quietly, looking in her direction. "Are you certain?"

She nodded but didn't look at him, instead busying herself with reorganizing their breakfast provisions into the box. "Have you always run the theater?" she asked, intentionally to divert both of them from any somber dialogue. "I mean as far as your general occupation?"

"I am not the only one who can state ownership," he said with a polite smile, yet he didn't elaborate on details. His readiness to say as much made her wonder if he didn't want to take away from Aylward's significance; at least she assumed he was speaking of the older man. "No, I was once wholly engaged in healing as far as profession," he further enlightened.

"You were a doctor?" she asked with piqued interest. He shook his head. "Not to the point of conventional certification," he explained, looking at her for comprehension. "I did not originate in this town, though I have occupied it for some time. The residents of my past location were inclined towards methods not employed here but our skills were effective nonetheless."

She was surprised by his story, not having assumed such a background. "Why did you leave?"

Taking the reins in both hands to maneuver the horse over a small hill, he smiled at her, relaxed again. "I followed my heart, as the actors say."

She smiled, understanding his decision. Though she had no details of her past, she knew that she had the principles of a leader rather than one that followed a predictable path.

Without any context to her background, they instead talked about the theater and he relayed many amusing stories about his life there. They were laughing so often that the time passed with considerable speed. His fob watch showed that three hours had passed since they ventured past the hills but she was sorry for how quickly their journey ended.

Chapter Ten

Olly was surprised at where Ehren stopped the horse. She had expected a great many tall stores and perhaps an active streetcar. Instead, three one-level stores faced a tidied and leveled dirt road. One army vehicle and two pony carts were in front of the store on the right; the large window was unlabelled and unadorned.

"They look like they could acquire more from us than us from them," Olly observed as Ehren returned his hat to his head and helped her down.

"This is closer to the city," Ehren explained, looking over her shoulder, seemingly for something in specific. "The food and supplies are driven from an airbase and that is where the soldiers first stop for food and petroleum for the automobile."

She turned to look over at the store and noticed two soldiers coming out from the nameless store, holding open the screen door for a third one. "There are some now," she pointed out.

The three of them, holding brown paper bags, of finger foods she imagined, suddenly looked over and waved at them.

She waved back cheerfully whereas Ehren seemed strangely reserved

"They look quite friendly," she noted, enjoying her good mood and the mild sunny weather.

He took his eyes off of them to look at her. "Yes, and in no small part due to their lack of female companionship for some time," he teased.

She clasped her hands in front of her and studied his expression. "I would hope you are a willing guardian should they accost us," she said lightly, though not in complete jest.

"You needn't be concerned with their conduct, Olly. I assure you." Walking around to the back of the cart, he pulled out a half-full bucket of horse feed and handed it to her. "Could you please take care of the horse, and I will bring him some water," he requested. "I am going to speak with them and start on the crates. I ask that you remain here," he insisted seriously.

She nodded. "Yes of course."

As he walked away and tipped his hat at the soldiers, a strange feeling overcame her and she realized he knew the men. Their skin was radiant like that of the beautiful young women at the theater. They seemed overly happy to see Ehren and were vigorous in their handshakes on his approach.

She patted the horse as he ate, but couldn't help but glance over at the men as they talked. Their smiles were wide, but even though Ehren was facing away from her, she could tell he suddenly addressed them somberly as their expressions turned serious and curious.

Two of them looked over at her and then back at him and she got the distinct feeling her situation was being discussed. She supposed he was warning them of her possible ignorance on some matters and that could only mean she might soon be meeting them herself.

After a minute passed, the four of them opened the screen door and entered the glass front store.

A light wind picked up and sent waves through the tall grass to her right. Tumbleweed rolled out from behind a large boulder and slowly jolted and spun until it was out of sight beside the store.

The horse lifted its head indicating it had had what it wanted and she moved the bucket aside, watching as a solider exited the middle store, an army checkpoint it would seem. In appearance he didn't look the same as the others and he did not glance over at her.

With papers in his hand, he approached the army automobile and got inside, starting up its motor and driving it past her cart and back onto the main road. She turned her attention to the street, the two pony carts and the lack of other appropriate vehicle.

Picking up the bucket, she walked it back over to the cart and lifted it up into it, noticing that one of the radiant soldiers was exiting the store. He had two large boxes balancing atop each other and he was walking it over to her.

She instinctively checked the chains on the cart and managed to get both of them unhooked so he could slide them onto the cart platform. He appeared to be in his early twenties, like the theater girls, and his smile was genuine as he nodded at her with some level of trained officiality.

"Lovely weather that blesses us today," he said, studying her curiously.

She smiled, getting the sense of genuine warmth from him. "Why yes, and much to our advantage too, for our cart has no roof," she said, pointing at the bench seat.

"Indubitably." he laughed and clapped his hands together appreciatively. "My name is Arthur and we will be riding back with you."

"Oh, do you reside in the main township?"

He seemed strangely surprised by her question. "No, not at all. The majority of our tenure is spent at the theater. It's been like that for quite some time now."

Before she could question him further, the other men, with arms equally full, exited the store, talking loudly and laughing. Ehren was the last of them, and seemed to be talking, with his foot holding the door open, to the storeowner inside.

Within minutes the cart was three quarters full and two of the equally young soldiers stepped over the boxes of provisions so they could rest against the back of the bench. Ehren finished up with giving a drink to the horse while the third soldier, Arthur, waited at the side of the cart.

When all was said and done, Olly was sandwiched between Ehren and the effervescent, Arthur, as the four of them caught up on the tales from Europe. Though jovially presented, Olly could tell they had witnessed some terrifying events, getting into quite a few close scrapes themselves.

The sun warmed up a little more and the soldiers pulled out their brown paper bags, sharing sweet crackers they had gotten from France. It didn't take long for Olly to realize that they were not involved in active duty rather they were at war in a secondary nature.

After one of them detailed a quick operation he had been forced into assisting with on the frontlines, Olly found the courage to join the conversation. "Are you doctors?" she asked as she turned her body so she faced Arthur and could see the two behind them.

The three of them exchanged a glance while Ehren shifted in his seat uncomfortably.

"Not as such," the blonde haired one answered.

"Not at all really," the one with broad shoulders beside him interceded. "Our interactions there are much more in an advisory capacity."

Arthur nodded. "Yes we counsel those that need it, point them in the right direction when required."

The blonde man nodded agreeably and then ventured to elaborate. "But we will help with hasty procedures," he said, musing on it. "We get involved with that often enough because we all have ability in healing."

Ehren shifted on his seat again. Admittedly, Olly was enjoying her closeness to him but he seemed dissatisfied with the direction of the conversation though she couldn't determine any rationality for it.

The broad shouldered man nudged the blonde man as discretely as possible. "We are just there to help like anyone else," he elucidated nonchalantly. "But we don't engage in the conflict at all."

"Oh I am glad to hear that," Olly said honestly. "Just the same, I imagine it's quite dangerous for you to be entrenched in the action."

They all agreed in their expression and she sensed the tension they felt and hoped they would be able to forget about a lot of it.

The blonde one suddenly piped up merrily and lifted his army cap. "Please forgive our manners," he said, looking at her with a smile. "We've had quite a long trip back. I understand you've become acquainted with Arthur there, but my name is Andrew, and this is Melly at my side."

"Short for Melvin," the broad shouldered one explained. "May I ask what your name is?"

Even without seeing him, Olly felt Ehren's eyes on her. "Well, I am afraid I have lost my memory and I can not recall my actual name," she explained, trying not to broach the subject too gravely. "But we have settled on Olly."

Melvin leaned forward, resting his hands on his crossed legs. "I encountered a few cases of profound memory loss over there," he said, looking at her concerned. "May I ask what preceded the impediment?"

She tried to lower her head a little to avoid the glare of the sun in her eyes, but there was no relief and her hat was purely ornamental. "I can not be sure how long I was lying out there," she began. "But it was evening and I was discovered unconscious behind the theater. We surmised that I was hit on the head and my purse was taken from me, as we hadn't found one on my person."

Melvin immediately looked at Ehren who was strangely quiet, but of course he had his eyes intent on the road. "A lady shouldn't be going out in the evenings alone," Melvin voiced to her quietly.

"I take that under good advisement, Melly," she said, alleviating the moment with a smile. "Just the same, you shouldn't fear a similar incident on my account. Should I find myself in equal predicament, I might just be concussed and fortuitously regain my memory."

The three of them laughed, even Ehren seemed to show signs of lightening up.

"You are a wonder," Melvin said with amusement in his pale blue eyes. "Where did you unearth this treasure, Ehren?"

"That would be Gilpin's find," he replied as he shook the reins for the horse to move a little faster over a dirt mound.

A big smile appeared on Arthur's face and he laughed. "Of course. I'd wager that sweet lad pays you good attention."

She nodded. "I am blessed by his friendship," she said honestly.

The cheerful topic of Olly's younger friend began a jovial conversation about the days when he was a boy and his many antics. The remainder of their journey was sunny and light hearted. Olly was happy to experience as much laughter on their return as her and Ehren had on their way there.

They arrived as the sun was setting and Ehren helped Olly down where she promptly stretched some of the aches out of her body from the ride.

Arthur took the remainder of his brown paper bag and brought it around to her. "There is enough here for you and Gilpin. I happen to know he likes these ones," he said with a wink.

"Thank you, Arthur. It was very nice making your acquaintance."

"Likewise," he said with a smile. "Me and the lads are going to set up camp in the rooms," he said to Ehren.

Ehren nodded. "Get some rest and I'll join with you soon."

The three soldiers tipped their caps and waved at Olly as they entered through the side door.

"Thank you for taking me along with you," Olly said to Ehren as he still faced her.

Studying her face, he looked like he wanted to say something but it was obvious he would withhold it, maintaining his air of intrigue. "I enjoyed your company greatly," he said honestly. "I hope you will journey there again with me, when next I go."

She smiled, wishing he didn't have to leave her side now, although she did feel fatigued. "I would very much like that. As long as I am still occupying the theater at that time," she added, regretting her words as she spoke them.

Simultaneously their expressions mirrored each other's somberness. "Yes, of course."

She ventured to correct her sentiment but there were no suitable words to offer.

Placing his hands in his pants pocket, he took out a small box and handed it to her. "I had to endeavor a great deal of flattery to acquire that for you," he said with a smirk. "Mrs. Lambton from the store bakes exceptionally good honey nut cookies and I am certain you will like it."

Smiling, she stared at the box, trying to calm her racing heartbeat at the same time. "I would like to share it with you," she suggested, deep down hoping he would see it as an extended invitation to spend more time together.

Looking over her shoulder at the full cart, he shook his head. "No, that is my gift to you, Ms. Olly. It is yours alone. Besides, I must perform the amiable task of unloading the cart and returning the horse."

"I understand," she said. "I hope you have a pleasant evening, Ehren."

He nodded, and turned away from her, contemplative again.

Chapter Eleven

Close to an hour later, Olly lay on her bed, half undressed but distinctly restless. Gilpin didn't appear to be in his room, nor was Gleda in the near vicinity.

The record she had put on was soothing but it didn't keep her thoughts from Ehren or the dream man that made her heart fill so quickly. Even though she was fatigued from the long day, she wasn't tired enough to battle her emotions and she decided she would seek out her friends.

Redressing now into the green princess dress that Gleda had loaned her, she hoped to find Gilpin. She would playfully present him with the French crackers in some ceremonious way to make him laugh. Now with the thought of it creating a giddy energy within her, she hurried her change in costuming.

For added novelty, she quickly fashioned a crown from a gold silk swatch, which she was now running out of, and pinned it atop her thick hair.

Leaving the light on and the record as it played the last song beneath the needle, she ventured out with enthusiasm. Closing the door, she found the hall to be quite dark; only one lantern offered her enough light to make her way to the heavy curtain divide.

Her basic flat white shoes still made a sound in the open empty hall space. She had heard a large group join together earlier to eat dinner but it was all packed up now. With the brown paper bag clutched in both hands in front of her, she took a deep breath and enjoyed the moment of anticipation.

Without certainty or love or understanding, she had much to be grateful for and right now she was relishing the quiet space. Standing at the room's center, she turned to look at the silent stage. One tall lantern illuminated the area, casting orange shadows over the antique furniture and broom.

In this time of contemplation, Olly wondered what would come of her but she wouldn't go too far into that thinking for fear of becoming melancholic. Suddenly she sensed someone and turned around to see Aylward standing beneath the archway that led to the backrooms.

"Oh, you startled me, I didn't know you were there," she said.

He clasped his hands serenely in front of his long white robe and tilted his head slightly to look her over. "Clarence and Esther sought you out at the restaurant, Questa. In one visit alone you created an impact in which others observed your absence."

She walked up to him, conscious of her childish crown, but he didn't stare at her in any unusual way. "You are very kind to express it that way," she said appreciatively. "Ehren insisted he wanted me along but I was sorry to have missed helping you."

The glint in his eyes expressed more than his stifled mannerisms. "The young men returned with you?"

"Yes."

"They possessed sweets from France?"

Olly smiled, seeing through his serious questioning. "I have some crackers here, would you like some?"

He smiled, but only slightly. "Two will suffice."

She opened the bag and held it in front of him so he could take two out.

Savoring the first one, he looked at her curiously. "I appreciate you stirring my lotion, it was an effective batch; perhaps your goodness aided it."

"It is doubtful but I am grateful to you for letting me tend to it," she said, taking a cracker for herself before closing the bag. "Do you know where Gilpin is in this moment?"

Finishing his second cracker then stroking his long beard, he peered over her shoulder and pointed down the hallway. The right hallway was where the ladies dressing room and side door was, but he gestured to the left hallway.

"You will find him down there. Be mindful that he is in the sewing room and may not hear you. I suggest you enter without notice."

"He uses a sewing machine?"

He nodded, without reaction. "The boy has many skills and has always requested to learn all that others are willing to teach him."

She looked back at the darkened hallway, the one that had the stairs leading up to Ehren's room. She noticed three rooms there and decided she would be able to work out which one he was in. "May I help at the restaurant tomorrow?"

He nodded. "I will come for you. Good evening, Questa," he said, walking away towards the curtains.

"Good evening," she returned, before walking with her bag towards the left hall. She stopped briefly at the bottom of the stairs and could smell the incense and for a moment wondered about Ehren, but then she remembered her mission.

Turning to face the three doors, she could clearly see the first one opened into a dark room so knew that couldn't be his location.

Venturing to listen in at the furthest door, she was distracted by laughter in the middle room. Assuming he had someone with him, and hoping it was Gleda, she did as she was instructed, and opened the door without forewarning.

Immediately struck by the large group of men in the room, she stood in shock and bewilderment.

Four electrical lights hung from the ceiling and all of the men were faced away from her, laughing and talking, playing a game of sorts. Over the noise, she hadn't been immediately detected.

As Arthur, directly in front of her, bent down to retrieve something, she was quickly able to see over him at the game in action. Instead of leaving the room like her instincts urged her to do, she found herself staring at the strange unearthly items floating in the air

Hovering above a glossy black marble table, were nine small bright lights, brighter than anything she had ever knowingly seen. She looked for something that held them up but there were no strings or stands, they floated independently in the air, unaided.

One of Clarence's goat-like friends quickly picked up a larger glowing circular ball and brought his arm back then threw it at the lights. Moving in slow motion, it hit four of the lights which vanished on impact then the ball fell directly down and stopped above the marble table where it hovered.

Olly gasped, knowing that what she had witnessed was something indisputably magical. Her intake of breath caused everyone in the room to turn and look at her. The goat men, Clarence, and the soldiers stared at her while Ehren promptly approached her with fear in his eyes.

Grabbing her arms, he led her out of the room and shut the door behind them. "What did you see?" he demanded, grasping her arms tightly, holding her close to him to look into her eyes for honesty.

"I don't know what it is that I saw," she replied quickly. Her heart beat faster and now she was scared he was going to throw her out into the streets.

"Did you see the obniongs?" he questioned as he shook her a little.

"What?"

"Did you see the lights? Did you witness what was played? The objects?"

She couldn't tell if he was furious or afraid but tears sprung to her eyes, she wished she had never walked in on them. "Yes, I did, I am sorry. I entered the wrong room."

Suddenly laughter erupted from the room; they had obviously continued to play. He quickly pushed her to the back of the hallway and held her there near the entrance of the scented stairway. "What do you make of it?"

Swallowing hard, tears threatened to fall but even though she was afraid for him to see her cry, she kept her gaze on his stern blue eyes. "It is a game I suppose."

"And the lights?"

She shook her head unsure of what response he wanted. "I've not seen them before, they seem very mysterious."

He brought his face so close to hers and just in that moment she could see that it was fear in his gaze. "Who will you tell of this?"

"I would not relay it to anyone," she said directly. "I would not breathe a word of it if you wish, not to anyone."

His expression softened but he was in incredulous, almost like he thought he had let her down by not locking the door. "Is this your solemn promise? Do you speak this vow from the heart?"

A strange sense of anxiety overtook her and she felt as if her body was burdened with shock. Lifting her shaking hand to his face, she touched his cheek ever so gently; fearful he might react without provocation.

"I would never betray you, Ehren, that is my promise and I am loyal to you and the people here." Tears now fell from her pain filled eyes as she placed her hand on his chest. "I am sorry beyond words. In my imagination I could not fathom being sorrier than this. Will you cast me out? Do you wish me to leave? I will never return here if I have injured your trust in any manner."

Surprising her, tears now fell from his eyes and he quickly pulled her into his arms and held her. "Never leave, mysterious angel. I beg of you, never leave," he said as she felt his chest rise and fall with emotion. She knew he had experienced loss but were his words for her or for a memory of another?

Returning his affection, she remained there, thriving on his warmth, holding onto that feeling. That yearning that was so strong inside of her was like lightning on her skin and beneath it. "I will never speak of it, Ehren. I wish I could offer you an insight into my heart so you knew this to be true."

He held her arms again, looking into her eyes with deep regret. "I do not doubt you, this I swear. I should not have reacted as such. Please forgive my wildish impulses. I protect the affairs within the theater walls with utmost precedence."

Clasping the paper bag in both hands again, she worried that he might have regretted his words as well as his affection towards her so she discretely created distance between them. "You feared, that because I had witnessed something of a shocking nature, I might unwittingly relay it to a person that did not reside here."

"Yes." He nodded then quickly wiped the tears from his face. He no longer wore his hat or jacket, and some of the buttons at the top of his shirt were undone, he looked tired.

Removing the ruby ring from her finger, she took his hand in hers and placed it in his palm. "This is my only possession and it is cherished by me. I will give it to you so you know that what I speak is truth. It does me great harm for you to hold my words in disbelief."

He quickly put the ring back on her finger and shook his head wildly. "Never part with this ring, Olly. If you must give me something, then let it be your forgiveness," he pleaded. He then pointed at her as if gesturing for her to remain where she stood. "Please, give me one moment."

With that, he returned to the room and closed the door behind him. It was quiet behind the door but she used that time to calm her heart and wipe her tears as she stared down at the ring.

Suddenly he opened the door and called her over. "We wish you to play with us," he said.

Hesitant to join a noisy group, she didn't wish to displease him and followed without resistance. As they entered and he closed the door, she was certain the men would seem unhappy with her participation but they accepted her warmly.

Melvin, who was nearest to her, stood and placed his army cap on her head. "I'd say it was your turn, Olly," he said cheerfully.

Clarence walked around and handed her the glowing ball, which seemed a little warm but not just from his grasping it. "With your thoughts, imagine hitting as many of those lights that you can, Duchess," he instructed. "Throw as hard as you can, it will not reach the other fellows here."

Unsure of the overall concept, she concentrated on what he had said; wondering if hoping for something could really accomplish much. Just the same, as she threw the glowing ball, it shot out towards the small lights and bounced back and forth, vanishing eight of them.

The group of men roared and clapped in immediate support. "Exceptional!" Arthur called out. "Try it again, you must show us if you can do it twice!"

As the ball was passed to her again, she glanced to her left at Ehren who now displayed great confidence in her. She sensed it in his face, he no longer doubted her and she would allow herself to relax and enjoy the evening.

Throwing the ball with the same intentions, she hit seven and nearly reached eight. Another raucous applause erupted and Olly laughed, in relief and joy. She was becoming one of them; she would not be turned away.

Chapter Twelve

Glancing at the thick record needle, Olly pondered venturing out in search of another album but didn't want to seem ungrateful for the one offered to her. Three nights had passed since she played the game with Ehren and the other men.

Since that time, she hadn't seen much of him but had concentrated her efforts on cleaning and working at the restaurant. Lying on her bed, she spun the ruby ring around her finger. Mindlessly staring out of the narrow window, she watched as the orange sun descended behind the building next to the theater.

Wearily closing her eyes, fatigued from the long day with the flu sufferers, Olly let her thoughts drift. Ehren was the first thing to come to her mind, he always was. It wasn't just his handsome face, his hair, his dashing countenance; it was something about his very nature, his soul perhaps.

Was she in love with him? She screwed up her face, annoyed that the thought entered her mind. She couldn't think about it. Once she used such a word as love, such a strong significant word, there would be no return for her.

She was no child, she reasoned as she tugged at the long sleeves of her nightgown. It was her responsibility to be sensible and rational and the ardor for a handsome, charismatic stranger would all in all be impractical.

A knock on the door came as a welcome distraction. "Yes?"

"Olly, are you presently engaged?"

She sprung up, her long braid flinging over her shoulder as she rushed across to Gilpin's door and quickly opened it. Startled, he stepped back in response.

"I am not engaged," she said hurriedly. "I am the opposite of occupied in any sense, whatever the opposite is, that is my current disposition."

A big smile appeared on his young handsome face as he ran a hand through his brown tussled hair. He was dressed in costume, royal-like as if he was a young squire in King Arthur's court. "Are you able to spend time with us?" he asked.

Ignoring her state of inappropriate attire, she opened the door a little further and reached out to touch his hand. "Gilpin, where have you been? I have not seen you for some time, nor Gleda, and apart from a brief encounter with Clarence, hardly has a word been spoken to me. Have I been shunned in some manner?"

His smile faded immediately, sincerely concerned for her assumption. "No, don't ever think like that. We talked about you the whole time," he insisted as he moved a little closer. "We had a matter that we all had to take care of—," he stopped before he finished his sentence. Once again, the mystery of the theater people was solidified. "We were all busy but it is dealt with at this time. I came to ask if you would like to be entertained."

"Here?" she enquired. "Will you dance for me?"

He laughed heartily as he pulled on his princely tunic top which seemed a little short for his tall slender frame. "Melly can tickle the ivories in such a fashion that you can feel like you are in the picture that you see."

"I enjoy the piano I believe. What picture do you speak of?" she asked curiously as she glanced over his shoulder to see that he had tidied his room.

"Oh, we wanted to take you to the picture theater in town. Gleda, me and Clarence are going in a short time from now. Andy knows how to operate the equipment and Melly plays the piano for the show."

"Yes please, I would like to attend with you, but I'm not dressed, how much time before you leave?"

Suddenly a knock came at the hallway door into her bedroom. "Ms. Olly, can I enter?"

"Please do, Gleda," she called back.

Gleda popped her head in; she was obviously wearing a queen like dress herself in a rich burgundy color. Her smile was sweet and genuine and Olly sensed that she had missed her in equaled strength. "Is that what you wish to wear? Can I at least acquire a robe for you?"

Olly laughed, crossing her arms against the nightgown and blushing. "I was just told of it, but I will quickly change now if time allows it."

"We are dressing as royals," Gleda divulged excitedly, her eyes lit up as she said it. "I have chosen a wonderful pink dress for you and it is in the powder room now. You have time to clean and dress; I will meet you both at the side door."

Olly suddenly remembered something and put her hand out, gesturing for her to remain a moment longer. "It is quite fortuitous that we should dress as such, I have a gift for you both."

She went to the walnut table beside her bed and took out two paper-wrapped packages, excitedly strolling barefoot on her floor to pass it to each of them. "Do not unravel them in my sight," she instructed and they both laughed at her childlike coyness.

"You have me on the verge of thrill, Olly," Gleda said happily as she started to close the door behind her. "Don't be too long, I wish to get us closer to the front."

Returning her gaze to Gilpin, she noticed how happy he seemed as he looked at her. "May I open mine now?"

"Of course, but please keep in mind to forgive my lack of experience. Hand stitching is quite arduous and I am an official novice."

"You make wonderful things, Olly," Gilpin said as he eagerly undid the wrapping and stared at it. Holding it up he could see that it was a gold crown, fashioned from layering velvet fabric and stitching it together.

Quickly pulling it onto his head, he stepped into her room to look into the Egyptian mirror that sat atop the green silk fabric that covered two crates.

"Oh, Olly. You make it look so real. Everyone will call me a prince now."

She laughed but agreed, she had done quite well on it. "I imagine you more as a squire because you are so young," she said. "A noble one of course."

He turned to smile at her. "Did you make one for yourself?"

"Yes, do you wish me to wear it?"

Returning to his door he appeared eager to get the night underway. "You should, then you can be our queen."

"I promise I will."

Before closing the door completely he peeked back in at her. "I got us some peach tarts, special for us to take."

Smiling, she watched as the door closed and she busily prepared for their evening out, one that was well overdue.

Taking her crown and name-labeled undergarments to the ladies room, she washed with her cloth and got dressed into the pink lace dress that Gleda had put aside for her.

Happy and excited, she sprayed some perfume on her hair and neck then quickly but carefully, pinned her braided hair it into a spiral at the back of her head. The crown was the finishing touch and even though she didn't know who she used to be, for now she knew she was part of a group of wonderful people.

Stepping out of the bathroom, she heard voices and recognized one of them as Ehren. Smiling, she thought she would surprise him, make a comment about being a princess or something of that nature.

But she ended up stopping outside of the door, standing briefly in the darkness of the dim lit hallway to listen to ensure she didn't interrupt a private exchange. Fortunately she was correct to do so, because there was a tone of intense seriousness in the air as he spoke low to a woman with him.

Resisting at first, she finally peeked in, standing enough in the shadows to be out of sight. He was with Gleda and they were facing each other, looking at each other with tears in their eyes, speaking close to each other.

He placed his hands on her petite shoulders and sighed. "I love you, Gleda. I can not fathom what I would do without you."

She in turn, wrapped her arms around him and closed her eyes. "I love you too, Ehren."

There was more to their words but Olly refused to hear them. Being careful to not make a sound, she rushed out into the empty theater, praying the heavy curtains would send away the thoughts of what she had just witnessed.

Suddenly her dress felt like led as it hung on her drained body. The blood had gone from her; her spirit had deflated in such a way that she was gaunt with sadness. Closing her eyes she admonished her reaction. He had made no assurances to her and her heart belonged to another, even if she didn't know whom.

Taking in a good amount of oxygen, she tried to force the color into her cheeks, imagining herself coming back to life, but to no avail. Why should she cry for him? Gleda was a beautiful wonderful woman and he was a kind charming man and they had both been so good to her.

Placing her hands over her face she prayed in that moment, hoping with all of her might to let go of the feelings she had. This was a good thing, she reasoned as she pressed her fingers into her skin and bent over, trying to stop the tears from falling. This was a rational and helpful occurrence for now she had no reason to feel conflicted.

The day she would meet again with her true love, when she would finally fall into his arms, she would be able to leave with him unburdened. She must have just been lonely for the man in her dreams and projected it onto Ehren somehow.

If only she could make herself believe it. She would *try*; she thought as she raised her head and crossed her arms, taking in a determined breath. No particular thing occurred between them that should cause that desire anyway. There was nothing to cause an emotional response; she would be the epitome of grace and decorum.

Hearing their voices, she realized they had come out of the kitchen and would soon be entering the theater. With the aid of her quiet white shoes, Olly quickly rushed across the floor to the right hallway, past the ladies dressing room and out of the side door.

Opening the door with a little too much gusto, Gilpin instantly looked at her in a way that she could tell he was going to question her. Fortunately Clarence was standing beside him, dressed in deep blue, also a prince like outfit, and she quickly thrust a gift into his hands. "I have made a gift for you, Clarence, Duke of the theater dwellers."

He laughed, enjoying her improvised title, but in his eyes she could see that he had noticed the somberness in her own expression too.

Not deterred, Gilpin appeared to reattempt his questioning on her state of mind, but Gleda now opened the door and came out to stand with them. She smiled wide at Olly and placed her hands on her own head, proudly showing off her crown. "You have talent in all endeavors you attempt, Ms. Olly," she said, taking a step forward and kissing her on the cheek.

"I am so glad you like it," Olly said, doing everything she could to not let her envy upset their friendship. "It looks beautiful on you, if only I knew how to work with real gold."

"The authentic head adornments are heavy and awkward," Clarence said from behind her. "This is comfortable whilst serving the truer purpose of ensuring the peasants are aware of my handsomeness *and* status."

They all laughed as Olly reached up to straighten his crown while enjoying the appreciative look in his eyes.

"It is a wonderful gift, Duchess," he said. "I cherish it beyond measure and wear it with undulated pride."

"It does emphasize your overall appeal," Olly said with a smile. "I'm sure you will be the favored topic amongst the peasant girls."

He smiled in response, enjoying a moment to entertain the idea. "Shall we go?"

She took his arm while Gilpin and Gleda talked happily between themselves. The four crowned friends were able to find seating in the front row of adjoining folded chairs.

Melly walked in wearing a toga and a false beard and stood in front of the piano, bowing for a sense of novelty. They all clapped, including the ten other towns' people sitting randomly on the chairs behind them.

Olly surmised that there were probably many more who were able to attend and in need of the morale but likely they were too afraid of contracting the flu.

The gray shadowed people in the moving picture appeared on the wide stretched canvas moving in a slightly unnatural jolted fashion. Melly lifted his arms up before bringing his hands down onto the piano keys and belting out an enthusiastic tune to match the mood of the scene.

Minutes later as Charlie Chaplin entered their vision, Melly twinkled the keys to represent the actors childlike waddle. Gilpin reached under his seat and took out a small box, opening it to share snacks with his friends.

Since Ehren's journey to the other town, their refreshments had been bettered. Along with two larger tarts that Gilpin had cut up so they could each have a portion, Gleda had spent some time that afternoon baking some savory squares with a mysterious meat within.

Nonetheless they were very good and as Olly rested beside Gilpin she began to feel better as they laughed together and enjoyed the lively show.

Olly moved a little closer to Gilpin so she could remark to Gleda on his other side about how well Melly played the piano. Clarence agreed and he smiled at her as he could see she was relaxing into the evening. It was then that she saw Ehren move in and stand beside him.

Clarence looked up and smiled, allowing him to take his spot next to Gleda.

Ehren was also dressed in noble theme; wearing his kingly outfit she had seen him in some time ago. He acknowledged Gilpin and Gleda with a smile and laughed at their crowns then gestured to Olly, showing he was wearing the crowned flower she had made him.

She swallowed hard and refused to let him see any hurt in her eyes, that burning sensation behind them threatening to betray her inner turmoil. She smiled and nodded, showing her gratitude then watched as he whispered into Gleda's ear.

Avoiding looking at them or displaying any concern over it, Olly leaned back into her chair and took a deep breath, clasping her hands in her lap. She could feel Gilpin's eyes on her but what could she say to him? He had been friends with them since he was a child. She was still a stranger in relative terms.

Not that she would say anything offensive about them, but how could she share these feelings with him? Who could she tell now?

Charlie spun around on the screen while Melly kept one finger on the piano keys and mirrored his action, causing the small audience to laugh. Olly tried to laugh, she wanted to, it was amusing, he was sweet and talented and she was amongst wonderful people.

Staring up at the screen she noted to herself how lucky she was to be there in that moment and concentrated on the plot and the wording on the screen as Charlie spoke. Just the same her sincere attempt was no match for her feelings.

Her thoughts turned to her sunny ride with Ehren. Why had he wanted her to go with him? He had at one point, tucked a wisp of her hair behind her ear, a gesture often perceived as more intimate than friendly. Closing her eyes she tried to rid her mind of it all.

No matter what had been said, even the day in Aylward's room, the way he looked at her sometimes, it was irrelevant. He was indisputably charming and handsome; perhaps he was naturally affectionate to all of the females there.

The audience laughed again, momentarily breaking her out of her ponderings but not for long. She was resolved to distract herself with thoughts of the man in her dreams.

Maybe if she concentrated hard enough now, maybe she could look around in her memory and see if there was anything else in the hills, some clue or word. That feeling, when she was with him, even now as she recalled it, it was an emotion that went through her whole body.

There was something about Ehren that was unlike any other man she knew. The way she felt when she was around him, she knew other women couldn't possibly feel as strongly about him as she did. His presence was strong yet gentle, but he was Gleda's, he said he had loved her.

Warmth bubbled up to Olly's cheeks and she knew that tears would soon follow. She briefly leaned towards Gilpin without looking at him. "I must go to the powder room, please excuse me," she said, emotion getting caught in her throat as she left as quickly as she could.

Locating the back door in the semi darkness, she rushed outside and let the cooler air placate her for a moment. Looking back down towards the tall lantern that stood quietly in front of the theater Olly considered not returning there.

Chapter Thirteen

Removing her hand made crown, Olly held it in both of her hands as she stepped down from the picture theater steps and into the cool night. Only three street lanterns were lit and no doubt there was no one left to relight the others.

The streets were mostly deserted. August was coming to a close and the evening temperatures were brisk without the kindness of being refreshing.

Not wanting to remain on the steps for fear of one of her friends coming to look for her, Olly made her way back towards the theater but intended on visiting the restaurant instead.

Adamantly walking slow to calm her emotions, she strolled in a small gait, her queen dress swishing around her white shoes.

Crossing her arms against the cold she did all she could not to think of Ehren and the memory of him telling Gleda he loved her. Nonetheless, trying not to think of something was a certain way to assure its presence in one's mind.

A gust of wind picked up and Olly hastened her pace but was suddenly diverted by something shiny in the alley between two vacant stores. Taking a few steps into the darkness, she bent to pick it up and studied it.

Holding it up to the crescent moon, which had little to offer in way of lighting, she found it to shine unaided. In that way it was much like the glowing lights in the game she played a few evenings ago. Another piece, another clue, yet this shiny unadorned coin-like object did little to enlighten her.

This town, these theater people, who were they? and more importantly, who was she? Yet regardless of it all, how lucky she was to know them and have them take her in as they did.

Even though her heart ached and she admittedly had feelings for Ehren, she would not let him or any of them down because of that. Sensibly, she would take some time to herself and go to the restaurant for now.

Straightening her stance in the dark alley, she held the coin and crown in her hands when she stiffened and listened to the sound of footsteps approaching. By the sound she identified it as a man's tread and when he appeared, passing her slowly, she could see he was upset.

He was lugging a small trunk, but he seemed deeply distracted and he had not observed her standing there at all.

Olly considered offering him assistance, not that she would be able to enlighten him much on town specifics, but one of Clarence's friends, she believed his name to be Adrian, approached him before she could.

Adrian was dressed surprisingly formal, for all of the theater dwellers usually wore costumes or white clothing for the restaurant. However, he was dressed in a vest and suit, small spectacles over his goat like face, distinctly reminding her of an apothecary.

She could see both men clearly, illuminated by one of the street lamps. The stranger was visibly taken aback on first sight of Adrian but was calmed by his clothing and passive approach.

"Good evening sir," Adrian said with a polite smile. "Please do not be alarmed. I have good references but I have not seen you here before. I had hoped to offer my assistance as you appear to be short on direction."

"I am aware of my location," the man said quietly, resting his trunk against his gray suit pants. "The only direction I am in need of is settling on a course of action. I can only suppose some manner of deliberation will present me with a solution."

Adrian tipped his hat slightly so the man could see his eyes, and then clasped his hands in a priest like way. "I acknowledge that we have not been acquainted before this encounter but these times have altered us all greatly. Please speak freely about your quandary for certainly as you look upon me you can presuppose that I have overcome much to become who I am now."

The man, perhaps in his sixties, tipped his hat also and studied the man as he contemplated his openness. "My daughter was taken by the illness a few months past," he said, sighing to prevent further emotion.

Adrian studied his somber expression and nodded. "It is very painful, I am sorry for you."

The man shook his head and then nodded excessively. "She married some soldier, nice fellow as far as they go, but he brought the disease back with the first ones and he died just about a week prior to her."

"And what of your wife?"

"She's been gone since we were in our youth. She tried to have another child but there was some complication and they both died so it left me to raise my girl alone."

Keeping still, Adrian looked him over compassionately. "Have you lost your business too? I know many have fallen on hard times."

The man shook his head as he placed his hands in his pockets and stared at the ground. "I shoe the horses and they seem to be living through this mess."

Olly studied Adrian's face and realized he was studying the man and presenting his own mannerisms accordingly. He must have been very perceptive.

"Martin Peel is coming for some of the townsfolk tonight to take them to the airbase. Will you journey out with him?" Adrian enquired casually.

The man reacted with surprise at his revelation but then looked down at his trunk and realized he had made a reasonable assumption.

"I've stood here three different times now waiting on Mr. Peel and I'm not sure I will get on his cart this time either."

"Does something keep you here?"

The man looked at Adrian, obviously comforted by his nature. "My daughter loved this town. She was going to marry in the church on the corner, she was going to have children and make me a grandfather," he said, with tears in his eyes.

"When her condition worsened, she asked me to stay here, here in *this* town because the other people here care about me. She wanted to make sure I had people around me so I wouldn't get too lonely."

Adrian nodded. "She sounds like a kindhearted girl," he noted. "But perhaps as you stand here with your belongings, there is something beyond this town that calls for you?"

The man swallowed hard then turned away, Olly suspected he might have shed a tear, he was visibly conflicted. "Years ago now, I went on down the road to tend to a horse and met up with a woman," he began to explain. "She is a good virtuous woman, bright and of considerable wit. She was helping her friend out there, but she originated from the other side of the state."

"You were impressed by her."

The man nodded. "I had been alone a long time without Livvy, and my daughter had already grown up by this time. I don't think my girl would have minded her, Eloise; the woman's name is Eloise. I just never got around to telling her. She was busied with her teaching and social gatherings. I just never told her."

Adrian, having listened attentively, smiled slightly but as an offer of solace. "Does Eloise wait for you now?"

He nodded. "I have told her to not expect me but she insists on waiting for me to accept that she makes me happy and go to her."

"And this conflicts with your daughter's request."

"Yes. She only asked one thing of me, to stay in this town."

"I understand you have made a promise that you wish to honor, but if you allow, I can advise a solution," Adrian offered gently.

The man appeared very open to the idea and nodded again. "I have given up hope so nothing you say will harm me, so please speak freely."

"Do you believe in Heaven?"

"Yes, of course."

Adrian shifted on the spot but kept his hands clasped, attempting to get eye contact. "Do you suppose then, when you die, you will see your daughter?"

The man's curiosity was piqued for it appeared he couldn't predetermine what Adrian was going to say. "Yes. She will be there when I finally die. I will see her then."

"I believe that to be true," Adrian said with a smile. "But you fear that her request will put her at ill ease if not obeyed. She asked you to stay in this town for a reason."

Pain appeared in the man's expression. "I wish to respect that."

"Yes, I do understand. However, she asked you to remain here because she believed it would make you the most pleased. What do you think was most important to her; you staying here or your happiness?"

The man considered his words thoughtfully. "She believed they were one and the same."

Adrian nodded and smiled again. "She believed you would be happy here because she did not know about Eloise. She was fearful of you leaving this town because she did not want you to be alone."

"She told me often she wanted me to be happy, such a kind girl."

"If she was able to speak to you now, she would be aware of your love for Eloise. She would tell you to take that ride on Martin Peel's cart because that is what she wants; she wants you to be happy. She only asked you to stay here because she didn't know that if you left here, you would be *less* lonely, not more."

The man's hands begun to shake a little as he looked at Adrian with tears in his eyes. "She truly wanted the best for me. I just loved her, she was my life."

"And she loved you so much she wanted you to do what made you happiest, she just didn't have all the details. The only way you can honor her is listen to her reason, not her words. Most of all she didn't want for you to be alone."

"In your belief, I should leave here."

Adrian nodded. "She will not want to see you lonely for the remainder of your time here. If you do not leave, and remain here alone, it would surely make her sad."

Suddenly a horse with an extended roofed cart approached the quiet street. The man looked Adrian over, still conflicted, fearful of making a hasty decision.

Adrian approached the horse and gestured for the man to walk towards it. Olly took a few steps to watch.

"Your daughter's soul is in heaven. She will watch you and be pleased that you are well and loved. Her spirit is with you, it does not remain in this town, and she will follow you. There is nothing keeping you here"

It must have been the reassurance he needed to hear. He reached out and shook Adrian's hand vigorously. "Thank you, my friend. God bless you."

"Safe journey," Adrian said as two women followed the man in and Martin Peel's cart turned to take them out of town.

Adrian turned and walked away and Olly was careful to remain in the shadows but was very surprised to see him return to the theater without delay. It was as if he had come outside intentionally for this interaction, but surely it couldn't be.

144

Olly entered the abandoned street and looked further down the road as a small group walked towards the end of the street. Three short men and one woman wearing long dark hooded cloaks talked as they approached the front of the theater.

There was something unique in their rigid gaits. A quick glance beneath the front lantern offered her a better look at their very small eyes and noses. So many people visited the theater but there were no performances at this time. Where did they sleep?

She gave the building more thorough observation and noticed there was actually a third floor containing many small darkened windows. Surely these many strange people stayed in those rooms. But where did they come from and why did they come?

It intrigued Olly no end but she was not concerned by them, more so fascinated by all that took place around them. As she walked slowly back, careful not to be seen as the door closed behind them, Olly pondered her good fortune.

Such a magical place with such kind people, so helpful and generous, and they let *her* live there with them, she would never forget them.

Her musings were suddenly interrupted by three shadows rushing out into the street. They had come from the side of the theater, the same place where they had assumedly attacked her. The three Hanley boys ran out, passing behind the streetcar and disappearing behind the five and ten cent store.

Olly's heart raced reactively as she realized that they were running from someone and it could have been another victim. Still holding her crown and coin, she lifted her dress and ran towards the theater, rushing courageously onto the cobblestones.

There was a lady lying there, she looked to be the same age as Olly and appeared quiet distraught. Olly rushed to her side, bending down to help her into a sitting position.

She wore a nice modern dress but she had no hat and was having difficulty with breathing. "Please do not draw near," she said, holding her hand out fearfully. "I am struck with the flu."

"I am safe from it," Olly said convincingly, though without the ointment she could not be sure of it. "Did they thieve from you?"

The woman could barely lift her arm to wipe the perspiration from her gaunt face. She did not look well but the war time had people out at odd hours when they should be at home healing.

"I fell. They had wanted to take from me, but they saw my condition and thought different of it," she explained. "Everyone knows they are orphans and I felt for them, having children of my own, so I threw them some of my money and they ran with it."

"You are kind to think of others in your state," Olly said honestly. "Where are your children now?"

She rested against Olly and tried to get more air into her lungs. Finally she spoke again. "They are with mother. I was going to remain in bed this night but I felt the cough rising, I had come to see if perhaps there was syrup available for it somewhere."

"Is your mother expecting you tonight?" Olly enquired, looking around to make sure she had not lost anything else from her person.

The woman's hair bun suddenly unraveled as if she had pinned it in haste. Olly felt sad for her. "No. She will check on me tomorrow morning though."

"Do you have a husband we should notify?"

Her lowered gaze caused Olly's heart to sink. "He is at war. I do not wish for him to worry for me but I do not believe he will return to find me here alive."

Olly placed her crown and coin in her left hand and tucked her free arm under the woman's arms, helping her to stand.

"I will not hear of it," she insisted. "I will take you now to rest in the restaurant. They have turned it into a hospital. They are my friends and are very kind and gentle and will help you."

The woman appeared so fatigued, her hazel eyes reddened and weary. Minutes later Olly found a bed for her and talked to Esther about her situation.

"Will you be returning to the theater, Milady?" Esther asked her with gentle eyes.

Olly shook her head, keeping her voice low as the woman got situated on the cot beside her. "I wish to stay with her for a while. Do you have some ointment and a mask, would you mind retrieving it for me?"

Esther gently pulled her aside. "I am glad to help you, but you look tired, are you certain you wouldn't rather retire for the evening?"

Olly smiled at her appreciatively, such a sweet young woman. "I have no where else I need to be, Esther. If I can presently remain and see her get well again, at least that is one happiness afforded me."

The pretty young woman with radiant skin and spirited eyes looked sadly upon her. "You are counted amongst us now, Milady. We take your happiness personally. I hope you know that we will always protect you."

Olly nodded, unable to speak for the emotion caught in her throat. "Thank you, truly."

The sick woman looked happy to be in more comfortable and protected surroundings. She turned to Olly and smiled the best she could. "Would you stay with me for a while?"

"Of course. I will remain until you wake. Please rest, no harm will come to you now."

The woman had fallen asleep not long after she lay on the cot. This allowed Olly time with her thoughts. The confusion, the gratitude, the loss, it was all too much to consider in one sitting.

Hours passed and she began to close her eyes. The room was settling, apart from a few people coughing loudly and sharply, most were asleep. Only three or four theater dwellers were there in attendance and they talked in respectful murmurs as they passed each other.

Olly's back was getting sore from sitting in that position and she pulled back her aching arm which had been kept at the woman's forehead.

Olly had fallen asleep for a short time, but not deep enough to satisfy her fatigue. This sensation of weariness at least diminished her emotional pain. She had felt she lost so much yet she didn't even know what it was she lost. How could she explain it to anyone? Who would understand a yearning to be with someone she couldn't even name?

Adjusting her lower face mask, she dropped the cloth into the bowl of room temp water and decided not to place it back on the woman's head for now. The woman's breathing had bettered, which she hoped was a sign of improvement.

As she stared at her with her thoughts elsewhere, she sensed someone standing nearby and looked up to see Ehren looking down at her. His expression was one of seriousness yet relief. He still wore his kingly outfit, but looking around she didn't see Gleda or Gilpin with him.

"We were concerned for you," he said quietly so as to not wake the sleeping patients.

She politely kept her focus in his direction but intentionally avoided his gaze, his warmth. "I had gone for fresh air and found this woman near the theater," she explained, equally as quietly. "The Hanley boys had gotten to her too and I promised to remain with her."

He crouched down close to her now, and she lowered her gaze to the tiled floor. "Did they cause her injury?"

"No. They were afraid she was ill but she gave them some money," she replied. "She has children, and I was hoping to get a message to her mother when she wakes."

He nodded; she could see his shadow on the floor in the dim lit room. "We will take care of it. I would like for you to return with me now."

"I want her to know she can trust me. I want for her to be comforted when she wakes and see that I have kept my word," she insisted, glancing up at him and his worried face.

"I can get Esther to explain for you. There is no need for you to remain."

"I would rather have a sense of purpose than not be needed at all," she remarked abruptly.

Looking at him, crouched down, close enough to emanate his warmth, he seemed saddened by her response. "Very well, if you so wish," he said before standing and walking away.

She immediately hung her head down and closed her eyes to stop the tears from falling. He had left, she had offended him. Yet only a minute passed and a cot was being put in front of her so she could lie next to the woman.

Gratefully she crawled onto it wearily.

There was only a small space left between the cots as the room was already congested. He flicked a clean folded sheet out and placed it over her, crouching down beside her cot and whispering to her. "I will also remain here, for then it is *my* purpose to be here when *you* wake."

She wanted to take him into her arms and hold his kindness in her heart. What would Gleda feel about him staying there for her?

He still looked at her, staring at her eyes, words upon his lips that he refused to say. Then before she could speak, to apologize, to thank him, she fell asleep.

Chapter Fourteen

A warm breeze picked up in the lush green hills as she stared at her closed hand. What had her love given her? She couldn't open it; she couldn't look up at him, but felt his breath on her neck. "What does it mean?" she asked aloud, but her words sounded like a whisper in the wind.

He spoke to her in another language. It was not one she recognized. "Forever," he said. She knew he had said that word, yet it was not in English, still she could hear the meaning inside of her. "What is forever?" she asked, praying for clarity.

"*We are*, my love."

He placed his hand against her face; she leaned towards it, pressing her skin against his, hoping to see his face, to see anything. The feeling of love consumed her, filled her heart so that it could barely be contained in one body.

"I will give you forever," she said as someone else came towards them.

A shadow was around but she wasn't afraid. She could feel someone watching her, she tried to look at her love, but he was gone. She suddenly jolted awake, realizing that the person approaching them was really someone approaching her in reality.

"It is me, Olly, please don't be afraid," Gilpin begged as he crouched beside her cot.

Her eyelids felt heavy, but he handed her an Altoids, knowing she liked to have one as soon as she woke. She placed it in her mouth and wanted to reach out for him to hold her, to give her comfort. "I am sorry, Gilpin. I had a dream; I don't mean to seem skittish."

He smiled gently as he got onto his knees and placed his hands on her hand, the one with the ruby ring he gave her. "Did you dream of the man in the hills again?"

"Yes," she replied, taking in a deep breath as she discretely stretched her body.

"Did you see anything else?"

"No, I'm afraid not. Has there been any word in town of me being recognized?"

"We tried, Olly, nothing yet, but please don't worry that you will always be lost. Every thing happens when it is supposed to."

She mused on his words as she lifted her pillow and folded it so she was sitting up a bit more. "Do you suppose that I lost my memory for a reason?" she asked seriously.

Contemplating the idea he nodded slightly but not committedly. "I have seen many blessings in the guise of tragedy."

She gazed at his youthful face, suddenly struck by his unblemished skin and the sincerity in his clear green eyes. "You are a blessing that is not so disguised," she said squeezing his hands. "I would intentionally suffer the same memory loss if it meant I was able to meet you again."

Touched by her words, he was unable to speak at first, with tears in his eyes he bent forward and kissed her hand. "I will protect you always, my sister. I will not allow your head to be violated any further."

"I should wear softer hats," she remarked as she laughed lightly, careful not to wake anyone. She sensed it to be early morning as light was peeking through the gaps in the fabric over the windows. "How is the woman I brought in?"

He looked over her to the woman in the next cot. "She is very well, Olly. She sleeps now but she had woken earlier and Esther said she asked for you to return home and not to wait for her."

"But I had wanted to stay and ensure her recovery."

Shaking his head, he appeared unexpectedly excited. "Clarence will return her home when she wakes next. They concluded she has not got the flu but she is fatigued and had gotten hoarse from rounding her animals."

"She does not have influenza?"

"No. They are certain and wish her to return home promptly so she will not be exposed to it further. She will need rest of course."

Olly sighed and rested into her pillow. "Oh I am relieved to hear it." Her eyes grazed over him briefly; he was wearing a white toga outfit so she knew he intended to work at the restaurant today.

Looking past him she remembered the previous night. "Ehren said he would remain here," she noted, hoping he would not derive any particular tone from her statement.

Not responding at first, Olly was worried when his expression registered upset. "Has something happened, Gilpin?"

"Do you remember the town where he had taken you to greet Arthur and the fellows?"

"Yes?" she responded, quickly sitting up and realizing how uncomfortable her body felt after having slept in a dress.

"He was beckoned there in the night," he replied quietly. He looked around seemingly unsure of who else knew.

Olly sat up and placed her shoed feet on the tiled floor as she leaned forward to look at him as he still knelt there. Though it hadn't been expressed, she sensed something ominous in his hesitant presentation. "Is he in danger?"

Getting to his feet, he decided to sit beside her on the cot. The open room was quiet and many hadn't risen yet and she sensed perhaps one or two weren't alive. "It is possible."

Olly closed her eyes for a moment, regretting her last words to Ehren, remorseful for her bluntness. "Why has he gone there?"

The worry in his young face was apparent as he looked upon her gravely. "A soldier had returned from the war yesterday and remained at that store you went to with Ehren. His time overseas had affected him greatly and he did not return the same as when he went there."

"In the sense of psychologically?"

"Yes. I was told that he hadn't wanted to go there to begin with but he was tormented by what he saw."

She nodded, sympathetic to his situation. "I am sorry for him," she said sincerely. "But what has this to do with Ehren?"

"The man, the one who returned this way, he threatened two other soldiers with guns. He thought they were German's going to kill him. The store owner summoned Ehren as he is the greatest of all counselors."

"Oh I wish I had been awake," she expressed with fear in her heart. "I wish I could have stopped him from going."

Gilpin placed his hand on her back and smiled comfortingly. "He is like you, Olly. He is stubborn in his ways and will not be deterred from heroic acts."

She smiled, enjoying his praise and observation. "I am sure Gleda is quite frantic. Is she very worried? Perhaps I should go to her to offer consolation."

Gilpin's smile turned to a frown as if he was confused by her statement. "She is worried for she is his friend but she believes he will be able to resolve the dispute peacefully."

Unsure of how much to express, but wanting to gain clarity, Olly persisted. "Certainly she has trust in him, but they are dearer than friends I know, that is why I enquire on her feeling particularly."

Gilpin looked around the room, likely to check for their privacy as he leaned closer to her. "Olly, no, they are friends like me and you are, nothing deeper in any personal way."

She now wondered if he was unaware of their attachment and was reluctant to expose their bond. "It is not my matter to discuss," she said nodding, thinking of something else to talk about.

With widened eyes, he surprised her by crouching down directly in front of her and frowning to the point he was almost scowling. "No, Olly. Tell me why you think otherwise, I insist."

She shook her head. "I had seen them," she began but then stopped to look at him for forgiveness. "Oh, Gilpin. I did not mean to see them, I had heard their voices and was going to approach them but then I noticed that their discussion was serious in tone."

He nodded. "They talk often, Olly."

"No, I did not mean to remain there but I was struck by the moment and he had said that he loved her and she returned the sentiment. Then he took her in his arms," she relayed shaking her head. "Perhaps you were not aware."

Sincere concern was in his face and mannerisms; he then took her hands in his. "No, he does not feel that way for her, Olly, I promise. I have known them for a long time. He lost someone so dear to him that he needs comfort from all of us," he explained quietly.

"You think she was offering him comfort?"

He nodded. "Yes, it is true, please do not doubt it. He has said he loved me, Gleda has said it to me too. We love each other as family. He loves her as he does a sister, like you love me as your brother that is all."

Olly couldn't hide her relief. "Are you certain?"

"Yes."

She smiled at him, not caring if he noticed. "And you believe I love you as a brother?"

He laughed, tickled by her teasing. "You do. You can not help it. Would you dispute it?"

She shook her head, leaning forward to kiss him on the cheek. "I do love you, silly boy. You are my brother; no one will take that from me."

He beamed with pride but then seemed to want to address more. "Olly, he doesn't think of *you* as a sister. He feels differently about you, he speaks of you often."

Her smile faded, she didn't want to invest her heart in such musings after the dream she just had. "Oh, I don't know that to be true," she said dismissively.

Before he could rebuke her statement, Aylward approached them. "Are you rested, Questa?"

She nodded, and stood, placing the sheet beside her, grateful for Gilpin's Altoids. "Yes I am thank you. I had wished to stay with this woman last night. I had found her near the theater and was concerned for her," she explained. "It has been made known to me that she will return home this day so I am able to clean the theater if you so wish."

He stroked his beard as his eyes lit up with a glint of appreciation. "You will return to nursing after you clean the theater," he stated without a tone of question. "Your presence is valued here; more people heal when you are in attendance."

She smiled, warmed by his flattery but then she pondered his statement. "Is that true?"

"A wise man never squanders his reputation by ways of deceit," he replied plainly.

"No I don't suppose he does," she agreed with a smile. "Thank you, Aylward; it is always pleasing to hear when one is considered useful."

She took a step forward and kissed him on the cheek which immediately caused him to blush. "Good girl you are," he said coyly. "Now be gone with you."

"I will hasten my duties so I can return speedily," she assured him as she began to walk away.

A sensation, a strong urge, held her back and she returned to them, suddenly placing her hands on Gilpin's thin arms. "All those that I have encountered here have spoken highly of you. You are the most praised amongst them, Gilpin. You make me proud and the fact that you call me sister is a significant honor."

The shock on his face was equaled by his quickly pinkened cheeks. He glanced at Aylward through his downward stare, as she left them there, sufficiently flattered.

Her good mood was no doubt attributed to Gilpin's divulgence on Ehren's feelings. Just the same, the woman's recovery and Aylward's kindness had also reignited her gratitude.

Once back in her room at the theater, she gathered her white dress and comb and went to the powder room. Minutes later she was attired for cleaning, and also for her nursing duties later which was easily performed in the same white dress.

After a spray of perfume and the tidying of her long pinned up hair, Olly went out into the theater and began sweeping quickly. The room was alive with activity. Adrian, Esther and some of the other regulars were merrily talking with the new small statured people who still wore hooded cloaks.

Most of them waved at her and she waved back, happy for their acceptance, glad to interact with them with her head held high. Another familiar face came at her from the long breakfast table.

Gleda glided across the shiny open floor in her white cleaning dress. Before Olly could speak, her friend had her hands clasped on her arms. "You had us worried last night, Ms. Olly. I am glad to see you safe and well."

"Oh, Gleda. Please forgive my leaving you, I found a sick lady and wanted to remain with her in the restaurant."

She nodded. "Yes all has been told to me, kindhearted girl that you are. But we were not informed of your location until much later and you had the four of us quite panicked."

Olly saw sincerity in her face and felt terrible. "I did?"

Gleda reached out and seized her free hand, the one that didn't hold the broom. A floral scent wafted off of her petite body.

"We tried to enjoy the entertainment but it was not the same without you with us," she said quietly. "You had created wonderful crowns for us, but your presence is what truly causes us to smile."

"I am blessed by your words," Olly said as she squeezed her hand. "I am sorry for leaving so hastily. I would have much rather finished viewing the moving picture and I had quite a restless night. The despondence amongst the people, I wish I could help them better."

Gleda nodded. "There is little for them to hope for," she said quietly. "If they have survived, most of them have loved someone who did not."

Musing on her poignant words; Olly realized that morale was absent from the healing of these people. "Gleda, I wish to propose an idea but I do not wish to offend you or your generosity."

Gleda tilted her head curiously. "Please do not fear my disproval, Olly. I am eager to hear your suggestion."

Olly was glad for her zeal. "Perhaps there needs to be some cheer in their vicinity," she began. "If you are agreeable to it, we could take the gramophone to the restaurant and play some quiet music."

"Oh yes, certainly we could do that," Gleda enthused.

"And," she whispered closer to her. "I had made some gifts for some of the others here but perhaps I could take them to the ill so they will feel they have been thought of. I can always make more for my friends here at a latter time."

"I do enjoy that idea, Olly," Gleda said, smiling with the anticipation of it. "When we are done with our domestic chores, I will come find you and we can get some of the boys to take the gramophone over."

"I look forward to it," Olly said, mirroring her excitement.

Gleda scurried back through the theater curtains, obviously having finished her breakfast.

Even though Olly was keen to get her work done, her stomach suddenly chimed in its protest. As if on queue, she looked up to see Clarence walking her way with a small tray of food. "Having made enquiries, it has been indicated to me that you have not eaten yet, Duchess."

He was wearing a black modern suit with hat and vest and she wondered where he might be going but thought it wise not to question him on it.

"Oh Clarence, you came just as my stomach was about to thoroughly berate me for negligence. You are worth your weight in gold," she said, taking the tray from him and placing it on a chair against the wall.

He smiled, happy for her appreciation. "I would say the same of you, but certainly your lack of consumption would put you at a lower weight and the comparison could not be made to your exceeding worth."

She laughed as she took a bite of a small peach tart and sighed as it went into her grateful stomach. Resting the broom against the wall, she decided to spend a short time concentrating on her food instead of trying to balance it all at once.

Apparently content to remain with her in the moment, he looked at her with a smile. "Tell me, friend, are you well?" he asked quietly so the larger group did not hear him. "We were told of your spontaneous heroics yet prior to that, your expression showed melancholic reflection."

Embarrassed about her reaction to what she perceived as Ehren's slighting of her, she shook her head, flustered. "I have a tendency towards becoming emotional at times, and there is no excuse really. I am in a better state now and I do apologize for my discourtesy."

His kind goat-like eyes studied her expression as if he could read more from her face than her words.

"What you have experienced would create utmost turmoil in the hearts of most of us if we were forced into such dilemmas as yours. Do not apologize, Duchess. Do tell me; have you any memory at all? Perhaps more than since the day Gilpin brought you in?"

She shook her head as she finished her tart and sipped the lemonade that felt very good as it entered her system.

"Not any particulars that can be verified," she replied honestly. "I have been experiencing dreams of a man and a place of lush green hills, a valley perhaps."

His curiosity had been piqued and he sauntered around to be closer to the wall as if indulging in a secret meeting. "Did you see him? Did he speak to you? What else did you see?"

She laughed as she finished off her animals crackers and sighed. "Oh, Clarence, so little has been offered to me in ways of specifics. I am not able to lift my head to see his face; it is a cruel irony that haunts me every time."

Now leaning against the wall, she could see pity in his face. Even though he wore a suit, certainly for some business he was about to venture, his concern was sincere and so he remained. "Poor girl," he said honestly. "And he has not spoken to you?"

She tidied the napkin and plate on the tray and held it in front of her. Studying his face, she was not sure if she should relay such romantic specifics to a man. Nonetheless, he did call her friend and she felt safe in his company. "He said *forever*," she replied quietly, staring down at the floor. "He said he and I were forever."

Quiet, she finally looked up to see a solemn expression looking back at her. "It is a rare love that endures always," he said seriously. "Then your heart is promised and I can understand your anxiousness to find him."

Having begun the morning in high spirits, this conversation had set her back a little. She nodded with sadness inside of her. "But such love, though it is achievable for me, Clarence, his existence is not assured. He could be but a dream, he could have gone to war, and it is even possible he stopped loving me in some past moment, I am not to know."

He shook his head, and took the tray from her but stepped closer, looking into her eyes.

"Forever is never expressed unless it is felt with all certainty, I assure you. Not only is he real, but he is not lost to heaven. God would never separate true eternal love; you are not destined for a tragedy. You are much too precious for such pain. Hold hope in your heart dear girl."

She nodded with tears in her eyes. "Thank you, Clarence. I will continue to hope but I will also cherish those who have befriended me with such kindness. You will never be forgotten by me."

Balancing the tray in one hand, he returned her broom to her while kissing her on the cheek. "I am easily found should you need consoling, Duchess. Fill your heart with joy for soon it will be a reality."

Smiling, she watched as he walked away. Now, even more determined to be exceptionally productive, and with renewed contentment, Olly got her work done much quicker than the last few times. Only an hour passed and she had even taken care of the ladies dressing room where she briefly spoke with Esther and Lillian who were glad to see her.

A short time later, she washed her hands and tended to her personal business in the powder room. She sprayed more perfume over her neck and white dress when suddenly she heard a commotion in the now emptied out theater.

Rushing out she noticed the gramophone in the center of the room and a large group of people. The small faced people and a couple of the soldiers were with Gilpin and Adrian, all in a state of joviality.

Olly picked up her small bag of handmade gifts for the restaurant and hesitated, standing back against her inconspicuous spot along the wall. A handsome man in a suit, tall and friendly faced, came bounding towards her with a large grin aimed in her direction. "Where have you hidden my love?" he asked cheerfully.

With her mouth hanging open, Olly was unsure of what to say, though he seemed the playful type, so she was thinking quickly on some remark to come back at him with.

Fortunately Gleda rushed out through the theater curtains and jumped into his arms.

He spun her around and kissed the side of her head, his eyes closed lovingly, breathing her in. "I am home, darling."

She held him back only long enough to look him over, then she fell into his arms again, tears in her eyes. Glancing briefly at Olly, she quickly seized the man's hands and pulled him away from her.

Olly had become accustomed to these actions. Being in polite society, she and her unusual dilemma were surely being discussed as if her actions would have to be pre-excused.

Unsure of whether she should attempt to walk across the room discretely, her discomfort was intercepted by Gleda's return. Still wearing her white dress, but looking fresh and pretty as usual, Olly had never seen her look so joyous, as if his return had revived the pink in her cheeks.

She was holding the mystery man's hand and pulling him along, though he needed little encouragement. "Olly, *he* has returned," she said, close to her face with unparallel excitement.

Olly smiled, warmed by her happiness. "So he has," she said teasingly. "And if I knew who he was, what name would I address him by?"

They both laughed, though the man studied her very curiously as if she was a unique oddity. "I am Nathaniel," he said, removing his hat, exposing a head of healthy red hair as he bowed courteously.

With surprise in her expression Olly was hit with a realization. "The man who was on stage with you that day?" she asked Gleda.

Gleda nodded excessively. "The very one. He is the epitome of dashing and every time he leaves, the thoughts of him keep me warm until his return."

"It is nice to meet you, Mr. Dashing," Olly said, offering him a quick curtsey. "How long will you remain here?"

His deep brown eyes were lit up but his smile waned as he looked down at Gleda. "I will not be leaving again, here I will remain indefinitely."

Gleda's smile now faded as quickly. "What do you mean, Nat?"

He took both of her hands in his. "I was surprised that it was Ehren who had sent the message—,"

Gleda shook her head as if there were certain things they couldn't discuss in front of Olly and he nodded then continued. "He said Andy opted to swap missions with me. I'll be working close to home from this point on. I am now a declared full time theater dweller; my heart is lost to my pretty actress and a stone building of fancy costumes."

Tears fell down Gleda's pale pretty face as she stared up at him, likely searching for assurance. "Tell me it's true, Nathaniel, please do not jest about it."

"No my darling," he said, shushing her as he kissed her forehead. "I am home to stay."

She suddenly sobbed into his jacket and he held her against him. The expression on his face showed that they had been apart for too long. Olly did her best not to get lost in the irony of her own predicament and she turned her gaze to the floor so as to not witness their private moment.

"Where are you both going, dressed so fancifully, Ms. Olly?" Nathaniel asked as if her name was natural to his tongue.

Olly smiled and Gleda wiped her tears, looking back at her friend. "We are taking the gramophone and some gifts over to the restaurant to offer the sick ones some good cheer," Gleda announced.

"Oh, isn't that a charming idea. And where did you acquire such gifts in these scarce times?"

"Olly made them with her hands, she sewed them," Gleda said proudly.

"Is that so?" He raised his eyebrows, impressed as he smiled at Olly with large and perfectly straight teeth. "You make gifts, Ms. Olly?"

She nodded. "Yes, well I attempt to do the best I can with fabric swatches and thread, it is all a matter of morale rather than something I can claim to be a talent," she countered cheerfully.

He laughed lightly as Gleda interceded, now very jolly herself. "She created these wonderful silken crowns for me and the men, even Ehren."

Nathaniel stared into her happy eyes. "How is he?" he asked shortly but seriously.

She shook her head as if not wishing to divulge too much. "He is a pillar of strength, as he always is," she remarked quietly. "The best that can be expected. Should we go to the restaurant now?"

"Yes of course, darling. Come now with us, Olly. I look forward to seeing you divide up your offerings of high spirits."

Chapter Fifteen

Minutes later the three of them entered the restaurant. All of the white-dressed theater residents quickly formed a small grouping near the doorway to greet the popular Nathaniel.

Gleda pulled Olly aside and kissed her on the cheek. "The angels smile on me this day, Ms. Olly."

"They certainly do, Gleda. I am glad for you. I am so happy to see your love returned," Olly said seriously.

Her eyes shone so brightly it was as if stars were within them, Olly mused.

"I must leave in this moment, Nathaniel is aware. I will speak with you soon."

Olly nodded and smiled at her as she watched her friend go back out into the street.

Gilpin briefly acknowledged Nathaniel with a handshake before taking the bag from Olly with a smile on his face. "Gleda had stopped by my room momentarily and told me how you were going to give these out. Would you like me to help you with that?"

"I would greatly appreciate it, thank you. I see you already have the gramophone ready for play. Hopefully it will soothe them somehow," she said quietly.

"You have a good heart, Olly. Don't fear it, your idea is going to change the whole room, you watch."

"Thank you, Gilpin. I can only hope so. We are all in need of reprieve at this time," she said as Aylward approached them.

Gilpin nodded at their older friend then rushed off towards the gramophone while Aylward gently pulled her away from Nathaniel's greeters.

"Traditional beings repair with potions and tonics, Questa, but you look inside yourself for remedies," he said quietly and seriously. "While the body needs to mend, it is what is found in the spirit that creates many ailments. Your gifts will bring about great healing."

She placed her hand on the long sleeve of his favored white robe and smiled appreciatively. "In my heart I am aware of the power of compassion. All of you have shown me such kindness that it is the very thing that keeps me alive now."

He seemed strangely saddened by her statement and turned to look back over his shoulder. Suddenly the music started up and startled a few people in their beds but then Olly watched as smiles appeared on some of their faces as they recognized the song.

It might have been that they had spent so long there, alone in their silent misery, that they had forgotten the special feeling one gets when hearing music.

Aylward studied her face, still looking contemplative. "There is a man who comes from the war this day. He has helped some of the soldiers there find their memory after injury. Will you be willing to try?"

She didn't want him to see the consternation in her face, for certainly that was not an easy decision to make. "Will you be in attendance?"

"I will not leave your side," he assured her.

"Yes, very well," she said, not wanting to displease him. "When will this take place?"

"After noon, on this day," he replied. "I wish for you to attend to a short errand if it does not conflict with any of your short term ambitions."

"Yes, certainly. I am grateful to you and for the hospitality of your people. I am indebted to you," she said sincerely.

Strangely, there was some level of poignancy in his face as he handed her a folded piece of paper. "There is no debt, Questa. Please take this across the road to the store beside the newsstand. The gentleman there has his wife cut the cloths for us and we are in need of more. There are other small items listed and he will not detain you long."

"Oh, I had hoped to give the gifts to the people," she noted.

"They will know you made them, my girl. You will see their smiles even on your return."

She nodded, taking the paper from him as she left the restaurant. The sun was stronger than it had been for the last week and she was glad for it, having gotten cold during the night prior.

Supposing that it might now be September, she looked around noticing that there were more people in the street than usual, perhaps because it was still early morning. Nonetheless, as she crossed in front of the abandoned streetcar, she noticed that no one else looked at her, even the old man who kept his gaze to the pavement.

The air was thick with unspoken fear, and all people were aware how easy it was to get the flu. Surely they would stay well away from her had they seen her come from the place of sickness.

The bell struck out into the atmosphere, loud and ominous. She looked back to see two sheet-covered bodies being carried from the back of the restaurant to Martin's yard by Adrian and a small faced man.

As she squeezed between two horse posts in front of the storefront, she mused on the mysterious theater dwellers. If anything they were charitable, all of them by nature and in manner. Perhaps that is why they took her in, she was another lost soul in need of help.

The older man in his musty brown suit in the untitled store, was very quick to fill her request and have her underway. After a short spell of chitchat, she ventured back out with a large brown paper bag of useful goods.

It was then that she noticed Gleda just a couple of stores down and the sight of her was entirely unexpected. Her hair was very nicely done in a pompadour bun and her dress was modern, a very lacy tiered dress much like Olly's.

Olly only caught a glimpse of her profile and fortunately Gleda turned away from her, allowing Olly time to think about what to do next.

A distinct feeling inside of her said to not bring attention to herself, so she discretely ventured to stand at the side of the tall unmanned newsstand. Only a few newspapers remained, dated from some weeks prior to now, the news then just as grim as it was now.

Masked by its shadow, Olly took a deep quiet breath, unsure of why she was being so secretive yet certain that she shouldn't get Gleda's attention.

The street had emptied out but now Olly heard more footsteps, hurried, smaller perhaps, coming from the other direction, and the other side of the newsstand. They stopped next to Gleda.

Olly froze but curiously bent just slightly to see some tattered hole-ridden boots, worn by three dirty young men. "You're lucky we don't get at ya," one of them said to Gleda. "We knocked that lady about, right? Weeks ago, the one who your lad took in, we got her good in the head."

Another one snickered while Olly's blood drained from her face. It was the Hanley boys, there was no mistaking it, and they were talking about her.

"I suppose you wish for me to be more frightened of you," Gleda said very formally in a precise theatrical tone that she no doubt usually reserved for the stage. "Will that you make you feel more respected perhaps? Do you wish all of the women to fear you as such?"

The third one, the middle one, by the look of his shadow, shifted uneasily on the spot. "He didn't mean to hurt her, right? She got scared and fell on the stones, but we got her stuff, threw it away after getting the money inside."

"Shut it, Ralph," the eldest instructed. "Why do ya keep hanging about like this, lady? We aint got time for yer preaching. Food aint going to come looking for us."

Unfazed, Gleda clasped her lace gloved hands in front of her and sighed, as if waiting for them to finish their diatribe.

"That lady who we took in has become quite close to us and she is well, so you need not be concerned for her," she said, mostly directing it at the more compassionate middle boy. "She has, however, lost her memory."

"Means she won't remember us, then," the snickering one chimed in.

"I remember you all with considerable accuracy and I have been in witness of enough of your torment to recall it clearly to the authorities if I so wish."

Her statement was met with silence before finally the eldest spoke up with less confidence. "That sheriff aint got a grain of good in him. When Hank went out with the soldiers, this one tried to sell us to the stockyards. He got wind of ma getting the flu and he then gone and took us but we got out of there in the night."

"I am sorry to hear that," Gleda said sincerely. "I have heard that he lacks scruples and I advise you to stay away from him, but you can not keep attacking people for your own benefit. Your lives are no more sacred than that of those you harm. I am here to propose a compromise."

"We aint no church boys and we aint going to be working at no stock yards," the eldest said.

"The bread was good you gave us Tuesday," the snickering one chimed in. "I'd work for bread but Johnny's right, no stockyards; we don't like what they do to them cows."

Gleda nodded; the sun, like a halo against the back of her pretty brown hair. "I am not here to offer you work. I have been keeping an eye on you because I was a friend of your mother."

"Were not," the eldest spat. "She aint had no friends since when pa died. It was just us."

"I am certain she loved the three of you," Gleda continued calmly. "She would come into town every Thursday and meet me in the five and ten cent store. She would always talk about your dogs and how good her sons were to chop the wood for the fire every week. She said you knew it was hard for her to do the laborious work and you had volunteered for it to help her."

The middle one sniffled now, obviously affected by the kind memory of his mother. "Why'd she tell you that stuff?"

"We became friends and decided to meet there every week. I would help her choose a small gift for each of you when she received payment for her embroidered doilies."

"And that's why you got yer nose in our business?" the eldest ask, a little more subdued now.

Gleda nodded. "I know Pamela well enough to be certain that she would be very disappointed in the harm you have been causing other people."

"We aint got nothing to eat," the snickering one explained. "No one's hardly about here to give us nothing."

"No, that is true, but how good are you, here?" she asked, pointing to her heart. "If you were given a choice, would you really choose to be good young men or do you enjoy hurting women?"

"The men fight back," the middle one explained while the other one snickered again.

"What would you do if given a choice?" Gleda continued, ignoring their remarks. "When you are older, if you were raised in a good healthy home, what had you planned to do when you became men?"

"He wants to be sheriff," the middle one said of the eldest.

"Shut it," he barked defensively.

"I suppose you think you could do a better job of it," Gleda remarked.

"Wouldn't be hard," the eldest replied affirmatively. "Ma said that's what I'd be good at and she knew I'd do good for this town."

"She did speak very highly of you," Gleda agreed. "But you have gotten off to a poor start I would say."

"I'm the man here," he said straightly. "I had to make sure we got fed, and I'd be no good if I didn't teach them how to work for it. I'd be a good man if I had food on the table."

Gleda didn't immediately respond and Olly could see she was perhaps looking him over. "How long until you are a man, Johnny, four years perhaps?"

By his silhouette, Olly could see that he was offended. "Just above three."

"Very well. Then I am going to make you an offer. I can get you food and the table to go with it, and I can also get you a start in with the policemen. I can even make sure that new man is not there when you do."

"What do you want from us, then?" Johnny asked, obviously suspicious.

Gleda turned away and Olly ducked back, afraid she would see her. "I can not be certain I wouldn't be wasting my time. I don't imagine any of you young men would truly be able to go through with it. I might have been mistaken to ask you to come to me."

"Wait, what you got to tell us?" the youngest asked. "We can be good, just tell us what we can do. I don't want to fight anymore for nothing."

Gleda made sure she had all of their attention. "There was a woman we took into the restaurant last night. I know you have abstained from there because of the illness. You had frightened her and she gave you money, but I will tell you she did not have the flu."

"What about her?" Johnny asked.

"Her husband is at war and she has small children. She is struggling to get the work done for all the animals. They are living animals; there is no harm to them. They need feeding and their housing needs cleaning."

Ralph's shoulders suddenly slumped. "So it *is* work. You just want us to clean up after cows and stuff and sleep in hay."

"Yes there will be some work involved but the people at the theater have made sure the lady has enough food, including peach tarts and sweet crackers, for all of you. Not only that but you will be sleeping inside of the house in beds and will be educated by her as she does for her own children."

"I don't need no lessons," Johnny insisted. "We don't need that part, but we'll take you up on it. But she can't be bossing us around about everything."

"The education is essential or no deal, Johnny, unless you are lying to me about wanting to be a sheriff?"

"I aint a liar."

"Very well, then that is part of becoming a man of authority, so you should accept the offer of a kind hearted woman, especially after you frightened her and she still agreed to take you in."

"What is her name?" he asked, this time without spite in his tone.

"It is Geraldine, and I expect you, *all* of you, to treat her very well and with great respect. No more running the streets, you will be catered for, I promise."

"Does she have a fire place?" the youngest asked.

"She has two and one is in the bedroom that you will share, out of the cold. We can find some of your belongings from your house with your mother and bring them there; you will not be cast out. You will be safe there."

"When?" Ralph enquired, trying to suppress his eagerness but not being fully successful.

"If you agree I will take you to the theater now where a buggy waits with one of our gentleman who will take you there directly."

Johnny pulled the other two aside, fortunately not far enough for them to see Olly though her heart was pounding wildly. They spoke for a matter of minutes before agreeing, but not enthusiastically, as obviously young men didn't like to appear eager.

"I will be checking on you regularly," Gleda said seriously. "Some of my gentlemen friends are able to get you into the right training when the time comes, Johnny but you must, without exception, treat Geraldine kindly, and always so."

"Yes, ma'am," he said, likely reverting to the way he responded to his mother.

"Good boy," she said cheerfully as she led them across the road and to the end of the street where the theater was.

The box felt very heavy in Olly's arms as she had been holding it ever so carefully so as to not be heard. She placed it in front of her feet for a moment and sighed once they were out of sight.

Her thoughts went in many directions as she made her way back to the restaurant with the supplies.

Whoever these mysterious theater people were, they were, without question, the best kind of people God had ever created.

Chapter Sixteen

The restaurant had calmed since she left to get the supplies for Aylward and it appeared that Nathaniel had already departed. She wondered if he went to meet Gleda in the theater, having been so long without her.

Her stomach tightened at the thought of love and reunion. Noticing Aylward beckoning her from behind the rag filled counter, she took the box of cloths over to him.

Only a short time later, he took her to a storage room in the back of the restaurant.

A rather average middle aged man in dress pants and white button shirt with sleeves rolled up, smoothed his mustache as he looked her over.

Clarence, still in his suit, was beside him, and she got the distinct impression that she hadn't known this man before this encounter. Nonetheless her friend smiled at her and she was calmed by his presence.

Aylward closed the door behind them, doing little to alleviate the mustiness in the apparently rarely used room. The four of them sat on crates, with Olly closer to the one that Clarence sat upon.

"I have heard of your predicament," the man stated, standing and looking down at her curiously. "My name is Mr. Santonio and I ask that you relax as best you can so we can begin."

Olly took the deepest breath she could, suddenly feeling self conscious in her plain white dress in the stale backroom. She shifted on top of the wooden crate and glanced up at him. "What would you like me to do?" she asked tentatively.

"Your positioning is not satisfactory for the procedure," he said shortly. "You," he said, pointing at Clarence. "Are you familiar with this girl?"

Clarence nodded as he glanced at Olly with a secretive yet amused smile. "Yes, she is my friend."

"Very good," the man said, revealing a slight lilt of British accent. "I wish for you to be seated on the ground, have you any resistance to the notion?"

"No, I am glad to assist Olly in any venture," he remarked as he sat on the hard tiled floor, lifting his pants slightly so he could cross his legs.

The proud-toned man pointed to Olly and then gestured for her to sit in front of Clarence. "If you will, Miss, I ask for you to dispense any discomfort regarding familiarity for the course of this process."

Olly nodded as she now got onto the floor and sat in front of Clarence, suddenly feeling compelled to snicker in spite of her nervousness.

He chuckled quietly behind her which caused her to smile rather mischievously at the serious mustached man. She was quite certain by the lines embedded on his brow that he was rarely, if not ever, amused.

"You must, without protest, lean back against the fellow behind you," the man instructed. "If during the procedure, you should feel faint or fall unconscious, we can not risk you injury should you be flattened against the floor."

Olly glanced at Aylward who appeared as trepidatious about the possibilities as her. "Will you be administering some form of inoculation?" she asked worriedly.

"Certainly not!" he barked, as his blunt voice bounced off the thick unadorned walls. "I am a man of mental intuitiveness. You will only need to cooperate and obey my instruction precisely."

She leaned back shyly towards Clarence who leaned forward to allow her head to fall back to his neck as he gently took hold of her arms.

"There is nothing to fear, Duchess, no harm will come to you," he whispered.

Squeezing his knee, she left her hand there and took a deep breath.

"Look at this finger, just this finger and do not take your eyes from it," the man instructed, holding his pointer finger straight and slowly waving it side to side. "You must do this for a short time and listen to my voice, slowly imagining my voice trailing away as if I stand in the distance."

Her lips partially opened, but as she grew tired, she thought it best not to speak in case her progress was ruined. He was correct, it did seem like quite a few minutes passed of this and not much was going on.

The room was very still, she could just make out the sounds of clanging metal bowls out in the restaurant and coughing but then her eyes began to close. Her eyelids felt so heavy it was as if a curtain was being closed.

Now the birds sang, such a beautiful sound, the resonance of a sunny cloudless day. She smiled, she couldn't help it. It was as if she had never smiled that way before, as if the happiness was so strong it was being forced to form in her lips. She was extremely joyful, and hope was in every blade of lush green grass.

The hills; she was in the valley and she could now smell the air, the flowers were so fragrant it was as if they were perfumed.

"Where do you stand?" the man's voice called out from a distant place.

"I am home," she replied. Her words trailed off and she wondered if she actually spoke them or not.

"What do you see? Tell us," he called out, so far away it seemed.

She tried to look around. Even though she felt invigorated standing there, so peaceful, she was tired, as if she couldn't keep her eyes open. "In the hills, and the birds are singing," she eventually replied.

"Think of my finger again," he instructed like a whisper on the wind. "Go deeper, fall and allow it. See all of it, discover where this is."

Releasing the tension, she obediently relaxed, fearless, just wanting to see what she could. So tired now, she was falling, literally reclining, her body was falling towards the grass but it was taking so long to land. "The hills are not far from the township," she recalled. "I can not see it; I want to find my love."

"Who is he? What is his name?"

She was laying on the grass now, it was soft and a tree appeared, its branches extended out, shading her from the sun. "He is— he didn't tell me his name."

"Look for him," he said. "Ask him what it is; ask him what *your* name is."

Her head was difficult to move but she managed to let it fall to the left and she stared out and spotted his leather slippers. Her heart began to race. "Oh I see him!" she cried out.

"You must settle down or you can not remain there," the man insisted.

"Please come to me!" she called out, fearful he would vanish. It appeared he was turned away, he wasn't looking at her. "Quickly, we must speak!" she called out.

He laughed as if he had been playing a joke on her but he didn't turn to her. Tears fell from her eyes as she lay there, unable to get up. "Please, quickly, I can not find you unless you tell me where we are."

"I love you," he said as he knelt beside her. His face hovered over her but the shadows darkened his features.

"Let me see you, please," she begged.

Suddenly she was jolted awake, her heart beating fast. Words were coming out of her mouth, strange words that she didn't understand. She watched as the mustached man quickly retrieved his bag and left the room hurriedly.

Her stomach was in some distress, as was her head, as the room appeared to be spinning.

"Why did he leave?" she asked wearily. "We had just gotten started."

"It has been quite some time," Clarence explained quietly as he stroked her damp hair. "He was frightened, Duchess."

"Whatever was he afraid of?" she asked incredulously, closing her eyes against the dizziness.

Aylward approached her, crouching in front of her, looking very upset, sincerely worried for her. He reached down and held her hand in his. "I am sorry he did not help you, Questa. He did not recognize your language and he took abrupt leave. Perhaps it was a personal distress that he would not divulge to us."

Allowing her eyes to focus, she felt clammy all over her body. In her vision she had only briefly glimpsed *him*, but she had sensed him there, warm and loving.

If only she had seen his face. "The words, I am not familiar with them. I was just asking him for his name," she explained. "But the words sounded different as if spoken from my throat, but I knew what they meant."

Reaching out, he placed his wrinkly hand on her forehead and gazed at her compassionately. "Your truth will find you, Questa. You are not destined for darkness."

She sighed, more confused and even less enlightened than before. "Would you mind if I rested for a short spell in my room?"

"Please rest," he replied, nodding. "Clarence, do walk with her."

Her friend lifted her up from beneath her arms and her body felt as if it wasn't completely attached to her soul, like she was floating at the edges of her skin.

Minutes later they were in the theater, walking across the long polished floor. Her fatigue was overwhelming and she had difficulty concentrating. She believed she thanked Clarence for getting her onto her bed, but she was not certain of it.

He covered her in the blanket and closed the door behind him. She fell asleep immediately, praying she would get to speak with her love again, no matter what the language was.

Chapter Seventeen

Opening her eyes, Olly stared into the darkness. She knew it was late, there was a distinct calmness in the air and the nearby street lantern would always extinguish before mid night. Her narrow window was closed but she was certain a noise had awoken her.

Suddenly she heard whispering, it was coming from Gilpin's adjoining room. Fumbling around, using her memory, she used her hands to blindly locate the pull chain of the electric standing light and covered her eyes as the room was illuminated by it.

Gilpin's voice rose excitedly for a moment while Gleda's voice came back at him, quietly. Olly got chills, were they in danger? Something was certainly in the air, because now more voices were sounding out from the theater.

She heard Gilpin's hallway door close and she wanted to stop him and ask him what was happening. Looking down, she saw that she was still wearing her white cleaning dress. It was crinkled and damp from her getting overheated beneath the blankets. She had slept so heavily, no dream had been experienced.

Quickly pulling the dress up over her head, she threw it onto the bed and reached for her long sleeved cotton nightgown and put it on over her undergarments. Without delay she opened her hallway door and peeked out, catching a glimpse of the back of Gilpin and Gleda, also in their nightwear, entering the theater through the heavy curtains.

Not wanting to witness one of their private interactions, she continued to follow them, worried because they too had been awoken.

As soon as she peered in through the curtains, her heart calmed and she realized they were happy; Ehren had returned. A small group, including Aylward, Clarence and Lillian, some dressed in day clothes, stood with him.

She entered, unconcerned if she was seen, even in her evening clothes. Eight people now gathered but she just wanted to glimpse him and be assured of his wellness. Gleda and Gilpin, looking like small children in their bed wear, approached the jovial group as they began to ask him questions.

Olly clasped her hands in front of her, planning on only remaining one more moment in hopes she would be able to get one more glance at him in the crowd. Finally Lillian moved aside and she got a good look at him. His suit pants appeared a little torn and his jacket was missing, his shirt looked well worn and she knew that he had been through some ordeal.

Taking a few steps, she considered approaching him. Gilpin suddenly turned and noticed her there, and she froze, worried she was not welcome at this reunion. Ehren followed his gaze and his smile faded.

Before she could turn to leave, he began to walk towards her and she stared down coyly at the floor. He didn't speak until he got close to her at which point he spoke in a low voice. "Olly, why do you appear fretful?"

She shook her head. "I was not certain I should be standing here as I am, but when I noticed you, I did not want to leave until I confirmed that you were unscathed."

"You were concerned for me?" he asked, seemingly pleased.

She gazed up at him and immediately placed her hands on his forearms, not caring what the others assumed by her action. "I will admit I was more than concerned for you, Ehren. You had me quite on edge and I can not express how relieved I am to see you here now."

Reaching for her hands and cupping them both in his, he moved closer and looked well into her eyes. "I am safe, I promise," he whispered as if they were the only ones in the room. "I am sorry for your anxiousness but I will confess that your worry for my wellbeing is something I had hoped from you particularly."

Flustered, most certainly blushing, she kept her eyes on him, studying his unshaven face and reciprocating his unyielding gaze. She opened her mouth to speak but the group had gotten to them and was now assembling around him.

"Let us get you cleaned up," Adrian said as he pat him on the back, then feigned disgust, which caused Ehren to laugh.

They, his true long term friends, were also obviously extremely glad to find him safe and he was suddenly lost in their fold, being led back to the stairway up to his room. Gilpin turned and smiled at her while she nodded at him and decided to return to her own room.

Leaving the light on, she stretched out on her bed and stared at the closed hallway door. All was quiet, no wind outside, and no laughter. Still tired, she was surprised that she could not so easily fall asleep again.

In spite of all that had happened with the serious man and his strange departure, her thoughts were more focused on Ehren. She wanted to get lost in a dream; she wanted to find her way back to the hills, hoping that now perhaps she would have more access to her love.

Nonetheless, Ehren was so real, so vivid, his slightly unbuttoned shirt, his intense gaze upon her, especially his words. He had wanted her to be concerned about him. Why would he want that from her? He had said her *particularly.*

There was no denying when she was around him; there was so much in his countenance that could not be determined by his words alone.

His strength, his confidence and his assured stance, but she could not drift off into that territory of mind, he would sweep her up and her heart would be irretrievable.

Her head now felt heavy on the pillows, and her scent, embedded in them over time, comforted her, like the feeling of family.

These people were her family now, she pondered as her mind drifted into many disconnected thoughts. Should her love find her soon, she could not part with these people so lightly, what would she do?

Just as slumber was ever present, a knock came at her door.

"Hello?" she asked, quickly panicked by the hour of the night and knowing Gilpin was not in the next room.

"It is, Ehren," he relayed quietly. "I do apologize. Are you awake or would you prefer me to speak with you at a latter time?"

"No!" she called out, a little too objectively. "No, please, I will be there momentarily," she added as she ducked her head under the walnut bed and located a small box of Altoids and placed one in her mouth.

Quickly hand-combing her long unbound hair; she rushed to the door but pulled it slowly inward so he did not detect any enthusiasm. He had shaven and washed and was presently wearing a long nightgown and burgundy robe, tied at his waist.

His mouth open, he seemed stunned, studying her long brown hair as it framed her arms and shoulders. "I will speak with you, Ehren," she assured him, her heart racing, pondering his presence and motives.

His eyes quickly took in her details as if the vision of her was new to him. "Perhaps me calling on you at this hour would be constituted as improper by the moralists, but I am not often a patient man, Ms. Olly," he said straightly.

"This time away has burdened me with freedom to contemplate. I did not wish for the clock hands to be the only obstacle that kept me from seeing you, so please indulge my imprudence."

She shook her head, offering a sympathetic smile. "A friend should be accessible at all times in my opinion," she replied gently. "The sun holds no claim over our interactions; the moon allows us an authenticity in our exchanges that can only truly be experienced in such silences as these."

Letting out an audible sigh, he nodded then shook his head as if strongly affected. "Your expressions are like lyrical prose, there is a simple wonderment when you speak that holds me awkwardly stunned without a worthy response."

In spite of the quiet hallway and the absent occupants therein, she drew a discrete breath and offered him to rest as he appeared fatigued. "Would you like to come sit a spell and talk with me?"

He looked past her into the warm semi-lit room and though his eyes said *yes*, his respectability kept him at bay. "Do you possess a robe?" he asked.

Suddenly conscious of the thinness of her nightgown, she walked back to the bed and placed the rectangular silk blanket around her shoulders and across her bodice. Following that, she slipped her bare feet into the white work shoes, knowing he wished to be away from there.

Smiling politely, he closed her door and he led her through the theater and surprisingly onto the stage. She stared at one of the chairs, but he pushed aside one of the heavy back curtains and opened a hidden door. It was painted in a way to make it look like part of the brick wall.

Following him up the dark unlit stairs, he held her hand, pulling her up so she would not fall over. She could sense that they were passing the floors, all the way up until he opened a door in the ceiling. This allowed the dim light of the crescent moon to illuminate the expanse of the wide flat roof.

A light gust of cool air emptied into the stuffy stairwell and he assisted her up so they now stood together, staring out over the entire town. She took in a deep breath, feeling liberated by the night and its rare discoveries. "Do you often come here?" she asked sincerely.

"It has been some time," he replied wistfully. Crossing his arms against his robe while a breeze played against his mid length hair, he gestured for her to join him on a wooden bench in front of a bricked chimney stack.

The chill in the air urged her to move closer to him on the bench, yet she hoped he did not think her too forward by the action. Lifting the blanket up over her ears, she regretted not bringing the velvet one instead. "Did that man threaten you?" she asked, enquiring on his dealings in the other town.

He nodded, but seemed distracted as if that wasn't what he wanted to discuss. "There was some physical conflict, but he is detained now and he will be counseled thoroughly," he replied vaguely.

"But were you endangered? Do you often get involved in such things?"

"I am safe, Olly, always, it is assured."

She wanted dearly to rest her head against his arm but instead she leaned back against the bench, keeping her face close to his shoulder, feeling the warmth from him. "What troubles you?" she asked him quietly.

He stared out in front of him, a general disquiet in his demeanor. "There are many facets that could be addressed in one reply," he stated solemnly. "At this time, I had wanted to approach you about your incident this afternoon."

Crossing her legs, she hoped he wouldn't turn back and see how she was looking at him. Certainly if he glimpsed her expression there was a chance he would suspect the truth.

He would assume correctly that she wanted to reach out and touch the fabric of his robe, simply because it was touching his skin. "You summoned me here in the cold to enquire of my brief episode with that silly man?"

"My concern for your condition is not feigned though admittedly if it were my only reasoning it could have kept until respectable hours."

Now he did look back at her and she wanted to speak, just to say anything to fill the tension in the air but he looked in her in such a way. It was as if in that one moment she wanted to take him into possession, protect him and own him.

Her eyes set upon his skin with a unique revelation, understanding its incalculable value. It was in essence, alike to a safe, holding within it, the most valuable treasure. It was the beautiful cocoon that carried his precious soul within it.

Swallowing hard, he looked back out into the dark night then lowered his gaze to the cold ground. "Clarence said that the man had left in great haste and that perhaps you were perturbed by it."

Feeling tired, she could not quickly muse on his reasons for addressing this now but she was glad to be with him. "I thought it strange that a man with prior experience would react so frightfully to a simple language difference," she replied.

"Yes, very odd, I agree," he said, as if pondering it. "I would not be concerned by his diffidence, Olly. It is likely he had assumed it to be the language of the enemy. Unfortunately these are trying times. Perhaps what he had been exposed to over there had given him cause to some level of mistrust."

Leaning forward, she registered his meaning. "He might have conjectured that I was a spy," she stated with great astonishment. "Did you ask Clarence? Had I been speaking German?"

Laughing he looked back at her, sincerely amused. "You were not and you *are* not a spy. A good soul does not derive from fresh perspective; you were always good, for this is your true nature," he reassured her. "Clarence was not paying much attention to your hurried verbiage rather he was trying to contain the response of your momentary overseer."

She leaned back again and sighed. "Not much was derived nonetheless. I am no more enlightened on my past than I was had I not met him at all."

He leaned back too, resting his head on the back of the bench, his face now inches from hers, his longing gaze a mirror of her own.

She wondered if he would kiss her. She would have ceased the universe spinning just to allow that one action to occur. Powerless to his charms, she would not stop him, but she prayed he wouldn't attempt it, yet she truly hoped that he would.

"You saw a man in your vision," he stated quietly.

The mention of her love, her potential man of forever, did little to diminish the sensation of yearning for Ehren as his blue eyes gazed at her now.

"I did not see his face," she relayed carefully. "I have dreamt of him, but I never see him properly."

"The dreams in the hills?" he asked, surprising her by his memory.

"Yes."

He looked upon her quite seriously now as he prodded her further. "What do you feel, please tell me. When you are with him in your dreams, what do you feel?"

There didn't seem any good reason for her not to be honest with him. Something in his countenance spoke of genuine interest and sincerity. She leaned forward a little but still remained close to his face.

"It is an indescribable kind of love," she said, watching as his eyes reflected back at her, intrigued. "I can not see him and his words are like whispers, in another language but I understand them regardless."

"What does he say to you, Olly?"

"He said that we would be together forever, always, sincerely always not some trivial expression, it is meant."

"I believe it," he assured her. "How do you know you love him? I would assume him to be real as you have dreamt it often, so how do you know these feelings are valid without seeing him?"

As if falling into a sense of comfort, she leaned back again, not wanting to feel that distance from him any longer.

"It is like I am a candle wick," she explained, considering her wording. "When I am in his presence, I feel the love as if it is prickling on my skin and deep into my body. And when I feel him near, he ignites my flame and then is the only time I truly feel the life flow through me."

Tears glistened in his eyes and she knew he understood that feeling. Perhaps the one he had lost made him feel that way and Olly was sympathetic while being honestly envious of her. "May I confide in you?" she asked quietly.

"Yes, always you can. Tell me all you feel and think and any tiny glimpse of any idea, but please stay with me now and speak all of it."

Swallowing hard, she felt so close to him that the sensation of her description was alike to how she felt now with him looking at her the way he was. "Two nights ago a woman died in my arms," she started. "She was my age and close to my appearance in some ways and her husband had died a year earlier in the war. Her pain for being without him was so strong that she was happy to be dying because she would be with him again."

"Do you wish to die, Olly?"

"No," she hastened a reply. "But I understand her, I feel as if in a way I am a widow because the man I loved I have lost. I am without him and I suffer. But her loss was different to mine for she had a memory. She told me of his words and his laughter and how he held her. I may as well love the misted vision of early morning dew for he bears no face or name. He resonates only in my heart but not in my mind."

Ehren looked back at her, she could feel his understanding and she regretted bringing it up knowing he too was suffering. "Could you love another?"

She was going to say no but as she looked at him, it would be a lie. She couldn't imagine loving anyone else, but Ehren was the exception.

As she opened her mouth to speak, he placed his hand on her face, so warm and comforting. She closed her eyes and sighed. "Ehren—,"

"Ehren!" Gleda suddenly yelled out as she ran up to the roof in her nightgown. She suddenly stopped in her tracks and Ehren removed his hand from Olly's face but not hastily or guiltily.

Gleda appeared flustered but lowered her gaze. "I am sorry to disturb you both," she said sincerely. "There is a sergeant lurking about town looking for Gilpin,"

Ehren stood quickly. "Why, Gleda?"

"One of the soldiers returned a few days ago and had seen him," she relayed quickly as she drew closer to them, shivering a little. "Just now the sergeant asked Adrian about Gilpin and his age. The returned soldier reported to him that he should be serving in the war and could see no physical reason why he wasn't."

"He approached Adrian at this hour of the night?"

She nodded, reflecting his astonishment. "He was visiting a man in the restaurant but I think he was quite drunk and riled up and was out to find Gilpin *now*. There was some kafuffle in the past with him rising up against any young men that aren't over there and I think he is going to make an example of him in no subtle way."

"I thought I had created some paperwork for him, Andy said it was approved," Ehren said, getting closer to her and seizing her arms. "Doesn't he have the papers?"

"Yes but I think this man is not concerned for it, I imagine he is out to do him some harm."

The three of them quickly made their way down the hidden stairs. All the while, Ehren held Olly at bay to ensure she didn't trip. "Where is he now?" he asked Gleda.

They reached the hallway and she shook her head, her long hair also unbound. Nathaniel and Clarence suddenly appeared beside them. "I think he is aware of the hunt," Nathaniel explained.

"He must have overheard," Clarence said apologetically. "I had told Arthur and then we heard a sound shortly afterwards so I suspect he was around and may not be in our midst at this moment."

"We must find him at once," Ehren asserted seriously. "If he runs out into the street most certainly that sergeant is not on his own. He is not safe out there."

They all separated but were quiet in their search in case any strangers had entered the theater uninvited. Gleda went to the restaurant while Ehren and Clarence ventured outside to see if they could find the sergeant.

Nathaniel went into the dressing rooms and backstage while Olly stood quietly at the center of the theater. No one was going to Gilpin's room but certainly they would have gone their first, nonetheless she went there to look for any clues.

Rushing back through the curtains she entered the dimly lit hall and ran into her bedroom, closing the door behind her. She then opened their adjoining doors and looked around. A candle was still burning in an old lantern and he had obviously accumulated a few more advertisement posters but it was quite tidy.

He didn't have a window in his room but a large piece of cloth was pulled aside, having come undone where it hung over a wide crack in the brickwork. She decided to get onto his bed and look out through it, hoping for a new perspective.

Stepping up onto his half made bed, she felt that the blankets were still a touch warm as if he had only been there very recently. It was night after all, she mused.

But when she took another step on his mattress she observed that it was very lumpy. Moving her feet back and forth it felt like something was hidden beneath the mattress.

Quickly jumping off, without hesitation she threw the mattress back.

"Olly, no!"

"Oh you gave us such a fright. I am sorry I stood on you," she said, taking the poor young man into her arms. "That is not a good hiding place for you, Gilpin."

"I didn't have much time," he said, shivering a little. "They made it sound like that man and his friends were looking for me right at this instance."

She held him back and looked at him, sensing his fear and feeling equally worried. "Nothing good can come from war," she stated straightly.

"I'm not in support of it either," he said with tears in his eyes.

She looked back to his closed hallway door, and was glad to not hear other voices yet. "Do you have access to a buggy?"

He nodded; comforted by her compassion. There is a small one that was left behind the old general store," he replied, thinking quickly. "There is a horse Mrs. Jenkins lets me use anytime I want. She won't even mind if it is gone because I take care of him for her and she said I could."

"Do you trust me, Gilpin?"

"Of course, Olly. Will you help me?"

"Yes, but you are going to have to put on one of my dresses so I can get you out of here."

Chapter Eighteen

A chill experienced in the open air held a bitterer frigidity than if it was felt in one's bedroom. Olly hadn't minded it so much when she was sitting on the theater roof lost in Ehren's eyes, but wherever they were now; there were no tall buildings to protect them from the wind.

She stared down at Gilpin, who was snoring lightly like an innocent child, his brown hair drooping partially over his angelic face. They had traveled quite a way in the dark night, and he knew of a good hiding place on an abandoned farm.

Unfortunately someone had died there of the flu, unbeknownst to anyone else, she supposed, and his body smelled retched enough to keep them from occupying it. Instead they had opted for a mid sized wooden barn beside one tree and algae filled well.

Having fearfully run from the theater, in their haste to get away from the soldiers looking for Gilpin, they had only brought one blanket with them. Gilpin had valiantly shooed a mice family away so they could climb up the partly rotted ladder to the hay loft where they settled for the night.

It was already past midnight when they left so now, as she cuddled up beside her friend for warmth, she noticed the first blush of daylight peeking through a crack in the wall. Nonetheless, it was a cooler day and the wind whistled through, ominous and eerie.

Gilpin still wore a dress and wig that she had used to disguise him to get him out of the theater. He must have sensed her movement and opened his eyes to look up at her. "Do you think we should have taken the buggy further away, Olly?" he asked, wiping his eyes and snuggling his face into her arm.

"I'm not exactly certain how far we are, so it isn't something I can answer with any great understanding," she replied honestly, yawning loudly as she lifted the blanket up to his neck and then to her own. "With that ringlet wig on, you remind me of a porcelain doll," she remarked quietly.

He snickered, tickled by the situation. "It does well to keep my ears warm," he explained. "It looks like no one else has been around here for some time."

She tucked her feet into the hay and felt the sticks poking into her thin stocking socks. "I agree, and we made sure to hide the buggy next to the house as it were, so I doubt those soldiers would think to look for us here."

"I'm cold," he noted, relaying his true vulnerability.

In spite of still being in her nightgown, Olly brought him closer to her and rubbed his arms as she held him. "Did you bring any food?"

"I'm afraid not," he said apologetically. "I was so concerned about them finding me, I didn't think of anything else. Oh but I have a small pack of Altoids and a handful of animals crackers in some paper that I had saved."

"Well that is better than none at all," she said as he reached beneath his dress and took it from his pants pocket. He handed them to her before returning to her embrace. Two crackers followed by one mint was their breakfast, which Olly was grateful for, and who knew when they would have something else.

"I will hold them at bay with a pitchfork if I have to, Gilpin. I will not let them take you there."

She sensed that he was growing tired again and she let the mint slowly shrink in her mouth as she pondered everything that had happened to her since he found her.

"Do you think they are looking for me? I mean Ehren and Gleda and such?" he asked, obviously having a lot on his mind as well.

"I'm certain they are quite frantic with worry for you, yes," she replied honestly. "They love you dearly, Gilpin. That is why they must have taken great measures to prevent you from going to war in the first place."

"I belong with them," he mused.

"I doubt the soldiers will be able to remain in town long," she consoled. "We will find a way back; we just needed to distance ourselves first so we could work something out."

He lifted his head and looked at her mischievously. "I've never been in a dress before, it feels so heavy."

She smiled then reached out to adjust his wig so the ringlets covered his ears. "You make for a very pretty boy," she teased. "Had you not worn one for a play at all?"

His smile faded quicker than expected and it was as if she had hit a nerve. "There have not really been many plays there, Olly."

Studying the strange look on his thin face, her heart beat quickened. She sensed that he might divulge something to bring clarity to the mystery that surrounded the cobblestone surrounded building.

"There are many people coming and going from the theater," she noted carefully. "Is there perhaps a reason for it, other than a meeting place for traveling vaudeville acts?"

He closed his eyes, strongly conflicted. "Olly I can tell you something but not everything and—, I really shouldn't say any kind of something," he added anxiously.

Closing her eyes, she felt for him, sorry to put him in that situation, so aggrieved. "I understand, Gilpin. I will not pry any further."

Sighing loudly, he clung onto her arm and pressed his head against her shoulder. "Maybe you can ask me something like 'what are your thoughts on what goes on there?" he offered with some hesitation.

She mulled it over in her head, wondering if she should further the topic at all, even though it did gnaw at her. "May I then express certain incidents that I have observed since being there?"

His green eyes lit up with the proposition of a reasonable compromise. "Yes! Yes, Olly, tell me about things that have happened to you since you arrived at the theater."

"I do not wish to go into too many specifics," she said truthfully. Even within their own grouping, she wanted to ensure not to betray a confidence, even if they were unaware of what she had witnessed. "I will say in summary that I have noticed many good deeds performed by the residents there."

Studying her face, he too must have been considering how much to say. "Everyone, all of them there, do good things for other people," he said carefully.

She nodded. "Yes, they are very compassionate people."

Shaking his head, he pressed up against her; she could feel his slender frame shivering. "No, Olly. I mean, all of them that come there, even the ones you don't know yet, they are there especially for that reason."

Looking into his eyes, she could see he was tense about his divulgence yet she detected a desire to say more. "The people who go to the theater stay there so they can help people outside of the theater? Like good Samaritans?"

Staring at the crack in the roof opposite them, a gust of wind whistled in as he considered his words. "Very much like that," he replied. "And when they leave the theater they go different places to help people there as well."

She knew there was something he was not saying, a missing piece that he would not express and she would not ask him about. The last thing she wanted to do is put him in an uncompromised position. "They look different from each other," she noted.

Pulling his hands out from under the blanket, he brought the long sleeves of the dress over them as he glanced at her. "There are groups," he confirmed. "Each group is from a different place but they come to help people. That is why we all get together."

Leaning back against a large wooden beam, Olly wished she had brought another blanket to place behind them. "How do *you* fit in, Gilpin? Do you help people too?"

He smiled but she could feel he was conflicted. "I do, but mostly I am kind of like an assistant to the leader of it all. I have more responsibility than a lot of them sometimes."

Now she too smiled, enjoying his pride in himself. "You must be very trusted."

His smile vanished as worry came upon his face. "Don't ask me about the leader," he said, more as a plea.

"I won't," she promised. "But when did they take you in?" She asked, attempting to veer the conversation away from his duties. "Did they find you outside of the theater too?"

Looking away from her, he stared off as if remembering back. "It was a long time ago," he said, expressing it in a way that he meant longer than she could have assumed. "They found me where we come from, not from here," he explained quieter. "None of us are from here; this is just where the leader chose for us to come. They said all the good people from different places need one home foundation to gather and have friendship and morale."

"That is very wise," she offered, even though she knew he hadn't given her all the details. "No matter who you are, you need to feel like you belong somewhere; you need to feel you have a home."

Melancholy rose inside of her and she could feel his gaze on her. "Olly, you have a home. You can stay with us, we all want you to; you belong with us too."

Swallowing her emotion, she reached under the blanket and squeezed his hand. "Perhaps I will remain, I would be happy to," she said, closing her eyes for a moment. "But I do not know if I could ever stop looking for my true home. I wish I could find it just so I could work out if I could leave it behind or not."

Suddenly she felt movement in the hay near her feet and she jumped up reactively. At the same time her foot jolted forward, it got caught on a protruding nail and she cut her foot through her sock. "Oh no!"

"What happened?" he asked, sincerely panicked.

She reached down under the hay, reluctant to check the damage. Instead she held the end of the blanket over her foot and pressed hard on the bottom of her foot near where it was cut. "I think there was a mouse beneath here," she explained. "I jumped and my foot came into contact with a nail I think. It is cut badly."

"Oh no, that could get infected," he said worriedly. "Let me look."

"I wouldn't recommend it," she warned. "We should just cover it for now. We might have quite a journey ahead of us."

Leaning forward, he brushed the hay away to expose her foot and she flinched anticipatively. "Will you allow me to touch it?" he asked, looking at her for permission.

"Yes, please be gentle, it hurts quite a lot. I think the nail might still be in it somewhat."

Removing the blanket from his own body so she was still covered, Gilpin crouched on his knees and surveyed Olly's foot. Blood had seeped through and she could see it pooling inside of her stocking sock.

Closing her eyes, she knew he was getting closer and she clenched her fists and teeth as he pulled the nail out. She could tell it was thick and without looking, knew it had to be aged and rusty.

Sensing him stop, she looked at him as he looked at her. "It was deep, Olly. You are not going to be able to walk on it."

The pain outweighed her anxiety, but not by much. There were no doctors in town and they were not close enough to approach someone knowledgeable as it was. "I honestly don't know what to do, Gilpin. But whatever it is, we are going to keep you safe from those soldiers. We can just wrap it up. I will walk on it if I have to."

He shook his head, giving it another intensive study, his hands were cold and she worried for him getting a chill. "Olly," he said, extremely seriously. "I am going to help you but you must give me your absolute word that you will never reveal what you witness."

Nodding, she clenched her fists again, anticipating some strange method of stitching up a wound. But he didn't remove a threaded needle from his pants pockets, he instead removed her sock.

Closing his eyes, he placed his hands together as if in prayer then took in a loud deep breath. Hunching his shoulders then lunging forward very slowly, he quickly clamped both of his hands on her foot.

She called out in pain but then the intensity of warmth coming from him was soothing. Looking down, she noticed a bright white light surrounding his hands so she couldn't even see her foot any longer.

Gilpin's eyes were still closed but she could feel the wound close up and the aching subside as if the pain was literally falling out of the bottom of her foot.

Then it was healed, completely. Gilpin fell forward, catching his breath. She quickly grabbed him and pulled him back into her fold, covering him with the blanket. "Did your action harm you in any way?" she asked, rubbing his arms.

He sighed but shook his head. "It makes me fatigued for a time, but I am not ill." He turned to look at her, still worried.

"We only do that inside of our groups," he explained. "That is not my gift to share with the people outside. Please do not tell anyone."

Kissing him on the cheek, grateful for what he did, and feeling warmth in her whole body now because of it, she held him close to her. "I knew in my heart that you were a miracle, my brother. You did not need to prove to me that you could perform them."

Returning her embrace, he sighed, still tired. "I would do anything for you, Olly."

She would not ask him about this gift but knew that it was something truly rare. "I would not ask anything of you, Gilpin, but I cherish you dearly."

All of a sudden a noise came from outside of the barn. It sounded as if a spade had been knocked down and fallen to the ground. She and Gilpin exchanged a panicked look.

"What if they saw the buggy?" he whispered.

"Just hide beneath the hay," she ordered. "Hurry. Just get under as far as you can."

He obeyed and the two of them madly dug into the high pile of loose hay and tried to cover themselves up. Then they listened, holding each others hands and taking shallow breaths so they could hear better.

Olly's heart was racing madly. She was willing to fight if she had to but was not certain there was any implement to aid her.

Someone entered the barn, she could tell by the sounds, and they kicked at the dirt floor beneath them. She wondered if they were looking up at the hay in the roof, as they had stopped walking.

Gilpin squeezed her hand tighter. The sudden silence was worse as now they couldn't tell what the stranger was doing.

Suddenly the person was up inside the roof with them and picking at the hay just feet from where they lay.

She thought she might just faint from the fear when out of nowhere a voice bellowed at them. "Stand up at once!" the male voice instructed.

The pair of them shot up without hesitation and within seconds Ehren let out a loud raucous laugh. "I have found them!" he called out to someone outside. "Well aren't you a sight for sore eyes," he said, crossing his arms against his warm overcoat.

Olly and Gilpin looked at each other and she could not help but smile. His ringlet wig was still on his head and now very much on a slant. The hay was all over it as well as stuffed into the bust of the dress he wore, making him look like a scarecrow. She assumed she looked quite a sight too.

Gilpin, noticing the amused look on Ehren's face, crossed his lacy frilled sleeves and frowned. "I would prefer it if this was not mentioned to anyone else."

Smiling, Ehren nodded. "You have my word and my honor on the subject but on occasion I will laugh out of turn and point at you and you will know why without provocation."

Returning a sheepish grin, Gilpin nodded.

Ehren quickly lunged forward and scooped him into his arms. "You had us frantic with worry, young one. We thought we had lost you."

Gilpin hugged him gratefully. "Olly was trying to hide me from the soldiers. She didn't want them to take me away."

"She was very brave," he said, as he squeezed him again.

Not finished with his expression of relief, Ehren suddenly turned and crawled across to seize Olly by the shoulders, then placed both of his hands on her face. "You had my heart in my throat all night," he said seriously. "I couldn't have lost you; it would cause me ruin."

"Where are you?" a female voice called out from below.

"Up in the rafters, come up, you must see the silly pair," he called back to her.

Rushing up the worn out ladder, Gleda's pretty face appeared and she was also wearing a thick fur collared coat, but even better, she was balancing an armful of blankets. She handed them to Ehren who in turn, gave them to his cold friends.

Gleda now got onto her knees and laughed. "Oh Gil, how am I ever going to get all that hay-stuff out of that wig?"

He crawled across, behind Ehren and hugged her. "I will do it, Gleda."

"I don't care," she said, kissing his cheek then looking him over. "I was so worried about you and Ms. Olly; I can finally breathe with some consistency now."

Olly wrapped a thick woolen blanket around her shoulders, relieved and happy as she covered her ears with it. Ehren was still looking at her and she was glad for his concern, truly grateful that they had missed her as much as they had Gilpin.

"Are you sure that sergeant didn't follow you?" Gilpin asked.

Ehren looked back at him and shook his head. "He has already been shipped out," he said straightly. "Adrian has a good friend of higher ranking and the sergeant's orders were to leave the township expressly and take a handful of his associates with him."

Gilpin sighed loudly. "I'm sorry I caused so much bother. I should have known you would know what to do about it."

"Never mind it now," Ehren consoled gently. "Are you hungry?"

"Famished," he replied quickly.

"Very well, Gleda will go back with you in the buggy you came in, and she has already put a box of food and a coat there for you," he said, gesturing for them to climb down. "I will take Olly with me in the pony cart. Is there any incidence to note that I should be aware of?"

Gilpin glanced at Olly and she quickly expressed in her face that she would not betray him and he smiled as if thanking her.

"No," Gilpin replied. "We are hungry and tired and don't want to sleep with mice tonight."

Ehren laughed. "We wouldn't wish you to. Now be off with you both so we can journey back and get our work done."

Chapter Nineteen

Ehren guided Olly down the worn-out ladder from the hay loft to the dirt floor of the old barn. As soon as she got all the way down, Gleda quickly rushed to hug her as well, while Olly returned it, grateful that her foot was completely pain free.

"You must never leave us like that, Ms. Olly," Gleda whispered, staring into her eyes tenderly. "I couldn't be without either of you and Ehren was more distressed than you can possibly imagine."

"I am sorry, Gleda," she said quietly. "I was swept up in the urgency of the matter and all I could think of was protecting Gilpin."

Gleda hugged her again, this time appreciatively instead of as an act of relief. "Your soul is a lovely one, just beautiful and bright, we do adore you."

Olly kissed her on the cheek. "Every thing you do is a credit to your loveliness as well." She glanced over at Ehren, who appeared tired and impatient to leave.

Gleda, noticing this as well, guided Gilpin out of the barn quietly. "I'm going to get the young one fed and we will meet you at home," she said.

"Be cautious on that third road, Gleda and keep him out of sight the best you can," Ehren cautioned.

She nodded and Olly watched as their shadows stretched out onto the grass beyond the door, because now it was very sunny outside.

Ehren picked up a pillow slip full of items and handed it to her. "I'm afraid we had no luggage on hand but I imagined, given the fact that you are a lady that you would want to freshen and change before we ventured back."

"There is a dress in here?" she asked, peering in and spotting velvet.

"I was told the last time you were seen you were in your nightgown which worried me a great deal out in the cold as you were. Nonetheless, there are some dampened cloths and Gleda packed your perfume and other necessities."

Returning her attention to him, she wanted to hug him, her gratitude was overwhelming. "Most people wouldn't have taken such specifics into consideration. It is as if you have reached into my heart and discovered its secrets. You have brought me exactly what I needed just when I needed it. I am obliged to you in all ways, Ehren."

Dressed in a modern suit, and with his hair tied back, he seemed to be keeping his distance but his expression was far from detached. "Finding you and bringing you back with me is the only compensation I seek," he said with a gentle smile. "I will wait for you outside."

Watching him leave, she experienced that longing for him that she had felt when last they spoke on the rooftop. Wanting to eat, and also hoping to return to him quickly, she rummaged through the pillow slip to study its contents.

A green velvet costume dress had been packed for her; it was long with oversized sleeves but no particular adornments. Gleda had packed her perfume and two Altoids, obviously not knowing Gilpin had some on his person already.

She put one in her mouth and smiled as she saw a small metal container, lifting it out carefully, she noticed it was half full of water and two cloths were wrapped around it.

A cold breeze blew in, even though the sun was bright, so she hastened to get finished. Minutes later she was in her dress and had tied her thick brown hair into one long braid with a green ribbon that had been supplied.

Collecting the items along with the woolen blanket, she stepped out and held the partially full pillow slip up to shield her eyes from the sun. Ehren was already in the cart, the same large one they had taken to meet Andy and the other soldiers in that time. He was very close to the barn, having stopped the horse outside of it.

Patting the horse as she passed it, she took Ehren's extended hand and stepped up on the bronze plate and situated herself on the bench seat. She wrapped the blanket around her shoulders and watched as he took a seat beside her, pulling on the reigns and guiding the horse back to the main road.

"That small box there has some food for you in it," he said.

She bent down and opened it up, glad to see two slices of home made bread and spreading butter. Also inside was a large glass of lemonade and a sweet roll with icing sprinkled on it.

Taking one of the bread pieces, she straightened and glanced at Ehren who had his eyes on the road. She could tell he had something on his mind but he appeared very tired. "I am sorry to have taken Gilpin from you like that," she said sincerely. "I have burdened you greatly and now you must sit and ride with me and valiantly remain cordial."

He laughed and smiled at her. "I would have done the same, had it been me who found him, Olly. Your courage and kindness are part of what endears you. You are not permitted to be sorry, but I do wish for you to eat."

She obediently took a mouthful of bread and then another before sipping her drink and sighing, glad for the nourishment. "You don't look as if you have slept much," she noted carefully. "I wish I hadn't contributed to your fatigue."

He turned his head and offered her a raised-eyebrow expression.

"Your cautious recounting of my forlorn physicality suggests that you believe me to be a horrid sight. Perhaps now, your late night actions have thus created a monster and you will be forced to cast me from the cart."

Smiling wide, she intentionally sipped her lemonade quietly whilst not looking at him. "I should never do such a thing," she said seriously. "I have no idea how to direct the horse."

He laughed heartily and loudly and she did too, so glad for him and his thoughtful rescue. "You always make me smile," he said, still laughing.

"I dare say that, tired or not, monster is not achievable for you." she continued, finishing her first piece of bread. "Even with earnest effort, there is no amount of alteration that would diminish your handsomeness. It must be a terrible encumbrance to be created in God's favor."

Studying her expression he looked away from her before speaking. "He has done well with you too, Ms. Olly. However, I have my suspicions that your brief admiration might be attributed to your hunger and my catering to this need."

Laughing, she took a bite of the sweet roll and sighed, enjoying its freshness. "You are exceptionally modest but now that you say it, this roll does certainly put you in a more favorable light."

Smiling he pointed to it. "Gleda was so restless when we first went looking for you in town, that she baked those for you. They are the favorites of everyone in the theater and she used the last of her sugar."

Olly swallowed her mouthful then held the roll down guiltily. "Oh, she did? I do feel terrible that she should use it for such a bleak occasion. Did *you* get one?"

He shook his head. "They were claimed hastily and in my absence," he replied with an intentional pout.

She broke off the side she had bitten on and made sure to offer him the more generous half. "Please take this; it will make me happy if you do."

Taking it from her he bit into it, showing he was truly grateful. "I have noticed that you are lax to accept a gift without reciprocation. There is something authentic and dear about you, Olly."

She shook her head and wiped the crumbs and icing from her hands then placed them under the blanket again.

"It is pure selfishness," she stated matter-of-factly. "I do of course enjoy the generosity of others, but I derive most pleasure from their appreciation. When you *give* something, the recipients' smile or surprise is truly a unique type of bliss. So you can not credit me entirely, for my motives are not without the incentive of its own reward."

His eyes glistened as he looked upon her warmly. They talked about many things on the ride back to the theater and she noticed that he kept the horse going at a slower pace than normal.

The more she spoke with Ehren, the more impressed she was with him. He recounted stories of the theater and the kindness of its residents as well as favored memories of Gleda and Gilpin's antics.

As the sun began to warm up, she recognized the main street and was sorry they had arrived so quickly. The empty streetcar reflected the cloudless sky as the cart went by and Olly was still laughing as Ehren finished an amusing tale about first meeting Clarence.

Just before they passed the church, Ehren's tone suddenly became more subdued and a sense of worry overcame her as she watched his expression change.

Without looking at her, he slowed the horse even more. "Olly, there is a matter I wish to raise with you, if you will allow me to be frank in my approach."

"You can always speak openly with me, Ehren. I ask that you never fear my reproach, I wish for you to trust me with your divulgences."

"I do, Olly, that is assured," he said quietly.

"Last night my worry for you was like a sharp pain in my chest and I felt as if the inside of me was an empty pit," he said looking at her. "I wish for you to know that my admiration for you is not of a companionable nature. There is a lingering that I carry with me throughout my waking moments and it only ceases on my slumber."

She hadn't anticipated him raising this subject, especially in such a forward manner. Her heart began to race as she considered whether to lower her gaze or not. The horse pulled up beside the theater and made its way around to the back, stopping in the shadows of the stone building.

Taking a shallow tense-filled breath, she reached out and placed her hand on his. It was warm, it was real, and the sensation was inexpressible. She could never imagine anyone touching another person and experiencing the same awe that went through her in that moment.

"I will not deny my attraction to you," she said, with her heart nervously pounding so hard against her skin that she was growing faint from it. "But there is a divide between us that has not been addressed. There is someone from your past that I fear possesses you and will not allow you to give your heart with entirety. Perhaps there is an element of loneliness that causes your eyes to fall on me thus."

Swallowing hard, his gaze was solemn and his lips parted to offer an explanation but instead he placed his hand on her face. "I promise to enlighten you on this, but I ask you first to trust that each revealing has its own time."

Placing her hand on his as he kept it pressed to her face, she leaned into it and considered her words. "We are both haunted, Ehren. You create in me a sense of magic and freedom that when you are absent, I am incomplete in my offerings."

"You have made similar declarations of the man you dream of," he whispered, close to her face.

Staring down at his suit jacket, she wanted to press her lips against the fabric of it just because it was worn by him. Even the air around him was sacred and he was right, she did feel the same way for him as she did for her true love.

"I promised him forever, Ehren," she said, with tears in her eyes. "I am compelled to trust my true self enough to know I would never make this vow without the sincerity of such devotion."

Leaning into her, she closed her eyes at the intense emotion he elicited within her. He kissed her forehead and held his lips there as she gently placed her hand on his chest, not pushing away, but getting as close as she could to him while not committing to her passion.

"After you have tended to any personal matters, Aylward had requested you to assist in the restaurant," he said straightly, pulling away from her and stepping off the cart.

Walking around to her side he helped her off and there was a sudden coolness in their atmosphere. "Tell me this," he said, looking down at her, refraining from any form of touch now. "What if your memory does not return? What if he has died in war or has not honored his vow?"

Staring into his blue eyes she pondered the scenarios, as she had done many times before. "I honestly don't know," she replied. She wanted to say more but there were no words to be said. How could she decide between the unknown past and the secretive present? "I know I love him," she added reluctantly.

Grinding his teeth, suppressing his emotion, he turned to look at the theater and then his expression changed again. It appeared as if inside of him he had chosen to be resigned and relayed this in his eyes. "Andy has suggested I go with them for their next term overseas."

"To the war?" she asked fearfully.

"Yes of course, I should do my part to help them."

Knowing he was saying it to get a reaction from her, she also knew that he would stand by his words if need be.

"I wish you wouldn't, Ehren," she said, looking at him pleadingly.

She could see his chest rise with tension but his stare remained determined and disconnected. "You have no claim on me to prevent it," he volleyed abruptly.

Tears fell from her eyes as she nodded, avoiding his steely gaze. "You are right to say so," she said, trying hard not to let the emotion break in her voice. "Please excuse me; I must prepare to help the others."

Avoiding his gaze, she hurriedly walked back around to the side door and rushed into her room. Falling to her knees, she placed her face into her velvet and silk blankets and cried.

Where would she find hope now? She had lost everything. Certainly her past was lost and all the love in it, and now possibly all the joy in her future too.

Gilpin and Gleda's voices sounded from the room next door and she wiped her face, even as more tears fell from her eyes. She didn't know how, but she had to change her story. Whatever had to be done, she could not remain in this state. There was a solution to everything and she would find it.

Staring at her hands as if seeing them for the first time, she pondered her situation. Her left hand just minutes ago had clutched Ehren's so lovingly. Her right hand, with her eyes closed, had held that of the man in her dreams.

Her suffering belonged to her and her alone. A decision would have to be made and she was the only one who could make it.

Placing her face into her hands she closed her eyes and prayed. If she was only allowed one miracle in a lifetime, she asked the angels to give it to her now.

Chapter Twenty

It had been twenty minutes since Ehren had discovered her and Gilpin at the barn and returned Olly alone to the theater. After all was said and done, time had passed quickly and it was already mid afternoon.

She was able to quickly acquire another piece of thick bread from the kitchen area to cover her hunger cravings before making her way to the powder room. She had started the morning in a hay loft in her nightgown, then Ehren had brought a dress for her to change into but now she wore her dreary white work dress.

Having tidied her hair into a neat bun and spraying some perfume, she still felt drab in all respects. Her conversation with Ehren had ended poorly and his indication of love for her thrilled but tormented her equally.

Out of tears from having cried so much, a distinct numbness filled her as she worked diligently and silently in the restaurant. It was a quiet afternoon and it appeared that some people had passed on, and the bell ringing outside supported her theory.

Nonetheless a couple of the patients had made improvement and there was a sense of something having been lifted from the atmosphere. Gilpin hadn't made it there and she assumed him and Gleda had either taken a detour on their return journey or were doing other work.

Lillian was the only face she recognized and she was tending to someone who was coughing a great deal and didn't look like they had much longer. A few of the small faced people who she hadn't yet familiarized herself with, were there as well as more new people who must have arrived in the night.

As she pressed a wet cloth to the forehead of a shallow breathing man, she looked over and noticed a man she had never seen before. He struck her as uniquely serene and beautiful as if he was truly an angel.

He was talking with one of the small faced women and then she nodded and left him, smiling as if she knew him well. Olly couldn't place why she was so drawn to looking at him and that was when her heart began to race.

Without any specific reason, she knew he was not her love but she wondered if he would know who she was. Suddenly he began to navigate around the occupied cots and out of the front door into the street.

He hadn't looked at her and she wondered now, if he had seen her, whether he would recognize her too. The man she was tending to had fallen asleep and Olly nearly knocked over her water-filled bowl to rush over to Lillian.

Quickly excusing herself with a vague explanation of unsettledness, she asked that Lillian tell anyone who asked that she would return soon. Within minutes she was outside on the street with the afternoon sun's rays settling on the church steeple in the distance.

With unique anticipation she scoured the area, knowing that if she saw the enigmatic man, she would not fear approaching him. Even so, when she finally spotted him, it was through the blurred glass of the abandoned streetcar.

Strangely he appeared to be hiding somewhat, standing against the side of an empty storefront and glancing ever so slightly to his left into the street. There was something ominous about his demeanor and though she couldn't rationalize it, she knew something was about to happen.

No one else was in the street and the breeze that had dominated most of the morning had ceased all together. The bell suddenly rang out and Olly jumped, startled, but she had to see him better and so got closer to the streetcar.

Positioning herself to the side of it and peering out, she consciously remained away from his sight. She kept her breathing shallow and watched him as he too stood still and glanced to his left.

There was a hint of worry on his otherwise serene face and she wondered if he was nervous about something. As the other times she had witnessed the theater people in their strange dealings, he too appeared to be on the verge of an intentional interaction.

Only a minute passed before her suspicion was confirmed. It was a younger man, perhaps in his late twenties and he had stepped out from an alley way and began walking towards where the other man stood.

His head was down and his hands in his suit pants but he looked distressed and he appeared to be in a hurry to get away from something.

Suddenly the angelic man came forward and pretended he had just incidentally exited his alley. He stepped out in front of this man and startled him. "My, I do apologize, excuse me," he said in a deep sophisticated voice.

The young man nodded and continued walking but the angelic man wasn't done. He reached into his pockets and pulled out a handful of money. "Excuse me! You seem to have dropped some of your money," he said.

The hurried man turned and glanced at his face and then at his hand. "No, I had no money with me," he said straightly. Olly could tell that he was in need of money, not only by his presentation but by the look on his face.

The angelic man took a few steps towards him. "I am quite certain that the man who was once in possession of this currency will not be returning for it. I have no use for it so you are welcome to it."

The young man with a gaunt face and deep dark eyes shifted then quickly took it. "Thank you, you are very kind."

Olly assumed that this particular encounter was over, that the angelic man had done his good deed but it was not to be, and that sense of dread still loomed in the air.

Perhaps it was a feeling within the frightened young man that traveled with him but it may have been more than that.

"Onward into that alley there, I had encountered a young woman selling fresh made bread," the angelic man added to him with a smile. "She indicated that she will stay there only for a short while longer so you may wish to go there now if you would like some."

The young man looked up towards the shadowed alley where the angelic man had come from but he reacted anxiously. Perhaps he was concerned that whoever he was running from might be hiding there.

He glanced into the street, and fortunately didn't notice Olly who was hidden well enough. "No, perhaps another time, I really must be going. I thank you for the suggestion."

"Please," the angelic man called out as the younger man stepped away. "You look quite hungry. There is nothing to fear up there. I believe you would benefit from some nourishment that is all."

"I can not, I am sorry," the younger man called back.

"I will buy it for you," the angelic man persisted. "You can keep the money, it is safe and warm there."

The younger man continued away and then suddenly a loud bang like a fire cracker rang out into the empty street. The young man immediately fell to the ground. He hadn't put his hands out to protect his fall, he fell flat on his face and there he remained.

Olly gasped and shook with terror. Turning around she saw an older woman holding a rifle. "If you hadn't come to our house, my daughter wouldn't be dead now. You and your flu ridden charity food. You can go see her now so she can spit in your face!"

With that she turned and walked away without fear of retribution. Olly had been on the other side of the streetcar so the woman had not seen her. But what about the angelic man?

Olly quickly made her way around to attend to the young man. She was surprised to see that the angelic man had returned to the shadows of the alley. As she passed him, she was compelled to freeze to the spot, stunned by what she saw.

Only being able to see half of his face by the light of day, she still recognized him. "Clarence!"

He was placing the money back in his pocket and he looked sad but then fearful as he saw her there. "Oh no, Olly. You can not be here, please return to the restaurant," he said, reaching out for her.

She studied his suit, it was the same suit, it was the same button that was undone at the top of his shirt, and he was the same man as the angelic man. But his face was transformed, he now appeared as Clarence, as if the angelic man was a costume, but one made of flesh not fabric.

"Clarence," she said, her voice wavering and tears springing to her eyes. "How did you change your face?"

She had never seen him the way he looked now, so frightened by her witnessing his transformation. He walked up to her and took her hands in his. "Please do not be afraid of me."

Shaking her head she looked into his eyes, to reassure and comfort him. "I am not afraid of you, Clarence. You are my dear friend. I ask you not to be afraid that I will harm your secrets."

Surprisingly he let go of her hands and placed them over his face. She knew he must have been upset over the man. "He has died, hasn't he?" she asked quietly.

He nodded and sighed deeply.

"You tried to stop him," she continued, close to him, placing her hands on his arms. She tucked her head into his chest and glanced up towards his hand-covered face, urging him to look back at her. "You came here because you knew that he might be harmed and you tried to stop it because that is what you do."

Lowering his hands she could see he had tears on his face and she wiped them away, holding his gaze so he knew he could trust her.

"Why do you assume I would know such a thing in advance?" he asked hesitatingly. He was obviously trying to derive what amount of knowledge she had and how much was supposition.

Glancing to her left, she noticed that blood was leaking out from the man's head and onto the street but no one else was around. She was surprised that her reaction was not more dramatic and she pondered her background given that she was not feeling panicked in this moment.

"I have witnessed others from the theater in their moments of good deeds," she explained, not wanting to expose Gilpin and what he had vaguely confirmed to her.

He too looked over at the young man and then towards where the lady had departed. "But I failed him," he said quietly with emotion in his voice.

Seizing his arms, she forced him to look at her. "Any attempt to help another is truly heroic, Clarence," she stated determinedly. "You tried to coerce an action from him but ultimately it was his decision where he went and what he did."

His gaze set upon her and contemplation was set in his green goat-like eyes. "Perhaps his free will negated the accountability of my counsel but it was my inability of persuasion that ultimately created his fate."

A strange sensation suddenly went through her as if there was a knowing inside of her that was overriding her confusion. Regardless of who he was, or who any of them were, ultimately he was her friend and all that was important was that she could comfort him.

"Clarence," she said, taking his hands in hers. "I do not know how you and the others are aware of situations before they happen but pray tell me, do you sincerely believe in fate?"

He nodded, relaxing in her presence. "It is not a belief, Duchess, it is a certainty. The path of destiny is indisputable, our people, all of us, we are fate's advocates."

Understanding that what he said was truth, she also realized in that moment that what she had witnessed confirmed Gilpin's divulgence. Indeed these people were from different places, but now as she looked upon him, she knew that their origins were not Earthly.

Despite her revelation, the importance now lay in his consolation and not her enlightenment. "I must ask you something in earnest. I have no preconceived notion of your response," she said seriously. "Does fate have its malleability?"

He nodded but then closed his eyes, considering it deeply. "There are possibilities in a person's journey that can be altered, certain details," he replied carefully. "However, there are greater events intended for each of us. No matter the slight deviations on one's path, their destiny is ultimately resolute."

Olly was fascinated by all that he said. It was surreal that the two of them should be standing there in an emptied town with a dead man lying a short distance from them. Stranger still was that all he said to her made perfect sense.

"Then perhaps you must alter your perception to see the truth," she said. "You are a man who works to alter one's path for their benefit but it had to have been inevitable that he must die at this time. As you have stated yourself, you can not alter his destiny; you can only change its intermediate course."

His eyes lit up in surprise and he squeezed her hand, shaking his head as if it was too much to comprehend. "Yes, Olly, most certainly you are correct. I do not know how you have witnessed what you have without questioning me in great length. Yet you stand here and offer me elucidation."

They looked at each other in a minute of pure silence, no wind outside, no voices, just staring at each other with fresh perspective.

A question appeared in his eyes and she was happy to let him voice it. "But what do you say about my role in this particular matter, Duchess? If he were in fact destined to die at this time, why should I have attempted to dissuade this incident at all?"

Filled with a sense of wonder at him, at their situation and at herself for her wisdom, Olly smiled as she knew she had an answer. "Destiny does not belong to one man only, Clarence. Perhaps this moment was providence but not for him alone."

He looked at the young man again and let out a breath that he must have been holding on to. "Then it is entwined with my own path?"

She nodded and laughed at the beauty of this knowledge, how clear and yet how fantastical. "Imagine with me for a moment, that you were meant to help him for your own progression," she said. "It might just be that you were meant to attempt to help him and learn what it feels like to not succeed. All people must experience heartache and happiness to mature in empathy."

Laughing loudly he placed his hands on her shoulders and his eyes widened with enthusiasm. "Yes of course! And Olly, do not discount your own involvement. Perhaps it was providence that you witness this act so you can gain some knowledge of your own. In so doing you could discover more about yourself and about your own beliefs."

Suddenly loving the wonderful person he was, her gratitude forced her to embrace him. "Of course you are correct, Clarence, and that is why such a horrid event has yet left us standing her in each others arms with appreciation. How fortunate we are."

He held her back with a smile in his eyes but then fear returned to them. "It has been requested of us not to speak of our truth to you, Olly. We are very protective of each other and can not have the outside world privy to our dealings."

Taking his right hand in both of hers she smiled. "I would never betray any of you," she assured him. "I can not offer any evidence of my loyalty, only my word that I am your true friend. I would never once speak of this moment or any others that I was in witness of. I am blessed to have been taken in by such kind hearted people. I am truly not worthy of my good fortune to know you."

Placing both of his hands on her face he sighed. "Do not discredit your goodness, Duchess. You belong with us and you have touched us all, our own souls have benefited from you being in our midst."

Smiling with tears in her eyes, she glanced over at the young man. Only minutes had passed yet it felt so long ago as if their conversation had altered her indefinitely. "Should we take him to Martin's yard?"

He walked over to him and effortlessly scooped him up in his arms, blood setting on his suit sleeve. "Return to the restaurant, Olly. I will take care of this matter."

She nodded, acknowledging that she was not to speak of the incident at all. "I am glad I spoke with you, Clarence."

"I am too," he said sincerely as he looked down at the man in his arms. "No happening can be dominated by regret when you understand the importance of its inevitable timing."

Watching him as he walked down the alley towards Martin's yard, she smiled. Many emotions went through her at once in this moment but she felt like the world had changed.

As she made her way back to the restaurant she pondered all that had happened to her. There was so much to appreciate and now she was grateful for losing her memory. Her truth, her past, was now altered in its significance to her. No matter who she once was, she was most certainly now a better person because of her loss.

Chapter Twenty One

Olly had worked at the restaurant well into the night so when she had finally returned to her room at the theater, she was certain she would have a dreamless sleep. Nonetheless as the night progressed, the mist lifted and she was standing in the green hills again.

There was a new sensation that filled the air and even though the imagery was clear in many respects, there was still a fog that permeated the borders of her sight. Fatigue was in her even there in her memory and yet she was gladly aware that she was dreaming and hurriedly looked for the man.

Sensing him near her, she tried to turn her head to the left but something caught her eye in the opposite direction, it was Ehren. He was dressed in a long white robe like the one Aylward often wore and he was looking at her sadly.

She loved him deeply, but what about the other man? If she were able to look at her true love would she change her mind? As she tried to move her head, urgently seeking him, she found him gone yet the sensation of him being there still remained. "Where are you?" she called out.

Afraid that the intensity of her voice would wake her up, she calmly sought him out but to no avail. Ehren stood there still, his handsome face serene, his love for her coming to her in waves that she could feel inside of her.

He was standing beneath a tree on a green grassy hill not far from her, beckoning for her to come with him. But should she? How could she promise someone forever and not endeavor to find him? But the pull of her desire had her taking steps, lifting her feet and moving towards Ehren.

Now fear set inside of her, he was starting to look very distressed and he was taking steps backwards. Ehren was leaving and she felt like she was losing him. He didn't love her now, she had rejected him.

She couldn't see him clearly anymore and now the feeling that her true love and Ehren were both quickly vanishing. "No, come back!" she screamed. "Ehren, come back!" She was screaming, full of terror, filled with a sensation of utter despair. "Ehren! Ehren!"

Her voice was so loud that she awoke to it , still screaming his name, her voice hoarse as she stared at the light flooding in. Gilpin had run into her room through their adjoining door and he fell to her side, taking her in his arms.

Holding him tightly she sobbed, completely distraught and hopeless. "Gilpin, please help me, what should I do? What should I do?"

He held her tighter, her screams must have woken him, his breath still sounding deep and fatigued. "Olly I am right here, tell me what troubles you. You are safe I promise."

Nuzzling her face into his thin night shirt, she closed her eyes and allowed his embrace to comfort her. "I am in love with Ehren," she stated fearfully.

The pace of his breathing changed as if he was thinking. "He professed his love for you," he stated straightly.

Pulling away from him but keeping him close by, she gestured for him to sit beside her on the bed. Reaching for a blanket that had fallen on the floor, she wrapped it around his shoulders. "He told you?"

Lowering his gaze he sighed. "He had spoken to Gleda in the afternoon and I overheard them in the kitchen," he explained. "He is truly honorable in all ways, Olly but he was in need of comfort and Gleda is his trusted confidant."

She nodded. "I do not fault him; I only wish I was not the cause of his dejection."

Clasping his hands in his lap, he glanced at her through the corner of his eyes as if not wanting to commit to seeing her reaction. "He also suggested he would leave with Andy."

Falling back onto her pillows she sighed. She was so tired and the screaming had hurt her throat but her heart still raced with worry. "Yes he had expressed as much to me."

It was obviously something that created great sadness in Gilpin and he hung his head but then he quickly turned to her. "But Olly, if you love him then you can just tell him and he will stay."

She wanted to agree with him and ease all of their suffering, but she still felt the obligation inside of her to someone else. Looking out of the narrow window to her right she could see the light of the full moon. "There is someone from his past," she said cautiously. "I feel he is withholding a truth from me."

Gilpin moved closer to her and placed his cold hand on hers. "I have sworn to—,"

Silencing him with a hand gesture, she shook her head. "I would not ask you to betray his confidence, Gilpin. It is just that we have much keeping us apart: his past and my own. I believe I have promised my heart to another man, this will always stand between us."

He waited for her to look at him before he spoke. His tussled hair was worsened by an abrupt awakening but kindness was everywhere in his countenance. "We all know how hard it is for you without your memory, Olly, but I promise you, there is a reason he has not told you about his own past. It is not something that would stand in the way of you being together. He truly loves you and you alone."

His words genuinely consoled her and she wanted to rush out and up the stairs and take Ehren into her arms but the conflict inside of her would not diminish. "Are you aware of the time?"

Glancing over at the light coming from his room he thought on it. "The fob watch that Esther gave me is unreliable but I am certain that it is past midnight. I believe somewhere in the vicinity of two or three in the morning."

"I am sorry to have woken you," she said honestly.

"No, Olly. I am glad that I can be here for you, I always will be."

She squeezed his hand and smiled. "I love you my dear brother."

Bending down he kissed her hand. "Do you promise you will always call me this?"

She laughed lightly. "No matter what truth is discovered, it is a solemn vow I make to you, Gilpin. Tell me, are the doors to the church kept open?"

Surprise registered on his face. "As far as I am aware they are, but it is quite cold this night, I can take you in the morning."

Shaking her head, she began to push her blankets away even though the chill in the room beckoned her to return to them. "I must resolve this now within me, it can not wait any longer," she said determinedly. "I will pray this night and I will make a decision on what to do one way or another."

Quickly standing, he looked around her room and then at his own. "That nightgown is too thin for you to go there," he said. "Do you have something warmer to wear?"

Thinking on it she remembered leaving the red velvet queen costume in the bathroom on a hook. "Yes I will change in the bathroom, I have a dress there and I can take a blanket with me."

"I am coming with you," he said, hurrying to his room.

"Oh no, Gilpin. That is not necessary."

"I am your guard and it is my job to protect you," he insisted. "I will meet you at the side door and I will take you the back way," he added enthusiastically as if they were plotting an adventure.

"Yes very well, I will not be long," she relented.

Minutes later Olly met with Gilpin at the side door. The queen's dress and equally red velvet blanket was not quite enough to combat the cold but her determination overrode her discomfort.

Gilpin had been wise enough to bring the Altoids and he now wore his every day suit and a thick dark trench coat. He took her the back way as promised, behind the restaurant and town center, and quietly past the large dirt mounds of the recently buried bodies at Martin's yard.

They walked quickly in the chilly early morning hours and a short time later they entered the dimly lit church. The door creaked loudly inward, echoing against the empty pews.

Many taper candles were half burned down, calmly flickering in misted glass lanterns on the wall. Someone coughed from the row closest to them and Gilpin rushed over to find the priest lying on the ground. "I have to take him to the restaurant, Olly," he said apologetically.

She nodded. "I am safe here, Gilpin."

They both got the priest to his feet, so he could then assist him out into the cold night.

She was alone, truly and utterly and the silence offered her an opportunity to really contemplate her situation. Wrapping the blanket around her shoulders and across her chest, she let the velvet warm her ears. She had not styled her hair; instead it hung down freely to her waist, giving her an odd sense of liberation.

There was something magical in this moment, she mused. To be in this place of God and angels, with flickering candles and astonishing serenity, she was on the verge of transformation.

Approaching the front, she had no particular religious beliefs that she knew of but she did know God had a hand in all things. Raising her eyes to the ornate golden candlestick on the wooden alter, she took a deep breath and spoke aloud.

"God, I am certain you can identify me without the name given to me at birth. I am at my wits end I must admit and I had hoped you would find the time to hear my plea," she said, before glancing behind her to make sure that she was still alone.

Turning back she sighed again, her eyes hypnotized by the flame. "I know that all things occur for a reason and that maybe I have lost my memory for my own benefit. But I find myself in a terrible position and I am praying to you now in hopes that you will have mercy on me."

Her words were met with silence but she felt as if someone was listening, someone out there in the universe was taking the time to hear her. "I am a good person and I have been taken in by a dear group of people and I care for them very much. In fact, I have truly fallen in love with one of them and he has expressed an equal admiration for me."

Sighing, she turned and sat on the plush carpeted step in front of the altar and stared out at the dim dark aisle in front of her. "I feel deep inside of me that my memory will not return soon or perhaps I will not regain all of it, but I have a dream that I have committed my heart to another man."

Suddenly a sensation went through her, a feeling of revelation and she realized that no matter what, she had to make a decision, even without all of the facts. "God, did you listen to my heart just now?" she called out, standing abruptly. "I am making a decision. I am not praying for you to return my memory, unless of course it is my destiny to regain it. Instead I wish for you to give peace to another."

Stepping down and clutching her hands to her heart, her body and face felt warm, a unique sensation of being alive for the first time.

"I know what to do!" she announced with joy in her heart. "All I ask is that you give me a sign that the man I leave behind will be happy and find love of his own."

Through the corner of her eye she noticed one of the candles as it suddenly went out, even though it appeared to be new and recently lit.

She walked over to it, not even caring if she didn't get a sign, she was just happy to have found a resolution. In this moment she understood that her destiny was now and that she was meant to make this decision, the one that felt right within her.

Cheerfully rushing over to the candle, she reached up and grabbed it, dipping it into the lit lantern beside it. Now reignited, she placed it back into its hold on the wall and froze in surprise. She hadn't expected to see what she did. Her prayer had been answered, her sign had come.

Below the candle was a framed oil canvas, small and antique. She stared dumbstruck at the painted landscape of a distant place.

She couldn't take her eyes from the hills in the painting, how uncanny that she should be looking at them now. The light illuminated the painting in a way that made the grass in the valleys look so vibrantly green, an unearthly green.

Gazing down at the ring on her finger, she remembered when he gave it to her. When *he* gave it to her. This ring had come from her beloved, she suddenly remembered. It had been found in the cobblestones where she had fallen. It must have fallen off of her hand!

A chill ran over her entire body, a physical realization, a confirmation, a sensation that was unmistakable in its arrival. How much time did she have? She had to hurry; she had never experienced such overwhelming panic, such urgency.

As she ran down the aisle with great determination, she prayed she would not forget. She had to quickly get out there before her memory, what little she had of it, would escape her.

She flung open the church doors only to run directly into Gilpin who looked extremely upset. His expression now turned to worry as he grabbed onto her arms to question her. "What is it, Olly? What happened?"

Quickly seizing his arms, she could barely contain her overwhelming excitement and overload of emotions. "Aylward is not the other theater owner," she stated, more as a question but with hopes he would confirm it.

He nodded, but he still frowned in confusion at her. "That's right, Olly. No one said he was."

She could tell that he was beginning to understand why she was raising the subject. She hoped he would smile with the revelation but his expression shoed that he had come to her in haste. "Did something occur?" she asked anxiously.

"Ehren is heading out with the Greesom lads as we speak. I saw him get into one of their vehicles. They plan on making their way to the airbase just now."

Panicked, she looked down at the end of the road, not quite being able to see the theater. "Please fetch Gleda at once."

Looking back, he shook his head. "She doesn't want to watch him leave," he said apologetically.

"Convince her with whatever words you must, but it is important that you get her out here, Gilpin."

"I will, but what will you do?"

"I am coming too, but I suspect that you can run faster than me. I have to stop them leaving."

Smiling he knew that all of their stories were about to change and she could see in his eyes that he wanted to hug her, but they would do that later. For now he nodded and then began to run as fast as he could.

Not far behind him, she was rushing with all of her might to get there.

She imagined the others might be surprised at his fast approach. Nothing was more important than talking to Ehren; she could not let another minute pass without him.

On getting closer to the restaurant, she could see the three army vehicles with the men inside and ran faster towards them. She waved her arms around, now her heart controlling her actions, begging God to allow them to see her.

She got the impression that the cloud in front of the moon prevented them from spotting her and they would soon rush past her, to be lost for months if not for good. Without concern for her own safety she ran onto the road and jumped in front of the first vehicle.

It came to a screeching halt, narrowly missing her, while the other two stopped just as abruptly behind it. The lantern that one of them held out of the window barely illuminated her. Ehren jumped out of the passenger side, at first not being able to identify her. "Olly? Is that you?"

"Don't leave!" she yelled, running towards him, wanting to stop him at all costs. "Don't go with them."

He met her half way, looking sincerely confused, unsure of her reasoning. He crossed his arms defensively against his soldiers, uniform. "I have to leave; I have already signed the papers. Why do you risk yourself like this? We will return in time and you can consult Aylward on any serious matters."

She felt pain emanate through his words and she was sorry to be the reason he felt that way. Everyone from the theater was outside, standing there to wave their friends off, but more so because one of their leaders was leaving and it was something that affected all of them.

Glancing through the corner of her eye she could see Gilpin pulling a reluctant Gleda by the hand but she stopped resisting when she saw Olly standing in front of Ehren in that particular manner.

Everything was about to change.

Chapter Twenty Two

Standing there in the chilled early morning hours, Olly was surprised by the silence around her given there were so many people standing outside of the theater. She couldn't remember much yet, her history remained hazy, but she knew she cared for all of them.

Ehren was standing directly in front of her. A small amount of light derived from a lantern that one of the departing soldiers held, allowing her to see the distress in his face.

She reached up and touched Ehren's soldier's cap, and then placed her hand at the back of his neck. He remained stoic and protective of his emotion but she held his gaze even though he frowned upon her. "Did you cut your beautiful locks?" she asked him disappointedly.

He shifted on the spot as if her wording piqued his curiosity. She could feel the eyes of everyone on them. The night was still, the lights on the car were bright in the dark evening but no one moved or spoke.

"There is an arrangement to have it done first thing tomorrow," he replied shortly.

Placing both of her hands on his face, which was so close to hers now, she spoke quietly but clearly. She didn't once take her eyes off of him, wanting to see the flicker of recognition as he came alive again. "I want to be with you, Ehren," she said openly. "You can not leave, I need you. I can not be without you, our hearts are bonded."

His breathing calmed but he maintained a protective resistance. Placing his hands on top of hers he stared at her. "I can't offer you promises when you have another man in your thoughts. Can you release him from your heart and give your love to me alone?"

"No" she said plainly, and he immediately took his hands from hers, shocked at her abruptness. "No, I will not, because *you* are the man from my dreams and I promised him forever."

With true shock on his face, he exhaled loudly; clutching the tops of her shoulders, shaking her with emotion in his voice. "Tell me why you say this."

She took his right hand in both of hers and kissed the top of it. "Tell me you love me, darling husband. Say to me, I promise you forever, Alarice, and I shall never cease my love for you."

"My dear, Alarice. Oh how I have prayed for you to return to me." With tears in his eyes, he pulled her into his arms and breathed her in. "Forever is not long enough, my love. No measurement of time can reward me with enough of you. Every second in your absence has been an eternity in itself; never let me lose you again."

There was an immediate shift in the atmosphere and somehow she felt the love of all of them in that moment. She had been home all along.

Nevertheless, Ehren's embrace still felt tentative. "I must go, my love. I have already signed the papers."

Pulling back slightly she quickly searched the sea of relieved faces for one of her oldest friends. "Clarence!"

Clarence suddenly appeared from the center of the crowd with a big smile on his face. "Yes Milady, Duchess Alarice?"

She laughed at his addressing her this way. Only a small portion of her memory had returned but she knew two important things; Ehren was her true love and the theater was the place she had designated for these people to congregate at, *she* was their leader.

"Oh that makes me laugh, Clarence. It will take a bit of getting used to," she said with a wide smile of her own.

Gilpin and Gleda quickly approached them, awaiting their own part in the reunion, but she gestured for them to stop for a moment.

"Clarence," she said seriously. "Please contact proper channels and let them know that the soldiers will not depart from here until tomorrow evening. Say what you must to convince them of the necessity of this delay and I will think of something to ensure that Ehren does not go with them."

He nodded alike to an official bow but smiled at her mischievously as he raised his gaze. "Your wish is my command, Duchess," he said, quickly turning to talk with the other soldiers and then to hurriedly contact the official channels to prevent an inquiry on them.

Gleda pushed Ehren out of the way and took Olly into her arms. "I have missed you, Ms. Alarice, Milady!" she exclaimed, teasing her with laughter in her voice. "Now you can sleep again in your bed and we can have our storage room back."

Olly kissed her on the cheek, sorry that Gleda was still in her night robe but glad that Gilpin had convinced her to come out to witness their happiest of moments. "I will even have it organized better for you my darling friend," she promised. "How blessed I am to have you as my eternal family."

Not able to wait any longer, Gilpin pushed forward, beaming with pure joy. He truly was her guard; he had come with her from their world as her assistant. She, Ehren, Gleda and Aylward had all raised him together

"May I hug you now?" he asked tentatively as if her remembrance prevented his informality with her. Taking him into her arms she kissed him on the cheek then pressed her face against his. "You may hug me now and any time you feel like it. I consider you my brother, darling boy, always. I don't recall everything but if I ever treated you less than that, I am sorry for not showing you how much I value you."

"You never made me feel that way, Olly," he said before appearing upset at his mistake. "It's going to take me a while to get used to calling you like I used to."

She took his hands in hers and smiled at him, feeling so much love. "I like it anyway; it is part of me now."

His smile lit up the joyous night and love was in his eyes. "I still remember when I was a small boy and I was abandoned in the valley and you were the one who found me," he relayed with tears in his green eyes. "You picked me up and held me and said '*I am going to keep you*'."

Laughing, she briefly recalled the valley in her mind, the green hills that she had seen in her dreams. Not knowing with any certainty, she sensed it was a long time ago. "And keep you I shall," she assured him.

She sensed another presence in their midst, and turned to see Aylward smiling at her. A glimpse of her own childhood returned to her and she remembered him holding her as a child, assuring her of his love and devotion.

She quickly embraced him and snuggled her face into his neck. "My prayers were answered, father."

Kissing the side of her head, he held her back and looked at her; she knew he was proud, he had always said so. "We have all been at the mercy of your bewildered husband," he said with a cheeky grin.

Ehren laughed heartily but did not interrupt them.

"I am glad to see you returned to us, Alarice, my cherished child. I have created a tonic for all of us so our minds and bodies are not so vulnerable to these Earthly ailings."

She nodded, reminded of all that she had gone through since she had been found on the cobblestones. "Thank you," she said, kissing him on the cheek. "These beautiful beings must all be protected. They must never be vulnerable to this kind of suffering."

The night had come to life as everyone in their presence began to talk amongst themselves. The vehicles were shut off and left as they were. The soldiers returned to the theater with some of their friends from their own world and others.

Olly yawned in spite of her excitement.

She could feel Ehren's eyes on her but she feared that if she returned his stare she would never be able to look away from him. "Are you tired, my love?" he asked.

She nodded. "Perhaps we should all return to slumber and celebrate in the daylight hours."

They all agreed and as they ventured back into the theater, Olly studied every detail of the building and all the decorations inside with new eyes. She could vaguely recollect where they had acquired some of the objects but there was still so much that she could not recall.

Gilpin, Gleda and Aylward hugged her numerous times before she was given the opportunity to return to bed. She would not be returning to sleep in the storage area beside Gilpin's room but instead in her own bedroom, the grandly decorated one upstairs.

Aylward walked up to the second floor with them and retired to his own room at the end of the hall while she followed Ehren into their room and closed the door.

Even though she knew they had been together a long time, she still felt like a nervous youth in his presence. She could feel the happiness from him, all the gloom had lifted from both of them, and she could barely contain her smile.

Walking past her, he stopped in front of an ornate wooden table at the back of the room. She shyly watched him through the corner of her eye as he began to remove his soldier's uniform. "How long have we been in love?" she asked, sincerely not being able to recall the information.

He removed his cap and his mid length hair fell to his shoulders and he smiled at her, knowing this was a physical attribute that attracted her strongly. "We are still in our beginnings, Alarice, but close to ten thousand years if measuring in Earth years."

She should have reacted with astonishment but there was something inside of her that accepted that he was telling the truth. She was enjoying her intermittent discoveries and placed her velvet blanket on the French antique armchair.

"It is no wonder that I am feeling so tired, I am older than I assumed," she remarked.

Fatigue was on his face too but she had never been more attracted to him than she was now. It was hard to believe that she could be loved as much as she was, by someone as impressive as him.

He handed her a nightgown, a pretty pink one with flowers on it and she recognized it to be her own, Gleda had made it for her on their first journey to Earth. Turning away, she removed her dress and put the pretty soft nightgown on, knowing he was amused by her coyness.

"Why didn't you tell me the truth about who I was?" she asked seriously.

He looked her over and she could tell it was a longer explanation than he was willing to give at this late hour.

"We wanted to protect our secret from the outside world, Alarice. We could not risk you finding out and then telling someone away from the theater. We could not ascertain if you would become afraid and inadvertently expose us to investigation."

She stood still for a moment and thought about it. "But I had seen things after a while, Ehren. Why didn't you tell me then, when I promised not to speak to outsiders."

A smile appeared on his face and she was surprised by it given the serious context of their conversation. "I will admit that when you started to speak of your dreams in the hills, I wanted to know how true your love was for me."

"You let me suffer in the end because you wanted to see if you could win my heart over the man in the dreams who was you anyway?"

He placed his hand on his chest, his long nightdress gathering beneath his hand as he laughed heartily. "I do regret the grief it caused you, Alarice. I succumbed to the romantic weakness of my character. I just wanted to know if I could draw you to me again, that it wasn't just a matter of circumstance that I captured your heart once."

She should have been upset but she understood and she was grateful for the strange events that led to this moment.

They were soon in bed together, one lantern flickering on a gilded wooden chair beside him. There were many things she wanted to say and ask him but for now she was content to lay with her head on her own pillow and gaze at him.

Reaching out to touch her face, he kept his hand there and tears sprung to his eyes, she could tell by his expression that his love for her was not only sincere, but truly eternal.

She wanted her soul to touch his if only it was possible. She moved forward so their bodies touched, so her face was next to his just inches away on his pillow. "You gave me the ring," she stated. "Tell me about when you gave it to me."

Smiling, she could tell that he had spoken of it many times before. "It was in our own world, a considerable time ago, Alarice. The day before, you had told me you wanted to create a place on Earth for people like us."

"We are like angels in a way?"

"Yes, we are alike to that. We come here to help people from our own worlds that are born as humans for a short time and we help guide them," he explained. "And so you came to tell me that you believed we should have a special place where our kind and the *angels* from other worlds could all collect together."

"I believe it is a good idea," she said, not quite remembering the particular time she had come up with it. "Everyone should have a place to call home while they are away from their worlds."

He smiled as if she had said that to him then as well.

"Did you like the idea personally?" she asked, as he placed his warm hand on her back and pressed himself up against her.

"No I did not care for it as we had only traveled to Earth for short spells to help our people here. So I was afraid if we committed to such an idea, then we would be obligated to stay here for lengthier times."

She smiled, knowing she must have had some hand in convincing him. "Did it turn out to be true?" she asked with a chuckle. "Have we stayed here much longer?"

He smiled too, not being able to hide his happiness. "Yes, in fact we have hardly returned home. Of course Gilpin went wherever you went. That is why Gleda and your father decided to come here too because they were growing tired of being without us so often."

Touching his face, she touched his eyelid and stared at his eyelashes, his nose, all of him that she could see as if viewing him for the first time. "And what happened the day you gave me the ring?"

"That night, I was quite upset with you but then I realized that my love for you would never leave me alone. I was quite certain I could not be without you and then I had a grand revelation."

Smiling she kissed his check and breathed him in, savoring his presence. "What was it?" she asked in a sleepy whisper.

Returning her affection by kissing her nose, he sighed as if having hungered for her so long; he was now finally fed again. "I realized that wherever you went I would have to follow and I would not mind it. For I belonged to no particular place or building, *you*, Alarice, were my true home."

Not being able to hold back any longer, she pressed her lips against his and he reciprocated passionately, she then wrapped her arms around him as they were immersed in each others love. "Do you still feel that way?"

He gazed at her with such adoration that she prayed he would always look at her that way. "Always, Alarice. You are everything to me," he replied, kissing her again. "And so the next day I took you into the hills and told you I would go with you on one condition. I said, if you accept this ring and you promise to wear it always, then I will go anywhere with you but you must promise me your love forever."

She pressed her toes against his and giggled. "And what did *I* say?" she asked with a childlike glee.

He laughed, amused by her. "You said, *'if I must'*."

She laughed. "Did I truly?"

"It is one of your favorite stories," he assured her with a smile. "How I cherish you, Olly girl. You make me laugh and love until there is no end to it. How blessed we are."

Smiling, she kissed him again, feeling every part of skin that touched him, feeling his heart beat, feeling his connection to her, true eternal love. The flame on the candle within the lantern was beginning to get low on the wick and fatigue was winning her over.

There were so many questions running through her mind. She knew that they were immortal beings, all of the theater residents were, yet why did her father look old and why did Gilpin look young? But she suspected it was a matter of choice somehow.

Just the same, her answers could arrive with the sun tomorrow. She only truly wanted to fall asleep in his arms but there was one thing left in her heart that she wanted to share before she closed her eyes. "Ehren, I want to tell you something I never want you to forget."

His eyes were slowly closing but she knew he was listening and he would not sleep until he heard her. "Your words will be engraved in my mind, dear one. Tell me what it is."

Wrapping her arms around him, full of love and gratitude in every way, she leaned back and touched his face. "I don't regret that it happened, Ehren. Because I lost my memory I got to appreciate all of you even more, truly seeing how valuable each of you are."

He smiled, understanding her, empathizing with her situation. "They are the most wonderful beings that God has created," he agreed. "They all adore you too."

"But there is one thing that I appreciate most of all," she said seriously, whispering into his ear. "I am the luckiest of all people, for I got to fall in love with you twice."

Made in the USA
Monee, IL
29 November 2019